Cast of C

James Hyde. A fifty-year-old retirea ~~tanner~~ ~~....~~ ~~~~

Hugh Selkirk. A British subject who has long lived in Argentina. He and James Hyde bear a striking resemblance to one another.

Robert Adam. Selkirk's very resourceful manservant.

Alexander Nairn. James Hyde's solicitor.

Mrs. Watson. Hyde's repressive housekeeper.

Ribbentrop. The Nazi whose stolen treasure started it all. He had several hundred thousand pounds stashed in an Argentine bank.

Bill Dodds. A plainclothes detective with an observant brother-in-law.

Manuel Varsoni. A member of the notorious Gatello gang. Italian by birth, he and the other members have been living in Argentina, with designs on the Ribbentrop loot.

Thomas Elphinstone Hambledon. A British intelligence agent.

Chief-Inspector Bagshott. Of New Scotland Yard, a friend of Tommy's.

Walter Race. Hyde's weaselly cousin, his only living relative.

William Forgan. A modelmaker who has a shop on the Clerkenwell Road.

Archibald Henry Campbell. Forgan's partner. Both are friends of Adam's.

Pietro Gatello, Giuseppe Mantani, Angelo Gatelo, Ramon Jacaro, Pacorro Pagote, Cesar Mariposa, and **Tadeo El Caballero.** The other members of the Gatello gang.

Konrad Hommelhoff. Another Nazi, with designs on Ribbentrop's loot.

Plus assorted servants, landlords, neighbors, and police personnel.

Books by Manning Coles

With Intent to Deceive

to Deceive

A Tommy Hambledon novel by
Manning Coles

Rue Morgue Press
Lyons, Colorado

ISBN: 978-1-60187-057-5

Rue Morgue Press
87 Lone Tree Lane
Lyons CO 80540
www.ruemorguepress.com
800-699-6214

Printed by Pioneer Printing
Cheyenne, Wyoming

PRINTED IN THE UNITED STATES OF AMERICA

About Manning Coles

Manning Coles was the pseudonym of two Hampshire neighbors who collaborated on a long series of entertaining spy novels featuring Thomas Elphinstone Hambledon, a modern-language instructor turned British secret agent. Hambledon was based on a teacher of Cyril Henry Coles (1895-1965). This same teacher encouraged the teenage Coles to study modern languages, German and French in particular, having recognized Coles' extraordinary ability to learn languages. When World War I broke out Coles lied about his age and enlisted. His native speaker ability in German prompted him to be pulled off the front lines and he soon became the youngest intelligence agent in British history and spent the rest of the war working behind enemy lines in Cologne.

The books came to be written thanks to a fortuitous meeting in 1938. After Adelaide Frances Oke Manning (1891-1959), rented a flat from Cyril's father in East Meon, Hampshire, she and Cyril became neighbors and friends. Educated at the High School for Girls in Tunbridge Wells, Kent, Adelaide, who was eight years Cyril's senior, worked in a munitions factory and later at the War Office during World War I. She already had published one novel, *Half Valdez*, about a search for buried Spanish treasure. *Drink to Yesterday,* loosely based on Cyril's own adventures, was an immediate hit and the authors were besieged to write a sequel, no mean feat given the ending to that novel. That sequel, *A Toast to Tomorrow*, and its prequel were heralded as the birth of the modern espionage novel with Anthony Boucher terming them "a single long and magnificent novel of drama and intrigue and humor." The Manning Coles collaboration ended when Adelaide died of throat cancer in 1959. During those twenty years the two worked together almost daily, although Cyril's continuing activities with the Foreign Intelligence Branch, now known as the Secret Intelligence Service or, more commonly, MI6, often required that he be out of the country, especially during World War II. Cyril wrote *Concrete Crime* on his own but the final two books in the series were the work of a ghostwriter, Cyril not wanting to go on with the series without Adelaide. While the earliest books had shown flashes of humor, it would not be until *Without Lawful Authority*, published in 1943 but set in 1938, that the collaborators first embraced the almost farcical humor that would come to be their hallmark. For more details on their collaboration and Cyril's activities in British intelligence see Tom & Enid Schantz' introduction to the Rue Morgue Press edition of *Drink to Yesterday.*

To Kenneth Corney of the police
department for his guidance through
the intricacies of police procedure

With Intent
to Deceive

CHAPTER ONE
Hyde for Leather

When James Hyde was a very small boy, he learned from his father to pause by the landing window on the way down to breakfast and sniff the morning breeze; when it brought with it a certain acrid tang it meant rain, for the wind was in the west. It was some time before he learned with surprise that the west wind did not smell like that always and everywhere, and that the scent was not, as it were, intrinsically west, but actually tannery. What is more, the faint aroma which hung about his father's clothes when he returned home in the evenings had the same origin, for old Tom Hyde was a tanner like his father before him, and intensely proud of a long-established and respectable family business. When James was six years old, which was in 1901, he was taken as a birthday treat, in the high dogcart his father always drove, to visit the works for the first time. The wind was in the west that day, and as they clattered through the streets of Yeovil the smell grew steadily till, when they swung through the yard gates, it was as strong as a sheet of color and nearly tangible.

When the dogcart pulled up at the office door James was lifted down to be introduced to elderly men who said, "So this is the young master. Well, well," and beamed upon him. James was dumb with embarrassment, for he was a shy child; he stared about him because it was easier to look at strange things than strange people, and the men laughed and said it was plain to see he was one of the noticing kind. After which he was taken through queer sheds with large tanks in the floor where skins lay soaking in dark liquid, across yards where more skins hung upon wooden frames to dry. There was a great barn filled with rough bark piled up and giving off a pleasant woodland smell.

"Oak bark, my boy," said Tom Hyde. "That's what we tan the hides with. We soak the bark in water to make tan liquor, very like the way your mother makes tea in the teapot. Then we soak the hides in the liquor; you saw that going on in those sheds with the tanks in the floor. When they come out of that they're nearly leather. Understand?"

James nodded silently.

"Not got a lot to say, has 'e?" said the foreman. "One of them as thinks a lot, like the parrot."

9

"Rather overcome by so much novelty, I fancy," said his father. "Chatters like a magpie at home, don't you, James? Well, what d'you think of it all now you've been all round? Eh?"

"It's—it's a very loud smell, isn't it?" said James, and was half pleased and half abashed to find he had said something funny.

"Very healthy smell, my boy. That's why we all live so long, we Hydes. Never get consumption when you work in a tannery."

There followed many other visits to the tannery as time went on; the high dogcart was laid aside for a car, and James went to school where the boys called him Sixpence because his father was a tanner and he would be one himself when he was old enough. He thought it strange that his mother would never visit the works; his father made excuses for her: the smell was too strong, the works were no place for a lady, she was not well enough to stand about or tramp from place to place. James pitied her for missing a treat and was dumbfounded when he learned that she hated the place. She was large and placid, completely devoted to her husband and the one child of their middle-aged marriage, but she would have no contact with the business. James discovered by degrees that she was a very innocent snob and amused herself by believing that the Hyde family was once great and had tragically fallen in the social scale. "My husband's ill-starred forbears," she would say, and glance sadly at purchased engravings of the saturnine faces of Laurence Hyde, Charles II's Rochester, and of the prim lawyer whose daughter was the wife of a Stuart and the mother of two queens of England. Tom Hyde laughed at her without unkindness and even allowed her to christen their son James Clarendon. " 'What's in a name?' " he quoted, feeling quite cultured for once. "She could have called you Shakespeare Tudor if she wanted to. I fear I am a sore trial to your mother. Women cherish these pretty ideas, boy, but men have no time to waste on them."

"Isn't it true, then?" said James timidly.

"True? Lord, no. My grandfather was a journeyman harness maker who married the tanner's daughter, wise man. My father always said the name of Hyde was a nickname because he dealt in 'em, I don't know. Nor care. It's a good name now, with a sound reputation for fair dealing, that's all I trouble about."

James left school and went into the business with a good deal of young enthusiasm. He had ideas about advertising; he invented slogans, "Hyde for Leather," "Say Leather, Say Hyde," and was immensely proud when they were printed on the billheads. There was a harness-making shop attached to the tannery; when harness declined in fashion and orders fell off, James persuaded his father to start a factory for fancy leatherwork: handbags, belts, wallets, and so forth. This succeeded, and another factory was opened to make luggage. James discovered a strain of his mother's romance developing in him at the sight of long shelves full of kit bags, Gladstone bags, cabin trunks, suitcases, and fitted dressing cases, ready to be taken down and go all over the world on errands of peace and war. War Office contracts for Sam Browne belts and leather equipment. . . . Sometimes luggage would come back to be repaired, plastered over with colorful labels from marvelous hotels beside dazzling blue seas.

James grew fidgety. Surely the world was full of marvels, and the years went by without his seeing any of them or going anywhere. One could not count the decorous annual fortnight spent at Eastbourne with an aging mother increasingly dependent upon him and still depreciatory of the noisome tannery. "I always wished you to enter one of the learned professions, my dear. A lawyer, perhaps; it is in your blood, you know."

"It may be in my blood, Mother," laughed James, "but I'm sure it isn't in my head. You want brains to be a lawyer."

"That may be. But I didn't want you to spend your whole life being a tanner. Now, suppose you were to stand for Parliament—"

James Hyde was beginning to think that he, too, disliked the idea of a whole life as a tanner. But old Tom Hyde, who had been forty-seven when his son was born, now leaned heavily upon him. As the old man's physical strength abated his strong will increased. James was trusted and beloved but also kept under and made to work, work, and keep on working. Since he was a key man in an important industry, even two world wars failed to open the doors of his prison. It was still a private business; no nonsense about a Limited Company for old Hyde, with annual meetings of shareholders telling him how to conduct his affairs, no. Never. It was much easier to keep a tight hand over the business himself and tell James what he ought to do, even after the old man became too infirm to go down to the office every day.

James's mother died in her sleep one night early in 1940, before the air raids became severe, before she had time even to miss the annual visit to an Eastbourne spoilt by barbed wire and mysterious <u>defense</u> works. She died, and James was still a tanner. He was getting very tired of it, but there in the background old Hyde remained, like a rock half submerged by the rising tide of years, but still hard and obstinate. "James, bring the order books home tonight, we must go through them. James, show me that contract before you sign it. James, have you answered that letter from Harrods? James—"

And James controlled himself till he thought he would never be able to relax even if the chance came. "Yes, Father, I'll see to it." He wondered sometimes whether his mother's spoof genealogies and borrowed heraldry were to her a means of escape from the same bondage in which he served; he wished he could believe in them also. If he had some other interest he might sometimes be free; music, photography, football pools, even wine, women, and song, but he cared for none of them. "Soon," he thought, "I shall be too old to learn to care," and panic seized him. "For all prisoners and captives—"

Tom Hyde, tough as the leather he made, was ninety-eight when he died; it was some weeks before James even began to stretch his stiff mind and think that now he could please himself. What finally awoke him to startled life was an interview with the family solicitor.

"I asked you to come and see me, James, to go through your father's estate with me and perhaps discuss what you would like to do about it."

"Do?" said James. "I don't know that it will be necessary to do anything particular, will it? Things can go on as they have always done, can't they?"

"They can, of course," said the lawyer with a laugh, "if you want them to. You mean to go on working the business yourself, do you?"

James nearly said, "Yes, of course," and just stopped himself in time. It seemed almost as though he heard rusty bolts being pulled back and a key rattling in a disused lock, and his first emotion was more terror than relief. "I— what had you in mind?"

"I suppose you know the extent of your father's estate?"

"No," said James, and his heart began to thump.

"You don't? Well, I am surprised. However, I have prepared a brief statement here which gives the outline in round figures, subject to correction in detail. After sundry legacies to old employees and men who have been in his service for a specified number of years—very generous legacies, too—the capital sum remaining, excluding the estimated value of the business, after payment of death duties, is in the neighborhood of half a million."

"Good heavens," gasped James.

"Say, fifteen thousand a year before, of course, payment of income tax and supertax."

"Good gracious!"

"Added to which is the annual income from the business."

"Great Scott!"

"You seem surprised," said the lawyer blandly. "Surely you must have known that the business was making profits at a far greater rate than could be absorbed by the very modest style in which you lived?"

"I suppose you think I'm a fool," said James humbly. "The fact is that until quite recently I did not handle the financial side, not as a whole, I mean. And being a private business, the accounts were never made public. Father employed an accountant who reported to him, and it wasn't my business—I mean, I didn't deal with it—I mean, if I'd asked, no doubt—"

"I know what you mean. I haven't had dealings with your father for upwards of forty years without learning what he was like. Let it go at that, he was an honest and good man, and it was, as you say, his business. I must confess, I was curious to see whether you would want to go on attending the office every day for the rest of your life, or whether you would—er—wish to make changes."

"I think," said James, rising to his feet and pushing his chair back, "I think I'll start by going for a walk. I feel I'd like some fresh air. No aspersions on your office ventilation!"

"My dear James, do you good."

"I'll go along the Fosseway to Sparkbrook, and round by Minchfield, and pick up the bus at The Jolly Sailor. By that time—"

"My dear James, I've known you since you were a schoolboy, so please don't take offense if I say something—"

"Of course not. What is it?"

"Walks are so much more fun, James, if you don't know exactly where you're going."

"Are they? I must try. Spontaneity is what you recommend, is it?"

James Hyde opened the office door and walked out into the sunshine, increasingly conscious, as he walked, of other doors which had opened wide for the first time in his life. He was free, he could sell the business, he could travel if he wanted to—he could live somewhere else, buy a house, run a car not merely for business, go where he liked—anywhere, so long as it didn't smell of a tannery. . . .

He sold the business and was startled by the price he received. Then he sold the house where he had lived ever since he was born. He had certain qualms over this; it was the home of his lifetime and he was attached to it if only from habit, for it was very ugly. But an inward voice warned him that he would never be free while he sat in the same rooms on the same chairs, and slept in the same bed. He looked for the first time with observant attention at the furniture and saw that it was bad; bought by the suite in the worst period of Victoria. He sold that, too, keeping only a few pieces which he cherished, and the portraits of Edward and Laurence Hyde, Earls of Clarendon and Rochester respectively. Not because he wished to claim relationship, but simply because they reminded him of his mother.

Then he went to London, walked into a house agent's office in Kensington High Street, and announced that he wished to buy a house.

"Er—in any particular district, sir?"

James had no very definite prejudices about the district except that it should be of a residential, not business, character. The house agent looked at the kindly, anxious face, the undistinguished figure, the sedate clothes, and said to himself, "Made his pile in the war, E.P.T. or no, and just retired. Wants a complete change." He offered James a photograph of a reinforced concrete house at

Sunningdale, with a flat roof, flat sides, and flat steel windows. Hyde looked at it without enthusiasm.

"Compact," said the house agent. "Easily run. Every modern convenience, central heating, hot and cold in all—"

"It looks like a golf-club house to me," said James, and dropped the photograph.

A gabled residence at Wembley. A castellated residence at Bushey. A tiled-fronted house at Wimbledon.

"I am so sorry," apologized James. "I suppose the trouble is that I have no very clear idea in my own mind of what I want."

"There is a house at Putney for sale, but it is furnished. It would be sold complete as it stands with everything in it, but perhaps you would not care—you have furniture already, perhaps?"

"No," said Hyde. "I shall have to buy furniture anyway."

He went to Putney and looked at the house, which stood back from the road with a short drive between laurels to the front door. It was built of brick and covered with stucco; it had a pillared porch and large sash windows symmetrically arranged. The furniture was excellent in quality if undistinguished in design; James was sure he would feel at home there. He bought it; the house agent introduced him to a firm which supplied him with a reliable staff of servants—money can do almost everything—and James moved in. He was happy for several weeks. Then it occurred to him suddenly one day that the reason why the house seemed homelike was because it was merely an improved edition of the old house where he was born, and the furniture looked friendly because it was the same sort of furniture he had always had. Plainer and better, but out of the same book. James could have cried.

His housekeeper gave him an inferiority complex, she was so very capable. She was the type who, desiring fresh employment, advertises for "a situation as housekeeper to single gentleman or widower," aware that a man is easier to manage than a woman, less knowledgeably critical about household matters or less courageous in expressing criticism. She managed James who, like the devils in Scripture, believed and trembled. She advised him about his clothes, she educated his taste in food, she chose his wines. Hyde began by being humbly grateful and became gradually exasperated.

He took to dining out at night to show his independence, trying one restaurant after another until he found one on the fringe of Soho where they grilled a steak as he liked it grilled, and the headwaiter recognized him the third time he came. It was not long before he had an accustomed table and the headwaiter would pay him a visit to see that all was well and to recommend what he thought Hyde would like.

"The Stilton, sir, is particularly good tonight. I should suggest it rather than the Gruyère; it is some time since I have seen such a fine Stilton. I think you would appreciate it. Nichols! The Stilton for Mr. Hyde. If you would excuse me, sir, there is a madeira upon which I should like your opinion. Not too sweet, no. Let me bring you a small glass as a sample. We have only just started upon this consignment, and I was very favorably impressed—"

When Hyde began to know the other habitués by sight and even to exchange shy and courteous greetings with them, the Café D'Artagnan seemed more like home than the stucco house at Putney with that female grenadier in possession. Besides, he had always loved the Three Musketeers.

There was one man in particular whose appearance always intrigued James because his face was definitely familiar, yet Hyde could not imagine where he had seen the man before. The stranger was bearded, and Hyde was sure he had never previously met him, yet there was this baffling familiarity in his face. The bearded man seemed to take the same guarded interest in Hyde; indeed, he was the first of James's fellow diners to wish him good evening in passing and remark that the day had been fine. Two nights later the Café D'Artagnan was unusually crowded—it was Boat-Race Night—and the bearded man sat at Hyde's table. They talked pleasantly; it emerged that his name was Selkirk, "not Alexander, but Hugh," and that he had traveled extensively.

"Have you been in England long?" asked Hyde, still wondering where he had seen the man before.

"No, only a couple of months. I've been abroad for nearly seven years and I thought I deserved a trip home. Not a trip, I think I'll stay here now. One can have enough even of the Argentine."

"I suppose so," said James, with a tinge of envy in his voice. "Must be rather wonderful out there, though. Marvelous climate, isn't it? Tropical vegetation, wonderful flowers, all that sort of thing?"

"Too hot," said Selkirk. "Yes, wonderful to look at, and mind you don't get fever. Flowers the size of cabbages and insects in proportion. Tropical languor and tropical tempers. I used to sit on my verandah watching the thermometer crawl through the nineties into the hundreds, and think of a nice east-wind haze creeping up the river to Westminster Bridge."

"Perhaps you'll change your mind when November really comes," said James.

"Then I can always push off somewhere else, can't I?" said Selkirk cheerfully. "Home to me is just the place where I hang up my hat."

"What a contrast," said Hyde impulsively. "Home to me has always been the place I couldn't get away from."

He found himself being encouraged to tell Selkirk all about his life, wondering at himself for doing so. "I can't think why I bore you with all this," he apologized.

"You must find it intensely dull. It is dull, and so am I."

But Selkirk did not agree with him. "You said yourself that there was a strong contrast between your life and mine. Surely contrasts make life interesting. Suppose one spent one's days leaping from one hazard to another—an endless chain of alternate frying pans and fires—that in itself would become boring after a time. I ought to know, I've tried it."

"I envy you," said James.

"And I you. A settled orderly life; to be able to make an appointment for next Thursday fortnight and to know, barring ordinary contingencies, that you'll be able to keep it; to start upon a course of study or take up a new hobby with a good hope of carrying it through, how wonderful."

Hyde laughed. "We ought to change places for a short time; it might cure you." He stopped, surprised at a sudden flush which rose to Selkirk's temples.

"Well, you suggested it," said Selkirk slowly.

"Then you could deal with my porcupine of a housekeeper."

"Is she so very prickly?"

"She's an excellent and capable woman, but I find her rather a trial. She wants to mold me," complained James, and Selkirk laughed outright.

"You think she'd have more difficulty with me, eh?"

Lights were tactfully lowered in other parts of the restaurant, and the two men became aware that they were the only guests left in the Café D'Artagnan.

"Our friends want to shut up and go to bed, I think," said Hyde. "I had no idea it was so late; I've never had an evening pass so pleasantly."

"I have enjoyed it too," said Selkirk, rising. "I suppose we must go, or Richards will be throwing us out. Eh, Richards?"

"I am delighted," said the headwaiter, "to find the gentlemen like this place enough to wish to sit here together when they want to talk. You know you are always welcome; it is only the law which insists that we close at this hour."

"Thank you, Richards," said Hyde. "Good night. Good night, Selkirk, we shall meet again soon, shan't we?"

"Oh yes," said Selkirk, "we'll meet again. I shall not be here tomorrow, but the night after, if you are here, we'll meet again."

CHAPTER TWO
My Man Adam

James Hyde walked out of the Café D'Artagnan that night with his head among the stars. This man Hugh Selkirk—how unlike anyone James had ever met. What a wonderful life, to walk freely and unfettered wherever adventure called, to—what was his phrase?—"to leap from one hazard to another, an endless chain of frying pans and fires." James paused at the corner of Shaftesbury Avenue and reflected upon life; it seemed to him as though he had never thought so vividly before. Men, he said to himself, were divided into those who made their lives into what they wished, and those who sat down and allowed their lives to mold them. It was a platitude, but Hyde had a tendency to platitudes and at least he thought them out for himself. Selkirk belonged to one division of mankind and himself to the other. The thought depressed him for a moment, then a reveler with a cardboard nose came and blew a cardboard trumpet in his ear and he cheered up again. Town seemed a very lively place tonight, with people cheering and singing; Hyde remembered suddenly that this was Boat-Race Night, the first postwar boat race, and all these young men who were capering about and assaulting the dignity of the Metropolitan Police were those who, a year earlier, converged upon death. Now death had been removed to his right place, a point so distant in age as to be beyond consideration; therefore, they climbed lampposts to address the singing crowd and one waltzed solemnly with an unwilling constable to the music of a friend with a saxophone. They also had escaped from compression in the mold of war and their lives were theirs to make. Hyde strolled on into Piccadilly Circus. Surely the lights were brighter than of old, the air fresher, and sensation more vivid. Was life like this all the time to a man like Selkirk?

Hyde stood still at the top of the Haymarket to consider this, and a young man circumnavigated him slowly and looked him in the face.

"Thinking about something?" he said.

"Why?" said Hyde, startled.

"Looked as though you were thinking 'bout something," said the young man gravely, and swayed on his feet.

"I've wasted my life," said Hyde confidentially.

"Well, don' waste it any more, then. Go an'—and do something," said the young man. With a wide gesture like a blessing he disappeared in the crowd.

By next morning the last influence of the last liqueur brandy had departed from Hyde and the world looked more natural and less Technicolor. The determination, however, remained with him. He would remove himself from the passive category to the active; he would—he blushed a little as he said it—he would, in future, be more like Selkirk. Adventures come to the adventurous. It was unfortunate that he had no idea where to begin, but in thirty-six hours he would be seeing Selkirk again.

That same evening Selkirk had a very private conference with his man Adam.

"Something drastic has got to be done at once, Adam. They nearly got me this evening. Giuseppe almost pushed me off the platform in front of a train at Charing Cross Underground. At least I think it was Giuseppe; I only caught a glimpse of him. A sailor hauled me back. Don't look so white, they haven't got me yet. I must slip them for a few hours somehow."

"Yes," said Adam, "yes. But they watch every exit from here like cats watching a mousehole."

"I know. But if they saw another man come in and leave again, and the watchers reported that I was still here . . . I'll show you something tomorrow evening, Adam."

On Monday evening Hyde went to the D'Artagnan half expecting, after so much eager anticipation, to be disappointed. Selkirk might be prevented from coming; a busy man with many interests must have unexpected calls made upon him. Or he might think better of it and not come. James was inherently modest and could not imagine what pleasure Selkirk could possibly take in his company. He was early, too; it was not yet the appointed time. He would tell the headwaiter not to serve dinner at once; "I am expecting my friend Mr. Selkirk. He may be here tonight." No, not "my friend," that would be showing off. "I am hoping Mr. Selkirk may be able to join me." However, when he pushed open the swing door, there was Selkirk already sitting at Hyde's table deep in consultation with Richards over the wine list, and immediately a door seemed to open upon a wider world. It was always the same simile which arose in Hyde's mind: a door which opened and let him out.

"Ah, there you are," said Selkirk, "good. You're dining with me tonight, you know. Richards has a dry sherry he wants to try on us. Shall we let him?"

"I have a lot to learn in the matter of sherries," said James. "I fear I have left it rather late."

"Not too late at all. You are not a heavy smoker; you still have a palate. Very well, Richards, and the soup ten minutes later." Over the sherry and the dinner which followed Selkirk talked about wines in their own countries in a way that surprised James, to whom wine was just something that came out of a bottle. "The Spanish wines take some getting used to, but one acquires a taste for them. I remember when I was in Seville . . ." and so on.

"You know Spain well?" said James.

"I have spent a good deal of time there on different occasions. I had to go there on business—various kinds of business," added Selkirk with a smile. "There is a strong link between the Latin-American countries and Spain, as no doubt you know. Very helpful to the Axis powers under the Franco regime. One did one's best without, perhaps, much to show for it."

"Do you mean intelligence work?" said Hyde, dropping his voice.

"No. Oh no. Not stealing plans of the latest battleship or the military dispositions round Gibraltar. Not in my line at all. No, just being tiresome to the wrong side in a business way. Spain is a poor country, you know, and a man with money can do a lot."

"I don't think I quite follow," said James.

"Of course it's all over now, so it doesn't matter. Spain used to buy a lot of goods from South America, particularly the Argentine, not for themselves but to pass on to Germany. Hides and tallow, silver and mercury—all sorts of things. The Allies tried to keep the supplies down to what Spain needed for her own consumption, but it wasn't easy. Quite a lot more slipped through one way and another. Well, I had quite a lot of money invested in this and that, and sometimes firms found they couldn't pay for what they'd ordered. Their shares dropped suddenly—all that sort of thing. Very financially embarrassing. Then the Argentine people didn't like waiting for their money. Oh, it was rather fun."

"But didn't it ever occur to them that you were responsible for their difficulties?"

"Not as a rule. I didn't act in my own name, naturally. There was a little trouble once in Malaga," said Selkirk with a laugh. "There was a sort of board meeting in progress, and a man came in who had known me under another name in Valencia. Rather awkward."

"What happened?" asked James eagerly.

"Oh, the meeting broke up in disorder and I dropped out of the window and ran for it. Fortunately, it was dark. The sale of firearms is not restricted in Spain. However, I got away and went to see a one-eyed cobbler in a back street who, I was told, might help me."

"And did he?"

"After a certain amount of misunderstanding. First he tried to knife me because he thought I was pretending to be a Communist to oblige the Falangists. When I disabused him of that idea he tried to do it again because he thought I was a Royalist trying to restore the monarchy. I suppose I overdid it, but he had a suspicious mind. Ultimately he proved quite helpful and I left the neighborhood. You are forgetting to eat."

"I'm so interested," explained James. "Nothing like that ever happened to me. Probably it's just as well; I should just be paralyzed with terror and get shot or knifed at once."

"Oh, I was terrified all right," said Selkirk. "But—I hardly know how to describe it. There's an exhilaration in it. You can dive through the terror and come up on the other side; if you see what I mean. Like diving into a mountain pool and it's a lot colder even than you expected. Then you think, 'Now I've done it!' and something rises up in you to deal with the situation. I think you have to be frightened to call up that something. Do you understand?"

"Yes," said Hyde slowly. "I think I do. Tell me, when this moment comes, when you're past the terror, do you see all light brighter, all colors more clearly, taste wine more keenly— Am I talking nonsense?"

"Not at all," said Selkirk. "I wonder, living the life you have described, how you knew that?"

James shook his head. "I suppose," he said, "that it's all over now."

"You sound regretful," laughed Selkirk. "No, it isn't all over, and I don't believe it ever will be, if you mean that men will live peaceably together now the war's over and that there will be no more knives in the dark, and all that sort of thing. I must break myself of that phrase. I'm always saying 'all that sort of thing.' Sign of a slipshod mind."

"I suppose there'll always be murder," said James.

"I fear there'll always be greed, and that lets in the rest. There are quite enough 'bad men' in the Latin Americas alone to prevent the world from going to sleep for the next few hundred years."

"Do you have much trouble with them personally?"

"I have had. Perhaps, if I go back to Argentina, I may have trouble again, one never knows." Selkirk's jaw came forward. "If they want some more, they can have it."

"You look as though they would get it," said James, and Selkirk laughed.

"Did I look so ferocious? Actually, there is a group of men out there whom I particularly dislike. I have been conducting a sort of guerrilla warfare with them for years." His voice became serious. "They killed my father, or at least they caused him to die. They kidnapped him for ransom." James made an exclamation and Selkirk smiled at him. "These things happen sometimes, you know, and this was some years ago. They did not deliberately ill-treat him, but they rushed him about from place to place. He lived rough and was cold and continually anxious and overtired. He was an old man and delicate—a diabetic—he could not get his insulin. By the time I got into contact with them and released him, the damage was done. He died three weeks later."

"Did you have to pay the ransom?"

"Oh yes, I paid it. They have regretted it since then." Selkirk looked down at the coffee he was mechanically stirring and there was silence for a few moments.

"What you must think of me," he added abruptly, "I really don't know. I entertain you to dinner and then talk about nothing but my own affairs. It is unpardonable; I hope you will forgive me."

"Please—" began James.

"It is largely your own fault, you know. You egged me on, you know you did. Let's talk about something else, or would you rather go to a show? It is not yet too late. . . . No? Well, let's stay here, then, or—I tell you what we'll do: would you care to come round to my place? We shall not then be acting like the dog in the manger with a table for which others are waiting. Richards! Could I have my bill?"

James Hyde strolled down Shaftesbury Avenue again towards Oxford Circus: the cheering crowds of Saturday night were quiet and orderly tonight and the policemen's dignity unassailed, but he did not miss the uproar. He thought that for the rest of his life he would have a special affection for those few hundred yards of London; it was the place where he had first begun to live.

"We'll walk, I think," said Selkirk. "It's not far. Near the top of Regent Street and then we turn off. I like walking in London at night, don't you?"

"It's wonderful," said Hyde. "I suppose the lights aren't yet what they were before the war, but it's a brilliant show to me."

"Of course, you had years of blackout. I never saw it; I wasn't in England at all during the war."

"I wasn't in London; I was at Yeovil all the time. Very quiet and dull and dark. I didn't realize at the time how dull it was. I wonder now how I stood it."

"You were working hard," said Selkirk.

"I was," said James briefly. "Never mind, that's all over now. I've escaped."

"What are you going to do with yourself?"

Hyde hesitated, and then: "Look for adventure," escaped him before he could stop it. "I suppose you think that's silly," he said apologetically. "It is silly, but it's the truth."

"I don't—" began Selkirk, but Hyde swept on.

"I'm turned fifty and I've never done anything but work like blazes at a job I loathed. My father—he was a good man, but he had no vision. He didn't realize I hated it and I never told him. I don't suppose it would have made a hap'orth of difference if I had. I don't want to blame him, my own fault entirely. If I'd had more backbone—"

"Were you the only son? You were in a difficult position."

"He was forty-seven when I was born. He was getting old when I grew up— Oh, it's not worth discussing. As I said, it's all over now."

"And you want a spot of adventure before it's too late. I don't think it's 'silly' at all—your word, not mine—I think it's very enterprising. There's fire in you. Most men in your position heave a sigh of relief, join the local golf club, and settle down to grow roses and fat. I think we'll have to put you in the way of something exciting—mildly exciting. You don't want to be arrested for murder or involved in crime. We'll consult my man."

"Your man?"

"My man Adam. He valets me, cooks for me when necessary, and looks after me generally, but he's more than a servant, a lot more. He knows all my private affairs and does a good deal of my business, but he's no ordinary secretary. He goes everywhere with me and I've known him all my life. In fact, we grew up together. He's just Adam, and you'll like him. Here we are. My rooms are on the fourth floor, so we'll take the lift."

Selkirk's place proved to be a suite of rooms in a hotel such as Hyde had never imagined. Presumably there were individual rooms let separately for the benefit of comparative paupers, but most of the vast building was divided into suites of varying size, each as self-contained as a flat. Selkirk's consisted of a large sitting room, a couple of bedrooms, and a bathroom of remarkable complexity and magnificence. The rooms were furnished with great comfort and considerable taste; only a certain impersonal uniformity in the furniture whispered, "I am a hotel—I entertain strangers." Selkirk led the way in, and a thin dark man came forward to meet them.

"Oh, there you are, Adam. This is Mr. Hyde, and I expect he'd like a cherry brandy. I should. Any letters?"

"One, sir," said Adam, handed it on a salver, and left the room. Selkirk murmured an excuse, tore the letter open, and read it without apparent interest. He pushed it into his pocket.

"Sit down, Hyde, and have a cigar. You do smoke cigars, don't you? When Adam comes back— Oh, Adam, we want your advice."

"Yes, sir?"

"Mr. Hyde has had an extremely dull life. No fault of his; in fact, his motives do him credit. He has at last escaped and wants a complete change with, if possible, some excitement. Any suggestions?"

Adam poured out the brandy, handed it, and said thoughtfully, "There are possibilities, sir, in travel."

"Heaven knows there are. Hyde?"

"I am stupidly handicapped by not knowing any foreign language," said James. "I should tend, I'm afraid, to stick to the beaten track and wander round looking at antiquities with other tourists. Besides, I have made some enquiries of travel agents and I gather that facilities are still very limited."

"You're right, they are. What's more, you don't really want to go and look at the Parthenon or even the Pyramids. You want something different."

"I was not thinking so much of a conducted tour," said Adam. "What I had in mind was something more like shipping as a steward on a liner going foreign."

"But that's damned hard work, Adam."

"Yes, sir, it is. But it's cleaner than stoking."

James looked rather alarmed, and Selkirk said, "Too drastic, Adam. Think up something else."

Adam looked at Hyde with a respectful smile. "I have heard, sir, that an entirely new life is experienced by putting on one's oldest clothes, taking only half-a-crown with one, and joining the down-and-outs. Doss houses, handouts, and so on. Very informative."

"Fleas," said Selkirk, "and worse."

"That is so, sir. But it has the advantage that one can always break off and go home, which is not the case at sea."

James laughed. "I think a humble steward who went to the captain and said, 'Please, I'm tired of this and I want to go home,' might meet some sort of adventure, but I don't think I'd like it."

Adam smiled and Selkirk laughed outright. "I'm sure you're right," he said. "Not so much adventure as catastrophe, with a lot of new words thrown in."

"Reverting to Adam's suggestion of turning tramp," said James, "he called it an advantage that I could always break off and go home. I call that a weak point, that so long as I have ninepence I can always wire to Nairn for money and all will be well. Nairn's my lawyer, by the way. I want to get into some predicament where I have to extricate myself by my own wits. You see, I want to find out if I've got any wits of that kind."

"You want to try some piece of defiance, like Buchan's John Macnab," said Selkirk. "He went poaching, if you remember." He looked thoughtfully across the room at a mirror on the opposite wall.

"Yes, but I'm no sportsman."

"Could the idea not be adapted, sir, to town life?" suggested Adam deferentially. "A brick through a jeweler's window, some trifle snatched as a trophy, and an escape carefully planned beforehand over a route previously studied. It would involve several changes of identity—and clothes, of course—becoming a bricklayer in the kitchen of some unoccupied house and changing again in a tool shed on some allotments into the appearance of a postman or a bookmaker's tout. The risk would be real enough; the police would see to that. If the escape were successful, the small trophy could always be returned together with compensation for the broken window."

"Now, that's an idea," said Hyde slowly. "That's more the sort of thing I had dimly in mind. The bare idea makes my spine go cold." He sipped his cherry brandy. "I wonder whether, at the last moment, I should heave that brick or whether I should keep it under my coat and go quietly home. I should feel a worm for the rest of my life." His face clouded.

"I don't think you ought to plunge straight into anything quite so violent as that," said Selkirk. "It's a fine idea and I hand Adam several silver-mounted bouquets for it. But try something a little quieter first. Give yourself a little practice."

Hyde's expression brightened perceptibly. "Yes—what do you suggest?"

"See that mirror opposite? Well, look at us two, sitting side by side. Eh, Adam?"

"I noticed it, sir, the moment Mr. Hyde came in."

"You mean—" began James, staring at their reflections. "Tell me what you mean. I may be mistaken."

"We are noticeably alike, aren't we? Apart from my beard, and nobody here knows what I look like without it. Except Adam, of course."

"That accounts for it. The first time I saw you at the Café D'Artagnan I wondered where I'd seen you before. In my shaving mirror, of course; I never thought of that. What a very odd coincidence."

"Odd that we should meet. Not so odd, perhaps, that we should be alike. My grandmother's maiden name was Hyde, though I don't know anything about her except that she was a Londoner."

"Then perhaps we are distant cousins," said James, beaming with delight. Adam, seeing he was no longer wanted, left the room.

"I shouldn't wonder. We'll go into the matter one of these days and find out. Incidentally, that was what first attracted my attention to you, the likeness. But I had a suggestion to make. Suppose you take my place here for a few days and see if you can get away with it. Adam will help you."

"I—er, I— What about your beard?"

"It's coming off. I'm tired of it, anyway, so you'll be all right. Nobody here knows me well; we've only been here three weeks and I've been away part of that time. I go down to the restaurant for lunch and dinner when I am in at mealtimes; breakfast and tea are served up here. See if you can bamboozle the waiters."

James turned his honest eyes upon his friend. "Suppose I let you down. I might, you know. Say the wrong thing."

"My dear fellow! No harm done if you did; they would only think I had answered absentmindedly. Besides, I'll coach you up in my habits, and you'll have Adam. I think you'd find it rather fun, actually. And, as I said, good practice for something a little more adventurous."

"And what will you do in the meantime?"

"Go down to your house at Putney and impersonate you, of course."

"Great Scott, no," said the startled Hyde. "That won't work. You don't know my housekeeper; you wouldn't take her in for a moment. She's got an eye like a gimlet. She'd bolt you into the bathroom and send for the police—"

"Then you shall come and bail me out."

"She'll stick her head out of the window and scream, and all the neighbors will come running."

"Oh no, she won't. Look here, I bet you a hundred pounds to a fiver I'll spend three days and nights in your house and she'll never spot it isn't you. Now then!"

"But it's impossible," said James.

"Easy," said Selkirk. "Simple. Have you got any sticking plaster in your bathroom cupboard?"

"In the second left-hand drawer of my dressing table."

"Splendid, that'll save my buying any. Listen, does she sit up for you when you're going to be home late?"

"Oh no. She always goes to bed at about eleven, never later."

"Good. You come up to town tomorrow night and have dinner with me here. Then you'll stay here as Hugh Selkirk and I'll shave off my beard and go off to Putney as James Hyde. I let myself into the house with your latchkey and retire to bed. In the morning I decorate my face with sticking plaster, make up a lovely black eye, and explain that I've had a fall. My eye hurts me, so I don't face the light. What did I tell you? It's simple. Much easier than your job, actually."

"Our voices—"

"Oh, I can imitate your voice. Listen," said Selkirk, and dropped into Hyde's gentle, slightly husky tones. "I have had a slight accident, Mrs. Watson. Nothing to worry about at all; the damage is more apparent than real. I slipped on the escalator at Charing Cross; a drunken fellow pushed me. No, no need for the doctor; I received professional attention last night. At a chemist's, to be exact. I have a large number of small cuts and my face is stiff and bruised, but that's all. A providential escape, as you say, Mrs. Watson. I shall not go out—"

"Stop, stop," said James, helpless with laughter. "You will convince me it has really happened in another minute. I give in. You win. But look here, I can't imitate your voice nearly so well."

"Come up tomorrow night and we'll practice. You can wrap a silk handkerchief round your neck, explain you've got a sore throat, and just hiss at people. Well? Are you on?"

"Of course I'm on. I wouldn't miss it for anything."

"Of course you wouldn't. Come here tomorrow night and tell me all about your habits—where you hang your hat and do you whistle in your bath—and I'll tell you all about mine. Is it a bet?"

"It is," said Hyde, and they ceremonially shook hands.

After Hyde had left, Adam came into the room and looked enquiringly at Selkirk.

"That's all right, he'll do it. He's a good fellow, Adam, take care of him. Keep him away from them for twenty-four hours and then let them have a good view of him. They'll know it isn't me when they really see him, but it'll be too late then."

"Will you really go to his house?"

"Certainly. One of 'em might be following me just in case. I shall leave first thing in the morning, though. I shouldn't think the housekeeper would intrude on his breakfast, would you?"

"No. What was in that letter you had tonight?"

"Oh, the usual threats," said Selkirk carelessly. "Three days and nights, I told Hyde; I shall be able to put in a lot of useful work in that time. I think we'll start with Giuseppe. I'll write to Ramon and Pietro at the same time. I'll ring you up and tell you where to meet me."

"If you could get clear of them, even for a short time, we can make a start."

"Yes. It's only another twenty-four hours. I should think I ought to be able to keep alive for another twenty-four hours, wouldn't you, Adam?"

CHAPATER THREE
Wanted, Manuel Varsoni

A "Wanted" notice was distributed to all the police of Great Britain and Northern Ireland. It was headed by a rather blurred and indefinite photograph; it had never been a very good photograph to start with and had not been improved by having been radioed from New York. The New York police apologized for it but said it was the best they had been able to do under the handicap of a camera-shy subject who must not know his portrait was being taken. The description was really more helpful. It ran: "Manuel Varsoni, a South American, exact nationality uncertain, age 28–30, height about 5 feet 6 inches, weight about 122 pounds, dark complexion, black hair, black eyebrows, long black eyelashes, brown eyes. Ears small, simple convolute, lobeless, set flat on head, once pierced for earrings. Face narrow, forehead low, eyes near together, slight glide in left eye, nose long and thin, drooping tip, nostrils widespread. Mouth small, full lips, deep cleft upper lip, lower lip slightly protuberant, rounded chin with deep dimple in center. Thin neck. Slim active build. Arms long. Small hands and feet. Dressed when last seen in blue cloth suit, shirt narrow purple stripes, bow tie navy blue spotted white, light tan shoes. This man is the associate of criminals in America and is also wanted by the Argentine government on a charge of bank robbery with murder. Suspected of being concerned in kidnapping case in Mexico in 1943. Believed to have made his way to Britain and is said to have been seen in London. Probably armed."

The New York police added that, according to Buenos Aires, this man was a member of the Gatello gang, and it was more than probable that others of this gang had accompanied Varsoni to Britain. Photographs and descriptions of seven other members were accordingly attached hereto, though only Varsoni was known to have come to England. The actual leaders of the gang were Angelo Gatello and his brother Pietro.

Among those upon whom rested the duty of taking appropriate action in this matter was a plainclothes detective named Dodds attached to the Putney district. He spent the whole of a lovely April afternoon and most of the evening going round the district to visit licensed premises, garages, restaurants, people who let rooms, and others whose walk in life leads them into contact with strangers. To all of these he showed Manuel Varsoni's photograph and description, asking each of them in an earnest if stereotyped phrase to communicate immediately with Putney police station if anyone resembling this man were seen at any time. The replies he received ranged from tepid indifference—"O.K., officer. Good afternoon"—through impatience—"Lumme, haven't I got enough to do without— Oh, all right. I'll ring up, but I don't suppose he'll come 'ere. This is a respectable 'ouse, this is"—to morbid horror: "Oh Lor', what an 'orrible-lookin' dago! Done a murder, 'as 'e? Looks it too, don't 'e? If I sees anythink like that you bet I'll ring you up. Quick an' lively. Gosh, I 'opes 'e don't come 'ere; fair gives you the creeps, don't 'e?"

By ten-thirty at night Dodds was more sick of Manuel Varsoni than any galley slave of his oar, but it was all in the day's work. He finished his round and went home to supper and bed. Being a bachelor, he lodged with his married sister and her husband, who was a tailor by trade. Dodds walked wearily into the house and dropped into a chair.

"You look tired, Bill," said the tailor.

"I am," said Dodds briefly.

"You sit quiet while I bring your supper in," said his sister. "You'll feel better after. I was lucky today, got a few pair of kippers. Like some tea with them, wouldn't you? That's right, and we'll all have a cup."

Dodds revived after supper and merely remarked in quite a mild voice that he supposed anyone who was idiot enough to join the police deserved to spend his days walking round Putney on his flat feet looking for a man who wasn't there and never likely to be, instead of having a nice quiet job like tailoring at which a man could sit down all day and watch other people rushing about.

"You must be tired, Bill, to talk like that. You know you'd hate sitting still all day, really," said his sister. "Look, don't think any more about it tonight. Have a fag and a look at the paper and then pop off to bed."

"Good idea," said Dodds, sinking comfortably into an armchair. "If I take my feet off when I go to bed and leave them in a bath of cold water for the night they'll be just right by the morning. It's been warm today."

At the breakfast table next morning Dodds said he had only a few more calls to make and then that job would be done. "They won't take long. Besides, it's cooler this morning."

"Somebody wanted?" said the tailor, who had acquired some knowledge of police procedure. "Who is it this time?"

"Manuel Varsoni," said Dodds, handing him the notice, now a good deal worn at the folds. "Though I don't think he's likely to call on you, but one never knows."

The tailor put on his spectacles, looked at the photograph, and read the description carefully. Then he went back to the beginning and read it all over again.

"I saw this man last night," he remarked.

"What!" said Dodds, and spilt his tea. "Are you sure? When? Where?"

"After you'd gone to bed. I remembered I hadn't posted some bills I got out last night, so I just slipped round to the pillar box to catch the midnight collection. It was just before a quarter to twelve; I heard the quarter strike as I came in at the front door."

"Where was he?"

"Walking down Putney Hill towards the station. I was standing under the lamp at the corner—"

"Upper Richmond Road corner?"

"That was it. I thought I'd dropped one of the letters and I was counting them to make sure. This man came down the hill and passed me under the light. I noticed him first because his clothes were a foreign cut. You know, coat opening longer than ours—"

"See his face?"

"Plainly. I can't swear to his ears being pierced, but most of the rest I'd swear to."

Dodds knew his brother-in-law was an observant man and not imaginative.

"You're coming along to the police station," he said. "Now, at once. We want a statement from you."

"Just a minute while I put my boots on," said the tailor placidly.

"Fancy me walking miles all round Putney," said Dodds, "and there was the information waiting for me at home."

"Not waiting," said the tailor accurately. "I didn't see the man till after you'd gone to bed."

"You'd make a better policeman than I do," said Dodds affectionately. "Come on, old sleuth."

Two hours later Thomas Elphinstone Hambledon, in his Whitehall office, was also reading the notice headed "Wanted. Manuel Varsoni, a South American."

"Any persons," said Tommy when he had finished it, "having any information about this man kindly communicate with New Scotland Yard, telephone number Whitehall 1212, and ask for Chief-Inspector Bagshott, by whom they will be rewarded with blessings or otherwise pro rata to the value of what they have to say."

Bagshott heaved himself out of his chair and said, "Yes, quite. And now we hear that a man, answering to this description more or less, was seen near Putney Station just before midnight last night. So we are driving down there to look into the matter, and as we go perhaps you can tell me what is all this fuss about a perspiring dago in a striped shirt and why you are mixed up in it."

"Certainly," said Hambledon, picking up his hat. "We'll start now and I'll tell you all about it."

"Putney Police Station," said Bagshott to the police driver at the wheel of the Vauxhall. "After you, Hambledon. Now then?"

"You will remember," began Hambledon, "that during the later years of the Nazi regime in Germany—during most of 'em, in fact—the Nazi leaders took a lot of trouble to export quite large fortunes to neutral countries just in case. Particularly South American countries. Ribbentrop was one who did this; he had a really large sum salted down in an Argentine bank, hoping, of course, that if the war went against them he could slide out of the country unnoticed, connect up with his treasure, and live happily ever after. Well, of course things didn't work out quite like that; Germany was invaded and surrounded, and Ribbentrop didn't get away. He had, however, some trusted German friends in the Argentine. He sent them a power of attorney, or some foreign equivalent, to hold these funds for him. If he could lie hid till the hunt died down he might be able to get to South America somehow even if it took him a couple of years.

"When Germany finally capitulated, Rib's friends in the Argentine toddled round to the bank with their legal authorization and demanded the boodle, but they left it just too late. Argentina came down on the winning side of the fence at the very last moment and froze all German credits, so the bank very rightly refused to part. Rib's friends went sorrowfully away. In the meantime, you remember that Ribbentrop was about the last of the Nazi leaders to be gathered in, and all the time that we were wondering where he was his friends in the Argentine kept on pestering the bank manager.

"When Ribbentrop was finally captured, they changed their tune but not the words. They produced a deed, under which they were trustees for Rib's heirs and assignees, and now might they have the money, please? But still the manager said no, and the argument went on for months."

"The Argentine government," said Bagshott, "probably thought that they had as much use for the money as anybody else."

"No doubt, but they didn't get it. The bank was broken into one dark night in January of this year, the caretaker had his throat cut, and the boodle disappeared. This is where our friend Manuel Varsoni comes into the story; the Argentine authorities say that he was one of the gang who did the job. The Gatello gang. I don't know what evidence the police have, but I'll take their word for it."

"Is this where you come in too?"

"Yes. You see, Rib's German friends howled to high heaven over having been robbed of their goods in the bank's custody, and certainly whatever else Manuel Varsoni is he's definitely not a German. On the other hand—"

"The Germans may have hired him to do the job and their howls may be camouflage," suggested Bagshott.

"Exactly. Or the Gatello troupe may have acted on their own initiative for their own advantage. Or even have been, as you say, hired by the Germans and double-crossed them. I don't know, do I?"

"Nor where the money is?" asked Bagshott.

"No. It may be safely in the hands of the Germans in the Argentine, in which case the howls will soon die down and cease. But, Bagshott, if that is so, why did Varsoni bolt to New York and from there to London? Who's chasing him? Or is he chasing somebody else, and what for? And is he alone or are the rest of the gang with him?"

"You want a little chat with Varsoni, don't you?"

"I do," said Hambledon. "If there's several hundred thousand pounds of German money heading towards London I want to know all about it. Germany may be beaten, but all Nazis are not yet dead. Unfortunately. Some of them may be chasing Varsoni. Well, here we are at Putney Police Station, and what shall the harvest be?"

The desk sergeant received them with respectful regrets that the superintendent had been called out: a man had been found dead in the garden of a house near by. The superintendent would not be long and begged them to wait for a short time. In the interim, the man who had seen the alleged Varsoni was in the station if they wished to see him.

"Please," said Bagshott.

The tailor came in and told his story.

"You saw this man quite plainly, did you?" asked Hambledon.

"Yes, sir, quite. There is a lamp there, and the light is good."

"What attracted your attention to him in the first place?"

"His suit, sir, it was a foreign cut. I am a tailor and I notice these things.

Besides, we don't have many foreigners of that type in Putney; it's not like Soho."

"No, quite. When you saw the description in the morning, there was no doubt in your mind that it was the same man?"

"No reasonable doubt, sir. I have always been interested in observing people, and perhaps having a detective for a brother-in-law has made me more so," added the tailor with a smile.

"It's a thousand pities you didn't see the description overnight," said Hambledon thoughtfully. "Still, we can't have everything. Rather a coincidence that he should have been seen by a relative of a detective who was looking for him."

"Not at all," said Bagshott firmly. "Look at all the thousands of people he must have met who weren't relatives of detectives. He must meet one sometime. Or some man who has been instructed to look out for him; that's how we catch 'em. When we do. You say he went on towards the station?"

"In that direction, sir. I soon lost sight of him. Besides, I put my letters in the box and went home."

"The man was alone, was he?"

"Oh yes, sir. Definitely."

"Well, I think that's all, thank you very much. Unless there's any other question you want to ask, Hambledon?"

"Only this," said Tommy. "Did this man—Varsoni or not—seem in any doubt as to his way? Did he hesitate at corners, for example, or look at the street names?"

"No, sir. Not while I was watching him."

"I see. Well, I think that's all. We are very much obliged to you, you know. If only more people were as observant as you, criminals would have a much thinner time than they do at present."

"Thank you, sir," said the tailor. "But what you call observant the neighbors might call nosy. Leads to unpleasantness sometimes, if one isn't careful."

He went out, and Hambledon said, "He's right, you know. What a nightmare life would be if all one's neighbors were really observant. Come, oh Night, and cover me with darkness—"

"Why not just pull down the blind?" said the practical Bagshott. "When you asked whether Varsoni knew his way—"

"Varsoni hasn't been in England long. I was wondering whether a knowledge of Putney was likely to be among his assets."

"Suggesting that this isn't our man. But he was presumably only going back the way he came, and nobody seems to have seen him arrive. Anybody who finds himself on Putney Hill and can't find the railway station must be a dope."

"Have it your own way," said Hambledon. "I wonder how much longer the superintendent will be. Why are we waiting for him, except out of politeness? I imagine we've got all there was to get from our friend the tailor."

"I'd just like to ask him," said Bagshott, "if anything is known of any dago having been seen about here. If it was before the 'Wanted' notice came through it wouldn't have seemed important."

The superintendent came in, apologizing for keeping them waiting. "People do choose such inconvenient moments for shooting themselves."

"Suicide, was it?"

"It looks like it at present," said the superintendent cautiously.

Bagshott abandoned the suicide for the moment and put his question to the superintendent.

"I don't think he's been seen here before," he answered. "That description has been posted here for two days now, and my constables would have reported before this."

"Of course," said Bagshott quickly, for there was a faint suggestion of rising hackles about the superintendent, and Hambledon hastened to change the subject.

"Not many suicides about just now, are there?" he remarked. "Not what you'd call a suicide season with the war victoriously over, the boys coming home, summer due at any moment, and an increase announced in the meat ration. Why did your poor parishioner shoot himself, or don't you know yet?"

"I haven't the faintest idea," said the superintendent. "He was a retired businessman who'd bought himself quite a nice house here about a year ago—not so long as that. He was very well off, apparently, and always seemed quite happy. I knew him slightly; he came in here with a stray dog he'd found, wanted to keep it, only the owner turned up. Quiet inoffensive sort of chap, I rather liked him."

"Perhaps he was bored," suggested Hambledon. "What was his name?"

"Hyde," said the superintendent. "James Hyde. A retired leather merchant. He just turned into his drive entrance and shot himself at eleven-thirty last night."

"What?" said Bagshott. "Before going into the house? That's very odd."

"I agree with you," said the superintendent. "Very unusual."

"Why?" said Hambledon. "I don't understand. Is there any etiquette about going indoors first, or is it just one of those quaint national customs that's made us what we are, whatever that is?"

"People don't kill themselves before going indoors," said Bagshott. "They either do it indoors or come out again to do it."

"Out of consideration for the carpet, I understand that bit," said Hambledon. "But why go indoors first?"

"Because there are always last things they want to do. Write a letter, or burn other letters, or telephone to somebody, or make a will—"

"Or wind up the clocks and put the cat out," said Hambledon, who had long ceased to be impressed by sudden death. "Any idea when he did it?"

"We know the exact moment. A man was coming along the road and heard the shot fired. The sound came from Hyde's drive; our witness turned in to see who was firing a revolver in a quiet street and found Hyde lying on his face— or what was left of it—still twitching slightly. There is no possible doubt that it had just happened. That was at about eleven-thirty, as I said."

"Nobody else about?"

"No one. The witness saw a light spring up in a window over the porch and shouted for help. The maid—it was one of the maids' rooms—asked what was the matter and said she would call the housekeeper. Then the housekeeper came out accompanied by the cook, both carrying electric torches, and said the dead man was their master. They rang us up at once, and we went up and took over. I've just been up there again now, taking statements. There's no doubt it could have been suicide."

"But you're not quite satisfied," said Hambledon.

"We have to assume it may have been murder and prove whether it was or not, as no doubt you know," said the superintendent. "In this case I certainly should."

"Where was the weapon?" asked Bagshott.

"Lying beside him, where you'd expect to find it. Queer-looking gun," added the superintendent. "I've never seen one quite like it. Here it is," he said, taking it out of a drawer and offering it to Hambledon. "It's been dusted for finger-prints."

"Any luck?" asked Bagshott.

"No. Only smears."

"I have seen a revolver like this before," said Hambledon. "They are made in Spain."

"I didn't know they made revolvers in Spain," said Bagshott.

"They make a few. Vendettas, local, for the liquidation of, mainly, but they do export some to South America."

"South America," said Bagshott and the superintendent in exact duet.

"Those who jump to conclusions sometimes land in the mud," said Tommy Hambledon. "I've done it so often myself that I've come to expect it. All the same, we'll bear it in mind. Did Mr. Hyde have a license for a revolver?"

"No," said the superintendent.

"Or was he known to own one?"

"No. His housekeeper said she'd never seen it before and that if he had owned it she would probably have seen it. That's one of the points which—"

"She's one of that sort, is she? I think the next thing to do, Bagshott, is to ask New York if they know anything about the gun Varsoni was alleged to carry about. What's the number on this? CEF*472776. I'll let you know, superintendent, as soon as I hear from New York."

"Thank you," said the superintendent. "In the meantime, I'll try to find out whether poor Hyde had any connection with South America. He was a leather merchant; he may well have bought skins from the Argentine. He may even have been out there at some time."

"Quite likely," said Tommy. "Some dark drama of jealousy and passion may have flowered beneath the scented southern stars. Romance. Guitars. Stilettos. Some black-eyed señorita sobs out her hopeless despair behind the whitewashed walls of the quiet convent beneath the lumba-lumba trees, while far away across the ocean—"

"Does he often talk like this?" asked the superintendent.

"Unfortunately, yes," said Bagshott. "But usually when things are getting nasty."

The superintendent raised his eyebrows, and Tommy said, "I should be very glad if I really thought this was a nice clean Technicolor drama like that. I'm still afraid it isn't. Superintendent, I feel it in my bones that you will soon be seeing me again."

CHAPTER FOUR
Seven Broken Matches

Tommy Hambledon telephoned to New York about the revolver and received an immediate answer. The weapon was of Spanish make and its number was CEF*472776. The New York police had searched Varsoni's room and found this gun; they did not remove it as they had been told not to let him know his room had been entered. Varsoni alone was of little use; the Gatello gang with their three million dollars were the real points of interest, and they had not been located. If Varsoni were carefully watched he might lead the police to find the others. However, someone must have noticed something for all their care, because Varsoni became alarmed and sailed for England at once.

Tommy frowned when he heard this and said, "Are you sure?"

"Sure what?"

"That he sailed for England because your attentions frightened him."

"Well, no. The guy didn't confide in anyone just why he was crossing the ocean just then. Guys like this Varsoni just naturally tend to leave a city if a cop looks their way, but maybe we're flattering ourselves. Why d'you ask?"

"Just wondered. It would be a great help to us if we knew the real reason why Varsoni came to England. There's plenty of other countries in the world where a man like that would feel more at home than here."

"Sure, I get you. You think he had some special urge to visit your country and maybe it wasn't to see Shakespeare's birthplace. Well, I think myself he hasn't lost interest yet in that little wad of notes from down south. Maybe the share-out's planned to take place in London; don't ask me why, for I wouldn't know. All I know is, it hasn't opened up over here, and even the U.S.A. would notice if about three million dollars suddenly broke loose. Any news of the guy your end?"

"Well, yes. That gun of his was found beside a dead man in Putney last night. . . . Yes, Putney, part of London. And a man looking like Varsoni was seen in the district at about that time."

"Well, well. So Manuel's started acting tough already, has he? Well, listen, Mr. Hambledon. I know we asked for him, but don't let that cramp your style. We don't want him that bad, and if you want to hang him for murder, that's O.K. by us. Carry right on."

"Thank you," said Hambledon, laughing. "I'm much obliged to you. I'll let you know what happens, in due course."

He replaced the receiver and rang up Bagshott. "That was Manuel Varsoni's gun. I still want to know why he went down to Putney and shot a retired leather merchant. I'd like to look in the leather merchant's safe; it might contain three million dollars, though I don't suppose so. . . . Yes, three million. Dollars, not pounds. . . . No, I can't do mental arithmetic; wait a minute while I write it down. . . . . Six hundred thousand, plus—er—twenty into one and a half million, say about six hundred and seventy-five thousand pounds sterling. Ignoring shillings and pence. . . . No, it won't be in dollars, of course; it will be in bearer bonds and suchlike, and I understand there are a few diamond necklaces and other comparative trifles. Coming to Putney with me?"

The superintendent at Putney heard their news with interest.

"Looks very like murder now, doesn't it?"

"It does," said Hambledon. "Of course, he might have borrowed Manuel's gun just for a moment, walked into his drive and shot himself, and Manuel was so frightened by the bang that he ran away. But I shouldn't think so."

"I know he didn't," said the superintendent. "Run away, I mean. Our witness would have seen him."

"Yes. Do you think we might go and have a look at the place?"

"Certainly."

"I should like to see the body, too, if I may. Where is it? At the house?"

"No, in the mortuary here. Come this way."

The superintendent withdrew the sheet from the quiet body of the murdered man, and Hambledon, hat in hand, looked down at the marred face.

"You say that his servants recognized him?"

"Yes, without hesitation. Coloring, general appearance, clothes, items in pockets, even identity card in the back of his wallet. Gold watch and signet ring; all complete. Besides, there's a good deal of his face left."

"Yes. Keys in his pockets?"

"Yes, they're on the table there. Underclothes all marked J.C.H., handkerchief the same. Cards in his wallet, James C. Hyde, all correct."

Hambledon wandered back to the slab. "I should like to know what he looked like when he was alive. Perhaps there will be some photographs at the house."

Bagshott bent over the body. "Curious wound, this; it's not often there's so much disfiguration from a single revolver shot. You see, the bullet entered under the chin and must have flattened against the bones behind the nose. I never heard of anyone being shot from under the chin upwards before."

"There's the doctor's report," said the superintendent, looking elsewhere than at the dead man. "Given in correct medical language, but he means the same as what you said. What's more, it was a soft-nosed bullet he was shot with. I've got it and I can show it you if you like. It's gone all shapes."

Bagshott replaced the sheet and the three men went out. "Not a pretty sight," said Hambledon. "It's nice to think that we have a fairly good idea who did it."

"We have certain indications pointing towards somebody who probably knows something about it," corrected Bagshott. "There's a long way to go beyond that. Varsoni will have to tell us how his gun came to be there. It was left there to make the case look like suicide, of course. We don't know that Varsoni himself did the job."

"Varsoni may have some associates over here," said the superintendent.

"Several, I expect," said Hambledon. "Would it be convenient for me to go up to the house now, do you think? Right, we'll take the car up."

Five minutes later the superintendent said, "Next turning right. . . . This is Clifton Avenue, and Mr. Hyde's house is the one next beyond that lamppost on the left."

The houses on the left side of Clifton Avenue were solid Victorian buildings, not all exactly alike but of the same date. They stood back about thirty yards from the road and each had a drive up to the front door. Some had two entrances with IN upon one gate and OUT upon the other. Some, including James Hyde's, had only one gate and room to turn in front of the door. High walls guarded their front gardens from the road and divided house from house.

"Curious passion the Victorians had for privacy," said Hambledon. "Anyone would think they expected to be besieged."

"Stop outside, please," said Bagshott. "Now, if you'd tell us exactly what happened so far as your evidence goes, superintendent?"

"At about eleven-thirty last night, a Mr. Coleman, who lives at Evandale on the other side of the road, just there," said the superintendent, pointing, "came along the road on his way home from spending the evening with friends. He came up the way we came, from Putney Hill, and just before he reached this house he heard the report of a firearm. He says he knew it was a revolver and not an automatic; he served in the war. The sound appeared to come from this drive, so he looked in when he came level with the gate. By the light of this street lamp here he saw the legs of a man lying on the ground just at the bend of the drive."

"I see," said Hambledon. "If Hyde had been lying a yard or so further round the bend, Coleman wouldn't have seen him at all."

"That's right. Coleman hurried up the drive and found Hyde lying here," said the superintendent, leading the way to the spot. "He was lying on his face with his head towards the house, and had only just died. The gun on the ground was warm, for Coleman touched the barrel with the back of his finger. Furthermore, smoke still hung in the air at that spot. Coleman jumped to the conclusion that it was a case of suicide. He saw a light go on in the window of that room over the porch, and shouted for help. The window was pushed up and Margaret Baxter put her head out. She is the housemaid. Coleman called to her that there had been an accident and her master was hurt—"

"Coleman recognized him, then?"

"Yes. Knew him well by sight, not personally. Baxter said she would call somebody, and disappeared from the window. Coleman stayed by the body, watching lights go up in the house, until a few minutes later two middle-aged women came out, with coats over their night attire, and carrying electric torches. They were the housekeeper, Mrs. Watson, and the cook, Ellen Patch. They also identified the body, and Coleman sent them in to telephone for the police; he remained by the body till I arrived. I then—"

"Just a moment," said Bagshott. "During the time when Coleman was waiting here, did he see or hear anyone?"

"No, sir. I asked him that."

"Although during the two periods when he was alone—before the women came out and again while they were telephoning—it must have been pretty quiet here?"

"Very quiet. He says he noticed it. But Mr. Coleman is slightly deaf, though he will not admit it."

"I suppose," said Hambledon, "one can get past the house into the garden behind, or whatever there is at the back of the house?"

"No, sir, you can't. There is a greenhouse this side that reaches from the house right up to the party wall. The further side of the house there's a garage that does the same thing. You can't pass the house on either side."

"Garage locked up?"

"Yes, sir. Mr. Hyde had no car."

"Any door to the greenhouse this side?"

"Yes, sir, but kept locked. I examined it last night and it hasn't been opened for some time. Thick with cobwebs outside and a strand of ivy stuck down across it."

"Do they employ a gardener? . . . Then how does he get into the garden?"

"In at the tradesmen's entrance and through the kitchen."

"I see," said Bagshott. "Then, if Hyde was murdered, it follows that the murderer must have stayed in this front garden all the time that Coleman was here and afterwards while you were here with your police."

"Yes, sir," said the superintendent woodenly.

"Since I take it he could not have gone out of the gateway after the shot was fired without meeting Coleman."

"That is so, sir."

"Where did he hide, do you know?"

"Yes, sir, here," said the superintendent, leading the way. "I think he ran along the narrow grass verge here, which would account for Coleman's not hearing footsteps. Besides, he wore crepe rubber soles; here's the print of them where the earth is soft. He dodged in between the bushes and stood here. The ground is trodden down, and he seems to have amused himself by breaking up unused matches. Here are the pieces, look. Seven matches altogether."

"I expect he wanted to smoke," said Hambledon, "and of course he couldn't, so he played with matches."

"Returning to your report," said Bagshott to the superintendent, "you arrived here—"

"I ought to have said that when the housekeeper rang us up she said that Mr. Hyde had committed suicide. I asked by what means, and she said he had shot his head to pieces. Accordingly, before leaving the station, I gave instructions for the ambulance to come up and for the police doctor and official photographer to be summoned at once. Actually, the ambulance picked up the doctor on the way as they passed his house, and arrived here only about five minutes after I did."

"Smart work," said Bagshott approvingly.

"When I arrived here I found Mr. Hyde's body lying as I described. Mr. Coleman standing a few yards away, and the two women together by the front door. They had switched on the porch light and this garden was well illuminated. When they saw us arrive they went inside and shut the front door. I looked about but did not see anyone else. I asked Mr. Coleman what had happened; before he had finished his story the ambulance arrived."

"You were talking here—you did not move from this spot?" asked Bagshott.

"No, sir. Actually, we were standing just across the drive from the body. The doctor came up, looked at the body, and said he would make an examination at the mortuary in the morning. He then went home. I told the ambulance men to wait until the photographer had finished and then remove the body to the mortuary. They stood in the gateway while I finished interrogating Mr. Coleman, then the police photographer arrived. I told Mr. Coleman he could go home and directed the photographer as to the shots he was to take. While these were being taken I went to the front door and rang; it was opened by the housekeeper. I took a short statement from her and the cook. The housekeeper sleeps at the side of the house; she was in bed but not asleep when she heard the sound of the shot, but took it to be a car backfiring. There is a car belonging to the house opposite which frequently backfires when the owner puts it away at night, usually at about that time."

"Owner providing for an easy start in the morning, I expect," said Hambledon. "I do that myself. Please carry on."

"She took no notice until the housemaid called to her, when she in turn called the cook, told Baxter to go back to her room, and the two older women came downstairs together. Their evidence after that corroborated Coleman's; they added that after telephoning they returned to the front door, switched on the porch light, and waited till they saw the police arrive. Then they shut the door, went upstairs, and got dressed."

"Their evidence was not very helpful," said Bagshott.

"No, sir. I then told them that I would come in the morning and take more detailed statements from them but would not trouble them further that night. Mrs. Watson—the housekeeper—asked what would be done about the body, and I told her it would be taken to the mortuary. They went in and shut the door, and I—"

"Did they lock it?" put in Hambledon.

"Locked and bolted it," said the superintendent. "I heard it. By that time the photographer had finished; he went away and I told the ambulance men to remove the body to the mortuary, which they did. When they had driven off I called to the police driver who was with me and told him to come and help me search the garden. I should say that I did this purely as a routine matter, because at the time it did not occur to me that it was anything but suicide."

"The porch light was still on?" asked Bagshott.

"Yes, sir. It remained on all the time we were there. It is switched on from inside the house. My driver and I went first of all to the garage doors and tried them—"

"Just a moment. You only had the one man with you?"

"Yes, sir. The garage doors are over there in the far corner, masked by those shrubs. We passed the front of the house, examined the doors, and looked about at the far side of the garden there. We worked round between the bushes, and my driver found the place I showed you just now, where someone had been standing and breaking up matches. But there was nothing to tell us when he was there; it might have been earlier in the evening, perhaps someone waiting for one of the maids. It might even have been the night before—the weather has been fine lately—but not more than that because there were no cobwebs there. We worked back to the drive again, seeing and hearing no one, and then searched this side of the garden. We found no more traces, and the greenhouse door as I described it. We then returned to the station."

"It's quite clear," said Bagshott, "that the first time the entrance was left unguarded was when you and your driver walked across to the garage doors."

"That is so, sir. I should add that when I left I stationed a constable on the gate all night until I arrived to make a further examination this morning. He saw no one inside or leaving the premises during that time."

"So it's obvious," said Bagshott, "that the man in the bushes, who was the murderer if Hyde was murdered, waited till the first moment when the coast was clear and slipped out of the gateway."

"Walked quietly into Putney Hill and down towards the station," said Hambledon, "passing our friend the tailor, Dodds' brother-in-law, on the way. A cool hand, you know, very cool. He stands there within ten yards of you—less than that—listens to all you have to say without more signs of emotion than destroying a few matches, and strolls out at exactly the right moment. When the tailor sees him five minutes later he shows no sign of agitation or excitement. He has a nerve, Manuel Varsoni."

"If it was Varsoni," said Bagshott.

"A very small 'if,' I think," said Tommy. "By the way, you said that window in the middle is the housemaid's room, didn't you? I wonder whether she saw him go. If I was a young girl sternly told to stop in my bedroom while excitements were going on, I should switch off the light and look out of the window, wouldn't you? Was her light still on when you came, superintendent?"

"No, sir, it wasn't. Would you like to interview her? I didn't ask her about anything except her speaking to Coleman out of the window and going to call the housekeeper."

"Bagshott will talk to her," said Hambledon comfortably, "and I will listen."

They went into the house, and Mrs. Watson showed them into the dining room; "the table being useful for you when taking notes," she said. She seemed a little annoyed when they wanted to interview Margaret Baxter first, saying with an air more of hope than conviction that no doubt they knew their business. She left the room, and Margaret Baxter came in; a young girl of seventeen, at once excited and shy.

"Come and sit down, Margaret," said Bagshott. "We don't want to bother you more than we can help, but there's just one thing more. You have told the superintendent about how you heard the bang and switched the light on, then you heard Mr. Coleman shouting and spoke to him from the window, and then went and called up Mrs. Watson. What did you do after that?"

"Mrs. Watson told me to go back to bed, sir."

"And did you?"

"I went back to my room, sir, and didn't come out again till the morning, usual time."

"Mrs. Watson is pretty strict with you, is she?"

"She—she's all right, but you has to do what you're told."

"Yes, I expect you do. Well, did you go to bed?"

"I—well, not exactly to bed, sir."

"What did you do?"

"Please, sir, I switched off the light and looked out of the window."

"I thought you probably did. I expect I should have done the same in your place. Could you see what was going on?"

"Oh yes, sir. Especially after the porch light was put on, I could see everything lovely."

"Not very lovely, really, was it?"

"No, sir," said Margaret, abashed. "It was ever so dreadful, really. I only meant I could see lovely."

"Yes. Well now, think back and try to tell me everything you saw as it happened, from the time the porch light was switched on."

Margaret gave quite a good account of the proceedings, rather interrupted by "Oh no, before that I saw—" and "No, that didn't happen next. The next thing was—" However, she got it all in at last, up to the point where the ambulance drove away.

"Then there was only the detectives walking about looking—looking for clues, I s'pose. This gentleman"—indicating the superintendent—"was one of them, weren't you?"

"Quite right, he was," said Bagshott. "How many detectives did you see walking about?"

"Three," said Margaret, thinking carefully. "Yes, three. But this gentleman was there, he knows."

The superintendent sighed, and Bagshott said, "Yes, but this is what we call accumulating corroborative evidence, so I want your story as well as the superintendent's. How were the detectives dressed?"

"Two in uniform, this gentleman and the one with him, and the other in plain clothes."

"How was the last one dressed—can you describe his clothes?"

"Oh," said Margaret. "Oh, I don't know. Just d-dressed in ordinary clothes. He had a felt hat on, and a coat—and trousers, of course." Giggles overcame her.

"Well, we'll leave that for the moment. What did this man do?"

"Came out of the bushes opposite the front door and walked down the drive towards the gate. I didn't see him again; I suppose he went out. I s'pose he'd been looking for clues in the bushes."

"When did he come out of the bushes?"

"Just when the uniformed co—policemen, this gentleman and the other, went across to the garage."

"Thank you very much," said Bagshott. "I think that's all we want to know at the moment."

"Yes, sir," said Margaret, and scuttled out of the room.

"Well, now we know," said Hambledon.

"Yes, don't we?" said Bagshott. "The man in the bushes was very lucky, you know. I wonder what he'd have done if the superintendent had started his search nearer the hiding place."

"Stabbed him, probably," said Tommy cheerfully.

CHAPTER FIVE
That Fellow Race

"Now," said Tommy Hambledon, "what about this safe?"

"Perhaps he didn't have one," said Bagshott.

"I'll call the housekeeper," said the superintendent.

Mrs. Watson came in and Bagshott asked her to sit down.

"You have given the superintendent a very clear account of all you did last night," he said. "What I want from you now is a little information about Mr. Hyde, if you can help us. Had he any relatives, do you know?"

"He had a cousin, but they didn't have anything to do with each other. Mr. Hyde didn't like him."

"Oh, really? Do you know his name and where he lives?"

"Mr. Race, he lives at Chartham, near Canterbury. I don't know the name of the house."

"And he is the nearest relative, so far as you know?"

"Mr. Hyde told me that Mr. Race was his only living relative. It was about wills we were talking; Mr. Hyde said he'd have to make a will or else 'that fellow Race'—that's what he called him, 'that fellow Race'—would get the lot, and he didn't mean him to. So I said, 'Would that be a relation of yours, Mr. Hyde?' and he said, 'Yes, my cousin.' "

"These family quarrels," murmured Hambledon. Mrs. Watson smiled toothily at him.

"Mr. Race had been rude to Mr. Hyde's mother, or so I understand. Mr. Hyde thought the world of his mother, anyone could see that. It was something about those pictures," she said, and indicated two engravings on the wall. Hambledon got up to look at them.

"Edward Hyde, Earl of Clarendon, and Laurence Hyde, Earl of Rochester," he said. "Ancestors, I suppose."

Perhaps old Mrs. Hyde turned in her long sleep and smiled.

"I couldn't say, I'm sure," said the housekeeper.

"I think we're rather getting off the mark," said Bagshott. "Did Mr. Hyde make a will, do you know?"

"I couldn't say, I'm sure. Mr. Nairn would know."

"His solicitor?"

"Yes. Mr. Nairn, of Nairn, Smith & Nairn; 75 Rood Lane, E.C. 3, is the address."

"I'll get in touch with him," said Bagshott.

"His telephone number is in the list on the study table," said Mrs. Watson. "Mr. Hyde always said I was to ring up Mr. Nairn if he was taken ill or anything."

"Have you done so?" asked Bagshott.

"Yes, this morning after the superintendent left," said Mrs. Watson reluctantly.

"What did he say?"

"He said he would come here and see me about things."

"When?"

"As soon as he could," said the housekeeper, and instinctively glanced at the clock.

"Did he not mention any time?"

"I—" began Mrs. Watson. "I—er, I cannot see how it can possibly concern the police!"

"Madam, sudden death always concerns the police."

"But these are private matters."

"Nonsense," said Bagshott, losing patience. "We must see Mr. Hyde's solicitor, and it will be convenient to see him here. Did Mr. Hyde own a safe?"

"A safe? Yes."

"Thank you. Now, when is Mr. Nairn coming?"

"I'm not sure," she said sullenly.

"Very well. It doesn't matter, I will ring him up and ask him."

"Half-past five," said Mrs. Watson.

"Thank you. It is now half-past four. We will return in an hour's time and meet Mr. Nairn here. Good afternoon, madam."

Bagshott stalked out of the house, followed by Hambledon suppressing laughter and the superintendent suppressing yawns, for he was hungry. A sandwich and a cup of tea had served him as lunch.

"Just time for tea," said Bagshott.

"What was all that about?" asked Hambledon. "Anyone would think the lady had a guilty secret regarding poor Mr. Nairn. I call him 'poor' because if she is regarding him at all I think he's to be pitied."

"What do you think, superintendent?"

"Pickings," said the superintendent darkly. "Contents of the house, or something like that."

"By the way, Superintendent," said Hambledon, "before we part there was something I wanted to ask you. This morning, when you first told us about this case, you said, or so I gathered, that poor Hyde was just arriving home when he was shot. How did you know that?"

"Because I saw him myself," said the superintendent. "I passed the railway station on my way to the police station and saw him come out and turn towards Clifton Avenue. That was at ten forty-five."

"Anybody following him?" asked Hambledon in a voice so low as to be almost a whisper.

"I didn't look," said the superintendent in an exasperated voice. "I've been thinking about that all day. He came out of the station just as I reached it; I was walking faster than he was and overtook him. I just wished him good night and walked on. If there was anyone behind him he was behind me too. There was nothing to make me look back; if only I'd had second sight or whatever they call it—"

"Don't think about it," said Bagshott. "These things happen."

"Yes, sir," said the superintendent. "Will you wish me to be present when you interview Mr. Nairn?"

"I don't think so, thanks."

Hambledon and Bagshott returned to the Clifton Avenue house in time to follow a neat gentleman up the drive to the front door. Mr. Nairn rang the bell; before it was answered Bagshott had introduced himself and Hambledon. "We are enquiring into this distressing affair," he said. "We shall be more than grateful for your assistance."

The housekeeper in person opened the door and admitted them. Nairn led the way to a room next the front door.

"This was poor Hyde's study," he said, "though exactly what he used to study in it I don't know. Except perhaps the *Daily Telegraph's* crossword puzzles. Poor Hyde! Such a good inoffensive fellow, what could have driven him to suicide?"

Hambledon, who had quick ears, answered, "His housekeeper, perhaps. She listens at keyholes," and was rewarded by hearing a definite snort outside the door and the sound of rapid footsteps departing.

"Now that we are really alone," said Bagshott, "we have to tell you something which we fear may be a shock to you. There is good reason to suppose that Mr. Hyde's death was due, not to suicide, but murder."

There was a sudden silence into which Nairn's whisper of "Murder?" fell like an echo. He stared at them in horror, and the color faded from his face.

"The New York police," said Bagshott, "asked us to look out for a man named Varsoni, suspected of murder. He carried a revolver. Varsoni was seen in this vicinity at the time of the murder. It was his revolver which was found beside the body. We assume that it was dropped there to make the death look like suicide."

"But," said Nairn, "what possible connection could there be between my poor client and an American gangster? Was the body robbed?"

"Not to our knowledge," said Bagshott. "Money, a gold watch, and other small articles were still in the pockets. But in point of fact the murderer had no time for robbery," and he recounted Coleman's evidence. "That is why we wanted to see you at once, to establish a connection if possible."

"I refuse to believe," said Hambledon, "that any sensible gangster would murder a total stranger for what might happen to be in his pockets."

"No. No, I agree," said Nairn. "You want to know—what?"

"This man Varsoni is a South American, not a native of the United States. He is said to be implicated in a bank robbery in the Argentine. Hyde was a leather merchant; it is reasonable to suppose that he obtained skins from the Argentine—I am informed that the best pigskins come from there. Can you tell me whether Hyde ever went there?"

"He told me once," said Nairn, "that he'd never been outside England in his life. Not even as far afield as Scotland. He said he would like to travel one of these days but had no idea how to set about it."

Bagshott smiled at Hambledon and said, "So much for your South American moonlight."

"Mere moonshine, evidently," said Tommy. In reply to Nairn's puzzled look he explained: "A fanciful suggestion for a motive, that was all."

"I cannot associate our poor friend with anything like that," said Nairn with a smile.

"Did you know him well?" asked Bagshott. "And for how long?"

"Answering your second question first," said Nairn precisely, "I have only known him for about ten months. No, twelve. He was in business at Yeovil in Somerset, and came to London when he retired about a year ago. His family solicitor in Yeovil recommended me to him; he came to me for advice about buying this house, investing his money, and so forth. I did get to know him fairly well. He used also to consult me about all sorts of matters not usually regarded as legal business; such as how to join a club in London and which club I thought he would like, and the name and address of a good tailor. The last time I saw him—I had dinner with him a fortnight ago—he wanted me to advise him about wines. Apparently his housekeeper chose them for him, and he was not quite sure— Poor man! I liked him and was sorry for him. He seemed so inexperienced and defenseless. Curiously innocent for a middle-aged businessman. I think he must have been, as we say in my country, 'sair hadden doun' by his father. Nose to the grindstone. Annual fortnight's holiday at Eastbourne with his mother. Told what to do and made to do it. Yet he was by no means the simpleton I seem to suggest; I am sure duty bound him, not lack of initiative."

"The picture emerges," said Hambledon. "But it seems further than ever from Argentine desperadoes and revolvers in the night. You can't tell me whether he had any South American friends, or enemies, or both?"

"No," said Nairn. "I never heard him mention South America at all; you must go further back into his life for that."

"Unless there's anything in his safe," said Hambledon bluntly, and looked at it pointedly. The safe was a fair-sized modern one with a five-figure combination lock; it stood naked and unconcealed in an alcove by the fireplace. "Not the sort of safe I'd keep fatal secrets in, and it isn't even covered up, but one never knows."

"I have a note of the combination to open the safe," said Nairn, pulling out his wallet. "Hyde gave it to me in case of trouble."

"Ah," said Tommy. "We progress. Will you open it for us?"

"Certainly," said Nairn. "I conceive it to be my duty." He unlocked the safe and swung the door wide open.

Inside, there were three vertical divisions and two drawers below them. The divisions contained papers, neatly tied up and docketed. The deeds of the house. Share certificates representing Hyde's investments. A fat bundle of papers comprising Mrs. Hyde's enquiries into the Hyde pedigree. A copy of her will and of old Tom Hyde's also. James Hyde's bank passbook. An inventory of the contents of the house. Nairn took them out and ran hastily through them, saying that he had seen most of them before. "I ventured to urge him to send the deeds and certificates to the bank; this safe does not pretend to be fireproof. He said he would, 'one of these days.'"

"These share certificates," said Hambledon. "You know about all of them, do you? They are ordinary certificates, not bearer bonds or anything like that?"

"No," said Nairn, surprised. "I should never advise a client to hold bearer bonds, especially if I thought he would keep them in a place like this."

"These are all shares which you knew him to hold?" persisted Hambledon. "No recent addition to his securities?"

"I don't think so. I brought with me a list of his securities, in case any question arose. I will just run through these and check them if you will excuse me a moment."

Nairn settled down at the table; Hambledon lit a cigarette and strolled about the room; Bagshott looked out of the window. More high walls surrounding a garden which backed against the garden of another house in the next road. A lawn with three rose beds in it, one round and two half-moon-shaped; hybrid tea roses in the half-moon beds, red and white standard roses in the round one. Bedded-out plants in formal lines filling a narrow flower bed which ran right round under the walls. Very uninspired, thought Bagshott, who fancied himself as a garden planner. He began mentally to abolish the center beds and draw out a screen of herbaceous border from the right rather more than halfway across, with another coming from the left further down. Break up the square and give the effect of distance. Take the grass right up to the walls and grow climbing plants over them, clematis, wisteria, jasmine—"

"Nothing new here, gentlemen," said the lawyer. "He has not added to his investments since I last acted for him eight months ago."

Hambledon said, "What's in the drawers?"

There was an old-fashioned gold watch in the left drawer, together with a two-guinea coin of George III wrapped up in a piece of tissue paper. The right-hand drawer held a trinket box full of oddments of Victorian jewelry belonging to old Mrs. Hyde, a silver double-extension pencil out of order, and two hundred and fifty pounds in English pound notes.

Hambledon sighed; Nairn put everything neatly back in the safe and locked it up.

"No letters there," said Bagshott.

"There might be some in the writing-table drawers," said Nairn. Only one of these was locked, and the key to it was on Hyde's key ring, which the police had returned. The drawers contained writing paper and other stationery, a checkbook and a book of household accounts, a file of receipted bills and a few more waiting to be paid. One drawer contained nothing but steamship companies' booklets, programs, and "deck plans showing cabin accommodation."

"Anything about South America?" asked Hambledon, looking over Nairn's shoulder. "No, there wouldn't be, would there? Mediterranean and the Holy Land; Egypt, Algeria, and Tunis. The Isles of Greece, where burning Sappho, etc.—Italy, Spain, and the Balearic Isles. Scandinavia and the Northern capitals. Anyone would think that the Americas had not yet been discovered. Unless we can deduce something from the deliberate omission, like the curious incident of the dog in the nighttime. 'The dog did nothing in the nighttime.' ' "That was the curious incident," remarked Sherlock Holmes.' "

"I know what I should deduce from this list of places," said Nairn. "That though Hyde was acquiring a fancy for travel, he was a little nervous about going too far afield."

"Doesn't look as though he'd ever crossed the Atlantic, does it?" said Tommy. "Let alone the South Atlantic, on the long trail to Pernambuco. But he might have had some South American visitors. I suppose I'd better go to Yeovil and see if I can learn anything."

"I can give you an introduction to the family solicitor there," said Nairn.

"Thank you," said Hambledon, "I should be grateful."

"One last question," said Bagshott. "Did Hyde make a will, do you know?"

"He did not. He intended to do so, and gave me his instructions, upon which I prepared a draft only last week. I intended writing to him today about it. He wished to leave the bulk of his estate to charity, particularly animal charities, such as the Lost Dogs Home, the People's Dispensaries for Sick Animals, and the R.S.P.C.A. There were legacies to servants and humble friends here and at Yeovil. He designed for his cousin Mr. Race," continued Nairn, smiling gently, "a legacy of twenty-five pounds and a printed copy of a sermon by a Georgian divine on Filial Respect, or Family Life Made Blessed by Courtesie; the text, of course, is the Fifth Commandment. It is in one of these drawers here. Hyde found it in a secondhand bookshop and showed it to me with great delight; he said it would do Race good. I think the subject of Race was the only one upon which poor Hyde was ever spiteful."

"Whereas now Race comes in for the whole lot," said Hambledon, "if Hyde died intestate, doesn't he? A fairly good motive for murder, isn't it, Bagshott?"

"If he knew about it," said Bagshott.

"I don't think Race had the least idea that Hyde had not made a will," said Nairn. "He would not expect to benefit by Hyde's death; he knew he was disliked."

"How much did Hyde leave the housekeeper?"

"Two years' wages to any servant still in his employ. No special mention of housekeeper."

"I think that's all I want to know at present," said Bagshott. "What about you, Hambledon?"

"I am surfeited with emptiness," said Tommy solemnly. "I shall go to Yeovil tomorrow, I think."

Nairn rose and picked up his hat. "What about the inquest, Chief-Inspector?"

"Tomorrow, at two-thirty. Evidence of identity only, and adjourned for further enquiry. Could you attend? There's no knowing what jurors will ask."

Nairn nodded. "I'll be there. I must communicate with Race at once, he may wish to attend; also, it is for him to make arrangements about the funeral. I shall ask the solicitors at Yeovil if they know anything of a will of Hyde's, but it's a matter of form; he told me himself he had never made one. Well, you know where to find me if you want me, gentlemen. Poor Hyde! Good-bye. I must just have a word with Mrs. Watson and tell her how things stand. Good-bye."

"One moment," said Hambledon. "Are there any photographs of Hyde, do you know?"

"I never saw one," said Nairn. "I'll ask Mrs. Watson, she'll know." He went out of the room.

"No very obvious connection with the Argentine here, Hambledon," said Bagshott. "Nor with Ribbentrop's nest egg."

"No. There's Varsoni's gun; but there may be some other explanation of that, though I can't think of one. There's Hyde's leather business, but that may prove a dead end. Why did I ask for photographs of Hyde, do you know? I can't think what impelled me to do it."

"Mere idle curiosity, in my opinion."

The curiosity, idle or not, was not destined to be satisfied. Mrs. Watson came in with an album which she said contained the only photographs in the house. There was "James, aged 4 yrs., Sept. 1899," in a sailor suit, and "James, aged 9, 1904," in a jersey and knickers. James cropped up again here and there among school friends; with a background of tannery; with a spaniel dog; but none was later than "James, aged 21," when they ceased. James, aged twenty-one, was hopelessly faded; moreover, the subject appeared to have moved. Hambledon sighed and shut the book.

"I feel that it's mere obstinacy," he said, "which takes me to Yeovil, but I shan't be happy if I don't go."

He went there by an early train the following morning and interviewed the elderly solicitor who had introduced James Hyde to wealth and freedom. The lawyer said that certainly James Hyde had never been to South America or, indeed, abroad at all. He himself knew nothing about any South American connection, but old Tom Hyde never confided business matters to anyone. Martin might know, Jack Martin, the works manager under James Hyde. He retired when the business was sold but still lived in Yeovil; Hambledon could go and see him. Poor James Hyde, what a tragedy, poor James. "An imprisoned life, Mr. Hambledon, and so brief a freedom. We must hope that it will be made up to him."

Jack Martin said that of course the firm bought skins from the Argentine, particularly pigskins, but the Hydes had no dealings direct with the suppliers; they bought through an agency. No dagoes had ever come snooping round the Hyde works; old Mr. Hyde 'ud ha' sent them off in short order. He didn't like foreigners; in fact, he didn't like visitors at all unless he'd known them for years. The firms which they supplied used to send the same travelers down year after year; it was Martin's belief that some of them were hauled out of retirement twice a year for that one purpose. Old gray heads, they were. Poor Mr. James, that was hard luck, now. All that money and no luck. . . .

Hambledon made a few more enquiries but had no luck either; he returned to town by a late train and went home to bed. In the morning he rang up Bagshott.

"Complete failure," reported Hambledon. "No connection with S.A. at all. Drawn blank. You'll have to find Manuel Varsoni somehow; he's our only hope."

"I've found him," said Bagshott in a flat voice. "You'd better come round here, if you will."

"What's the matter? Won't he talk?"

"No. Not to us, anyway. He's dead."

"Oh, *caramba!*" said Hambledon.

CHAPTER SIX
The Stand-In

On the first night of James Hyde's great adventure he took some considerable time to drop off to sleep in Selkirk's extremely comfortable bed; he was excited, and bright pictures of the past evening paraded before his eyes. Adam cutting off Selkirk's beard, shaving him carefully, and rubbing into the skin a mysterious brown liquid out of a bottle to conceal the absence of sunburn on jaw and neck.

"What's that stuff?" asked Hyde. "Something special?"

"No. Just good old walnut juice. Nothing like it. Adam will make you up a bit in the morning to look as though you've just shaved."

Hyde and Selkirk changing clothes right down to the skin. "Not that all this elaboration is really necessary on this occasion," said Selkirk, "but we may as well do the job properly."

"It is necessary," said Hyde. "If Mrs. Watson saw American-pattern under-wear hanging over the back of a chair when she calls you tomorrow morning, she might wonder what I'd been up to."

"You've got the idea," said Selkirk approvingly. "Do you always hang your things over the back of a chair? Which chair, and do you fold them?"

"A ladder-back chair with a rush seat; there's only one like that. No, I don't fold them. I just throw them over in order as they come off."

"Shoes?"

"Outside the door, on the right."

And so on, throughout every customary action of the day. James lay awake trying to remember whether he had told Selkirk everything he ought to know. After all, there was always the post; he could write, provided he disguised his handwriting, or got Adam to address the envelope. His mind turned to his own doings on the morrow, but he was getting too sleepy to worry. Besides, there was always Adam ready to be consulted. This was going to be fun.

He was awakened in the morning by Adam with a cup of tea and the rattle of blinds pulled up to admit the sunshine.

"Eight o'clock, sir. Your bath will be ready in ten minutes. If you will be so good as to call me when you have finished, I will shave you, sir."

"Oh," said James, "but I always shave myself."

"It would, perhaps, be better if I did it this morning, sir. It is also necessary to produce the effect of a beard having been removed."

"Of course, of course. I'd forgotten that for the moment."

"After that, sir, if you will retain your dressing gown and enter the sitting room, I will ring for the coffee and rolls."

"I'd rather have tea and bacon and eggs, Adam."

"I regret, sir. We always have coffee and rolls. Sometimes we have grape fruit also, if obtainable. Shall I enquire, sir?"

James looked at himself in the glass when Adam had done with him. There was an unbecoming pallor round his jaw and chin.

"I look like an unevenly baked loaf, Adam."

"I trust you do not consider I have overdone it, sir. It seemed advisable to make the change quite noticeable. It can be toned down by degrees."

"You are perfectly right, Adam."

"Thank you, sir. I will ring for breakfast at once, if you will allow me. We are five minutes later than usual, already."

Hyde awaited the arrival of the breakfast with some nervousness; this was, so to speak, his first public appearance in his new part, but the waiter betrayed no interest in him beyond a momentary stare at his chin. James grunted, "Thank you—thank you," in a fair imitation of Selkirk's deeper tones, and the man left the room without a backward glance. A murmur of voices came from outside the door, and a moment later Adam entered.

"Did I do that all right?" asked Hyde anxiously.

"Perfectly, sir. The man remarked upon the loss of the beard, as was natural, sir. He will tell the other hotel servants. It will make things easier, sir."

Selkirk was not in the habit of entering into conversation with porters and commissionaires; they showed no surprise when Hyde barely spoke to them. He went out in the morning and enjoyed a sense of mischief such as he had not experienced since his school days. Once an attack of something like panic seized him; people were staring at him, he noticed it. Then he caught sight of his parti-colored face in a shop-window mirror and ceased to be alarmed. Any intelligent person would look twice at that. He returned to the hotel for lunch and simulated a tiresome cough and a troublesome throat to mask his voice. No one seemed even faintly interested in him beyond what was necessary to serve the meal with courtesy and attention. Hyde expanded his chest and stalked out of the restaurant with a careful imitation of Selkirk's longer stride.

Hyde habitually read the *Daily Telegraph;* Selkirk's paper was *The Times.* Unfamiliar with its arrangement of news, James missed completely a small paragraph about an unimportant suicide in Putney, and Adam did not point it out. If the servant was gray in the face, heavy-eyed, and even more formal in manner than usual, James did not know him well enough to notice the difference. The day passed without event, with Hyde gaining confidence every hour. Dinner, coffee perfectly served by Adam, and a peaceful evening among Selkirk's books rounded off a successful day.

"Will you take cherry brandy, sir, or would you prefer a benedictine?"

"Cherry brandy, thanks."

"Will you be wanting anything more tonight, sir?"

"Nothing, thanks."

"Good night, sir."

"Good night. Oh, Adam?"

"Sir?"

"Do you think I am managing to speak more like Mr. Selkirk?"

"Yes, sir. Very like. Good night, sir."

Adam shut the door rather less quietly than usual; he appeared to be in a hurry, thought Hyde. Perhaps he was going out for a time, why not? But when Hyde passed the servant's door ten minutes later, there was a light showing beneath it.

James retired to bed rather late for him, nearly midnight, with the idea that if he was thoroughly tired he might go to sleep at once. Again, however, his mind revolved upon the past day and planned for tomorrow. Selkirk, apparently, had managed to deceive Mrs. Watson since he had not returned. Tomorrow, Hyde must induce Adam to let him practice Selkirk's voice; give him a critical audition, as it were. The voice, Hyde felt, was his weak point.

There was a clock with chimes somewhere in the immediate neighborhood. It saluted the quarter past midnight, the half-hour, a quarter to one. When the full chimes sounded for one o'clock James lost patience. So tiresome to lie awake when he would be so much better asleep. He would find himself a not too interesting book and read for a time. He got up, slipped on a dressing gown, and walked quietly, in order not to disturb Adam, along the passage to the sitting room. The door was closed but not latched; he pushed it open and switched on the light.

The bottom half of the window had been pushed up, and the head and shoulders of a man appeared in the opening. He had both arms over the sill and was obviously in the act of climbing in. He was a black-haired man, dark-skinned, with dark brown eyes; as he stared at Hyde the eyes opened till the whites showed all round the iris. He did not speak, but his face turned a dreadful greenish-white, his hands relaxed their grip, his arms slithered across the sill, and with a crash of breaking glass he fell from sight. An unbearable moment later there was a heavy thud upon the concrete path below.

Hyde leaned against the doorpost, sickened and shaking; immediately, it seemed, Adam was there beside him with a hand under his arm, a different Adam in pajamas, with ruffled hair but somehow more alive and comforting, no longer aloof behind his mask of formality.

"What happened? Are you hurt?"

"No, no," said Hyde. "There was a man on the window sill, climbing in. I switched on the light—I wanted a book to read—he saw me, looked as though he was going to faint, and just fell of backwards. I heard him hit the ground—" Hyde shuddered violently.

"Come and sit down," said Adam, steering him to a chair. "You are shaken, and no wonder. I'll get you a little brandy." He went first to the window and leaned out; there were people looking out from windows all along the side of the hotel and from the block of flats only a few yards distant. Voices were heard asking questions; down below someone shouted and a distant voice answered.

"It's all right now," said Adam, "the police are there." He went away and returned with a glass in his hand. "Drink this and sit still for a few minutes." He waited until the color returned to Hyde's face. "Did you see him plainly? What was he like?"

Hyde described the man's face in considerable detail. "I can see it now," he said with a shiver. "Eyes near together and one of them squinted a bit. Hair growing low on his forehead, a long thin nose and a little round chin, a silly little chin, you might say." He paused, surprised at the look of savage delight on Adam's face.

"There's one of them," said Adam in a low tone as though to himself.

"One of who?" asked Hyde, and, getting no answer, repeated, "Who was he, Adam, do you know?"

Adam appeared to awaken suddenly to the fact that Hyde was still there, and reverted at once to the perfect manservant.

"A cat burglar, sir, without doubt. There have been a number of cat burglaries lately reported in the papers. If you are feeling restored, sir, it would be as well if you returned to bed, would it not?"

James sighed. It was as though he had been taken up like a piece in chess and set down again a great distance away. He felt old and tired, and vaguely hurt.

"Very well," he said, and rose from his chair. "I will do as you suggest."

"A very unpleasant experience, sir," said Adam in a more friendly voice. "If you will allow me, sir, I will go downstairs and make enquiries as to what has happened."

"Yes, do," said Hyde, getting back into bed. "Come back and tell me about it, Adam."

"Certainly, sir," said Adam, expertly tucking in the bedclothes. "I will be as quick as possible."

"Thank you," said James, and smiled at him.

Adam returned twenty minutes later and said that the man, who had died at once from his fall, was undoubtedly a cat burglar. It was supposed that he was after some emeralds which belonged to a widow lady resident in the hotel, "in the rooms exactly below ours, sir. It is to be supposed he mistook the window."

James warmed to that "ours" and said in a cheerful voice that he supposed the man had realized, on seeing him, that he had come to the wrong place, and the surprise had caused him to lose his balance. "Not much loss to the community, by the look of him."

"None at all, I should say, sir. Some sort of dago, by your description."

"I suppose I shall have to give evidence at the inquest," said James, and at that a horrid thought struck him. "Adam, I should have to declare on oath that my name is Hugh Selkirk. I can't do that!"

"No, sir. Certainly not. I think if you will leave it to me I can manage to avoid that. The police are coming round the hotel at once to interview everyone who may have evidence to give. If you would permit me to deal with them—"

"I wish you would," said James fervently.

"Very good, sir. I see no need to tell them that we saw him—that he came to this window at all. If he was after the emeralds, it was an accident that he came here and can have no evidential value. I will just say that we were aroused by the sound of breaking glass and looked out, like everyone else, to see what had happened."

"Yes," said Hyde. "I should think that would do very well. It's better than committing perjury in a court of law, anyway. By the way, what glass was it that broke?"

"The window below ours, sir. He kicked it in falling, I understand."

James made the noise usually written "Ugh!" and Adam advised him kindly to go to sleep and not worry about it. He himself would attend to the matter. Hyde thanked him and put out the light, not expecting to be able to sleep at all that night, but anxious to show himself willing to collaborate in any suggestion Adam might make. In point of fact he fell asleep almost immediately and did not wake until Adam called him in the morning.

"Eight o'clock, sir. Here is your tea."

"Oh—ah! Thank you— Gosh, that fellow last night! Do you know, I fell asleep at once and never heard another sound? Did the police come?"

"Yes, sir. I told them what we arranged that I should tell them, and they accepted the story without demur. After all, it is the same story as they will have heard from everyone else within earshot. I enquired, sir, whether the attendance of either or both of us at the inquest would be necessary, and they said it was very unlikely."

"That's a relief. Will they want to interview me, too, do you think?"

"I think not, sir. They asked if you were in the flat and I said yes, but that you had retired. I offered to call you, sir, if necessary, but they said there seemed no need to trouble you."

The inquest on the body of Manuel Varsoni took place in due course, and the emeralds of the lady on the third floor received all the credit for relieving society of an undesirable. New York, when informed about it, said that one way was as good as another for a guy like Varsoni, and everyone was satisfied except Hambledon, who said there was something wrong somewhere, and Bagshott, who agreed with him. The police who interviewed Adam and other tenants did not think it necessary to supply a complete list of people who had no evidence to offer, so the name of Selkirk did not arise.

Three or four days passed without any particular incident, and Hyde began to be a little bored. This was a wonderful life, but without Selkirk it was like a cocktail without gin. The three days and nights which he had wagered to spend in the Putney house were up, and Hyde was looking forward with pleasure to paying up the five pounds which he had lost. Still Selkirk did not return, and James began to feel vaguely uneasy.

"Oh, Adam?"

"Sir?"

"Have you any idea when Mr. Selkirk expected to come back?"

"He did not tell me, sir."

James wondered whether it was merely his fancy that Adam's voice sounded suddenly flat.

"I understood," said Hyde, "though he did not actually say so, that he would return here when his three days were up. You remember the bet."

"Yes, sir. Perfectly."

"It's rather odd, isn't it?"

Adam shifted his tray from one hand to the other.

"Not necessarily, sir. Mr. Selkirk's plans are sometimes rather uncertain."

"What do you think I ought to do? Go back to my own house?"

"I think—" began Adam with an unusual hesitation in his manner, and then cleared his throat and spoke more decidedly. "I am sure Mr. Selkirk would wish you to remain here, at least till you hear some news. Unless, sir, you have any reason for wishing to return home at once?"

"No. Oh no, I haven't. I was only thinking, I don't wish to inflict my presence upon—that's not the right phrase; I can't inflict my presence on him when he's not here, obviously. But—"

"I can assure you, sir," said Adam earnestly, "there is not the faintest reason to fear that."

"Thank you," said Hyde, and Adam left the room.

James settled back in his chair and thought it over. All this welcoming courtesy was quite delightful, but he was coming increasingly to believe that there was something behind it which was withheld from him. It was odd that Selkirk didn't return, whatever Adam might say; it was deuced odd. Hyde felt like a child staying in a house where something was happening about which it was not told. The child had a wonderful time and everyone was kindness itself, but something was happening, it was in the air. Besides, there was that business about the death of that man Varsoni. James had been shocked and confused at the time; when he came to think it over he was sure that Adam knew more about it than he would admit. "There's one of them," he had said, or "That's one of them," speaking like a man who doesn't realize he has spoken aloud. Then his interest in what the man looked like. What does it matter what a cat burglar looked like after he was dead, unless you thought you knew him?

"There is no earthly reason," said James, trying to clear his mind by putting his thoughts into words, "why Adam should confide in me. Why should he? If he's had cat burglars in his past, it's no business of mine. But the man was getting into this window, and one can't imagine a cat burglar climbing up one floor too many without noticing it. The first thing Adam said was, 'Are you hurt?' Why? Was he expecting Selkirk to be attacked?"

James got up and walked across to the window, which gave him only a view of the wall of the adjacent flats and a saucy-looking maid in a window opposite who gave him the glad eye. James frowned at her mechanically, on principle, and went on pacing the room.

"Selkirk has enemies; he said so. Was Varsoni one of them? If so, where are the others?"

After this, three things immediately became obvious: (a) that he must know more about this business in case these thugs pursued him by mistake, (b) that it was no good asking Adam; one might as well ask the lions in Trafalgar Square, and (c) that therefore the only person to ask was Selkirk.

Hyde paused to observe with astonishment that the thought of being pursued by thugs, even by mistake, didn't make his knees knock together as he would have expected. That slightly cold feeling amidships was almost pleasurable, but perhaps it would be different if the pursuit became intensified. "It's easy to be brave," said James contemptuously to himself, "in a room on the fourth floor of a large hotel in daylight with a manservant within call. You wait till you're alone in the dark, my boy."

There seemed only one way of even trying to get in touch with Selkirk, and that was to go down to Putney and ask for him. Hyde glanced down at his clothes, so different in cut from those he usually wore. It was a chilly day with a nasty east wind blowing dust round corners; a light overcoat would not look remarkable, and he could muffle his neck and chin with a handkerchief. One of Selkirk's hats, slightly wider in the brim than was usual in London, and a pair of dark glasses ought to do the trick, together with a different walk and the new voice he had been assiduously practicing. A passing idea of dressing as a brick-layer or a postman he abandoned at once as theatrical and overdone. Besides, it would take too much time and he wanted to start at once. Besides again, Mrs. Watson would never admit a bricklayer.

"I'll just go straight down to Putney," said James, "walk up to the house, ring the front doorbell, and ask for Mr. Hyde. If he's in, I'll give the name of Selkirk and be shown in. If he's not, there's no harm done. Or I could hang about on the chance of seeing him."

Hyde went to his bedroom and put on a coat, stuffed a silk handkerchief into the pocket, picked up his hat, and called to Adam that he was going out and probably would not be in to tea. Adam said, "Very good, sir," and opened the door for him.

James arrived at Putney Station with the muffler almost over his mouth and dark glasses—bought at Charing Cross—to shade his eyes from the glare. As the day was brilliantly sunny with a wind like a knife, there was nothing remarkable in his appearance. He walked up Putney Hill and turned the corner into Clifton Avenue.

He saw at once that there was a group of people along the road near his house. When he came nearer he saw that the group was nearly big enough to be called a crowd. They were not merely near his house, they were outside it, round the gate, in fact. They were waiting for something.

Hyde advanced, slowed down, and mingled with the outer edge of the crowd. He edged up to a messenger boy and said in what he hoped was an American accent, "Say. What's goin' on here?"

"Funeral," said the boy without turning round.

Hyde felt as though someone had hit him in the waistcoat.

"Funeral? Whose funeral?"

"The gent who lives there. Mr. 'Yde."

"Is he dead?" gasped Hyde.

"Dead? Course 'e's dead. Ain't I just said it's 'is funeral?"

Hyde could not speak, and the boy turned his head and glanced at him. "Did you know 'im?"

"Slightly," said Hyde.

"Committed sooicide. Shot 'imself."

"Good God," whispered Hyde, and drifted blindly away.

CHAPTER SEVEN
Ticket to Chartham

Hambledon said in a discontented voice that they didn't seem to be getting anywhere in this case. Ribbentrop's money had gone to earth somewhere, Varsoni had killed himself by falling from a third-floor window in an expensive hotel he did not inhabit, and James Hyde appeared to have been murdered just to make it more difficult. "What was Varsoni trying to do, anyway?"

"A little cat burglary, apparently," said Bagshott. "He climbed up a waste pipe until he reached a window in a suite of rooms occupied by the elderly widow of a patent-medicine manufacturer. She is extremely well off and has some very fine jewelry, mainly emeralds. She keeps the jewelry in her rooms because she likes to wear it, and frequently does, in public. It is quite well known, and the only wonder is that nobody has had a try at it before. The window—it's the ordinary sash type—was latched. Varsoni went up the pipe till he was level with the window, and then stepped onto the sill. He had a jemmy like a tire lever with the thin edge sharpened; he pushed this in above the top sash, trying to force it down and break the latch. At this point he slipped, smashed one of the windowpanes in falling, and went straight down about forty feet onto a concrete path below. The jemmy fell down too. This was just after 1 A.M. Several people heard the breaking glass and Varsoni's fall and looked out of their windows at once; there was nobody in sight except Varsoni. The path runs between the hotel and a block of flats next door; it is about seventy-five feet long and quite straight. There is no doubt Varsoni was alone, confound him."

"Nobody saw this gymnastic performance, I suppose," said Hambledon.

"No, why? If anyone had seen him, the alarm would have been given."

"Of course. No, what I meant was that you had described his actions so very graphically."

"There were marks on the pipe all the way up. There is a deeply indented mark on the upper sash of the window where the jemmy was forced in. There is the broken window, and finally there was Varsoni. It's as clear as a comic strip."

"There's nothing in any of those New York reports about Varsoni's mental state, is there?" said Hambledon. "He is mixed up in the robbery of that Argentine bank. He comes to England and murders an inoffensive leather merchant at Putney for no reason at all that we can gather. Later he is killed trying a cat burglary on a pill fancier's widow near Regent Street. Bank robbery, murder by shooting, cat burglary. I thought criminals always specialized; this doesn't make sense. Was he a sort of criminal-general, or just plain batty? Or are there several Varsonis, all exactly alike, in the Gatello gang?"

"Heaven forbid," said Bagshott. "No, there's a connection between these crimes and we shall find it—I hope. In the meantime, we have put out a routine enquiry for any car driver, a taxi driver possibly, who picked up a man on Putney Hill on the night of Tuesday, April the second, between 11:40 P.M. and midnight. If a man commits a murder, he usually wants to get away from the neighborhood as quickly as possible."

"It isn't a good idea really," said Tommy thoughtfully. "It's much better to dodge round behind, join with the gathering crowd, and impede the police by asking silly questions."

"It's as well you were brought up to be honest," said Bagshott. "We are also arranging to interview Race. He is coming to town today from Chartham; he is seeing Nairn this morning. He is coming here at two o'clock if you'd like to be present."

Hambledon returned at two o'clock, not expecting much help from Mr. Race, but clutching at any chance which might lead him to some indication of what had happened to Ribbentrop's treasure chest.

"I rang up Nairn a little while ago," said Chief-Inspector Bagshott, "and asked him how he got on with Race this morning."

"Anything interesting emerge?"

"Nairn said that Race naturally wanted to know how much money there was. When he heard that there would be several hundred thousand, he was pleasantly surprised."

"Who wouldn't be?" said Tommy.

"Then he wanted to know how long it would be before he could handle it. When Nairn explained the process of proving intestacy and told him how long it would take, he was very cast down. He asked if he couldn't have an advance, and when Nairn said no, Race was seriously annoyed. He said it was absurd that a man who was coming into all that money couldn't have a couple of thousand if he wanted it."

"He did, did he?"

"Nairn said, 'But suppose we find a will leaving the money to somebody else? There is no certainty yet that you are the legatee to any considerable extent.' Nairn said he was thinking of the twenty-five pounds and the sermon on family courtesy, but naturally didn't say so. Race went scarlet in the face and said that of course these legal tomfooleries were arranged so that lawyers could keep their clients out of their rights while they—the lawyers—ran up long bills for their clients to pay. Nairn said that if Race felt like that perhaps he'd prefer to employ some other firm of solicitors, and showed him out."

"Good for Nairn. I think our Race is a fool," said Hambledon. "He must know he can't be sure of the money yet."

"Either that, or he's very eager to obtain some," said Bagshott.

"Are you going to ask him where he was on the night of Tuesday, April the second?"

"Not yet," said Bagshott. "At least, not in those words."

Race turned out to be a weaselly little man with a long nose and a sharp manner. He said he did not know his cousin James Hyde at all well; in fact, he had seldom seen him in the last ten years. "We used to go to Yeovil in the summer holidays and stay with the Hydes when we were children," he said. "I and my sister, she's dead now. We didn't like it much; too many rules and regulations. Early to bed, early to rise, good plain food, and Sunday school on Sundays. Country walks with our cousin James, virtuous little prig. Watching cricket on Saturdays, helping Auntie arrange the flowers—oh, gosh. Finally, when I was seventeen I decided I'd had enough, so I got myself disliked and wasn't asked again. I did spend a weekend there about seven years ago; yes, it was in May '39. I was in the West Country and thought it would be fun to see if the old place was just as awful as ever. It was. Auntie a bit gaga, Uncle an old tyrant, and James circling round both of 'em saying, 'Certainly, Mother,' and 'Let me do that, Father.' I only went twice more: that was once to each funeral."

"You were Mr. Hyde's cousin?" asked Bagshott.

"Yes, his mother and mine were sisters."

"Are there any other relatives of Mr. Hyde's alive, do you know?"

"None, I believe. We were supposed to be the only cousins James had. I've got cousins on my father's side, but no more on Mother's side."

"I see. Did you keep up any sort of correspondence with Mr. Hyde?"

"James used to write and tell me any important news. The family deaths; that he'd sold the business and come to London; and so forth. He came and lunched with me in town once—last September that was. I thought he was a trifle more human, seemed to have come alive a bit, if you know what I mean. Still, we hadn't much in common."

"Mr. Nairn has told you," said Bagshott, "that if your cousin didn't make a will you come into the whole estate?"

"Yes. Well, that was obvious, wasn't it? The only thing that surprised me was that he hadn't made a will. I should have thought he would, if only to keep me out of it," said Race.

"Tell me," said Hambledon, "did your cousin ever mention South America to you?"

"South America? Never."

"Thank you," said Tommy, and leaned back in his chair.

"Was that the last time you saw your cousin?" asked Bagshott. "Last September, did you say?"

"That's right," said Race, glancing at his watch. "Look here, if there isn't much more you want me for, I could just catch a train."

"I don't think there's anything else," said Bagshott with a glance at Hambledon, who replied, "No, nothing more," in a tired voice.

"You're going back to—er—Chartham, is it?" said Bagshott. "You will be there if we should want you?"

Race nodded. "I shan't move, believe me. One doesn't lose touch with all that money, you know."

He went away, and Bagshott said, "Well?"

"Don't like him," said Hambledon sleepily.

"No. But I don't think he knows anything, do you?"

"About South America? No."

"I meant about the murder," said Bagshott.

"I daresay not, but he did talk rather a lot, didn't he? All that rice-pudding-on-Sundays stuff. Rather anxious to dissociate himself, I thought, but perhaps I've got a suspicious mind. It didn't strike you that way?"

"I think he's worth keeping an eye on," said Bagshott. "If only somebody would come and tell us that he knew his cousin was just going to make a will. Or that Race knows Nairn's office boy."

"Who tipped him off it was now or never, and borrowed Varsoni's revolver for him to operate with," said Hambledon. "I don't care about this case much, do you? What do we do next, engage a spiritualist to interrogate the ghost of Varsoni?"

"We wait. What's your favorite phrase? 'Some scheme will probably present itself.' "

Bagshott's telephone rang and his face lit up as he answered it. "Yes. Send him up at once." He replaced the receiver. "There you are, faint-heart. A taxi driver."

A man was shown into the room who gave his name as Robert Northam and an address in Walham Green. He said he was a taxi driver and displayed his badge. He had picked up a fare near the bottom of Putney Hill at a quarter to midnight or thereabouts—he couldn't be sure to a minute or two either way—on Tuesday last. He heard the police were enquiring about it and thought he'd better come along.

"Thank you," said Bagshott. "Very good of you. Tell me all about it, will you?"

Northam said that he had picked up a party in the Haymarket and driven them to a house on Putney Heath, arriving there about half-past eleven. When he had set them down, he thought he would drive slowly through Putney in the hope of finding another fare back to town. "Not much chance, but worth tryin'. We strike lucky sometimes." He saw no one till he was nearly at the bottom of Putney Hill, when he saw this gentleman cross the pavement towards him and signal to him.

"So I stopped," said Northam, "and the gent asked me if I could drive him to the West End, and I opened the door and said, 'Get in, sir.' He seemed in a bit of a dither, I thought. So he got in and I drove off. When we got near the top of Brompton Road, I asks him where to, and he tells me a hotel just off Kingsway. So I drives there and stops at the door and he gets out. Then he starts an argument about the fare, sayin' my flag was down when I picked him up. I told him I didn't play them sort of tricks and that was the fare, what he saw on the meter. He said it was too much and I says, 'If you think so, we'll consult the law,' I says, and points out a fla—a policeman on the other side the road. So then he pays up, all of a fluster, and gives me sixpence tip. Sixpence! Then he went in the hotel."

"Can you describe the man?" asked Bagshott, expecting a word picture of Manuel Varsoni. "You saw him quite plainly, I suppose."

"Oh, quite plain, especially when he was arguin' the toss about the fare. But as to describin', I don't 'ardly know. Ordinary-lookin' chap, 'bout my height. Gray suit, brown felt hat. Gray eyes, rather near together. Got rather a high color. Long thin nose, sharp at the end. What you'd call a weaselly-looking chap."

Bagshott wrote down these particulars with no sign of emotion, and Hambledon merely crossed his knees, leaned one elbow on them, and covered his eyes with one hand. The description was nothing like Varsoni, but very like Race. There are, however, many men answering this description.

"Anything else you can remember about him?"

"No, sir, I'm sorry. Very ordinary-lookin' bloke."

"Do you remember the hotel you took him to?"

"Yes, sir. The Octagon Tower, in Kemble Street."

"You're sure he went in there?"

"Yes, sir, sure. I watched him in."

"Thank you very much," said Bagshott. "I'm very much obliged to you for coming here."

The taxi driver went towards the door and turned, with his hand on the knob.

"I've just remembered. He left the near-side door open an' I had to get out and shut it. I picked up a ticket on the step; he must 'ave dropped it out of 'is wallet getting the money out to pay me. I says to myself, 'I'm hanged if I run after you with it, mean old so-and-so,' I says. So I stuck it in the windscreen of my cab and I s'pose it's there now. It was this morning."

"What sort of ticket?"

"Railway ticket, sir. Return half."

"Where to?"

"I couldn't say, sir. Shall I go and see if it's there now?"

"I'll come with you," said Bagshott, and left the room. He returned a few minutes later and handed Hambledon the return half of a ticket on the Southern Railway. The station of origin was Chartham.

"Are you going there," said Hambledon, "or having Race brought back here?"

"I'm going to Chartham," said Bagshott, "as soon as I've had a word with the

Canterbury police and paid a visit to the Octagon Tower Hotel. Are you coming?"

"I don't think so. I cannot see any connection between Race and Ribbentrop except that their names begin with the same letter. Much as I love gamboling after murderers with you, work is doubtless accumulating in my office. Besides, the department doesn't pay me to inspire the C.I.D. Let me know what transpires, won't you?"

Race owned a market garden at Chartham to supply fruit and vegetables in their season to the inhabitants of Canterbury. He was not by nature or training a market gardener; he employed a manager to look after the technical side of the enterprise and himself attended to the business side. He visited greengrocers' shops and hotels in the city, obtained orders, and undertook contracts. He ordered whatever was necessary for the garden, engaged labor, and paid wages. He also kept the accounts. Race had a habit of saying that all businesses were alike to a businessman; it didn't matter whether it was a market garden, a Chinese laundry, or the Army & Navy Stores, it only wanted running on sound business lines and there you were.

Unfortunately for Race, Nature has no business sense and even seemed to have taken a dislike to him. Race liked to place his seasonal contracts early to forestall his competitors and also in order to arrange his budget for months ahead. Foresight, he used to say, intelligent foresight, was what was wanted, not just muddling along from week to week like these mutton-headed locals. Race was not a countryman, and proud of it. So he contracted for the supply of so many score of lettuces as soon as his seedlings were well established, but Nature sent wireworm to bite them off two inches below ground and many of them leaned over and died a fortnight before deliveries should have started. He had to buy elsewhere to fulfill his contracts at a price which swept his estimated profits into the dustbin. When it wasn't wireworm it was blight on the potatoes or mold on the strawberries or early frost on the plums; not, of course, all at once, but alternatively; till Race began to think of Nature as a very large witch with black hair, a churchwarden pipe, and an expression of malign intelligence. The fact was that he had not enough capital behind him.

Bagshott heard something of this from the Canterbury police, since there is far less hidden from the local police force than their neighbors hopefully imagine. He whistled softly between his teeth and went to Chartham.

He knocked at Race's door and it was opened to him by a harassed woman who looked at him with distrust.

"Mr. Race at home?"

She took two steps backward and called over her shoulder, "Mr. Race! A gentleman to see you," for Bagshott was in plain clothes. A voice answered indistinctly; the woman said, "Excuse me," to Bagshott and went down the passage to a room at the back of the house. A few minutes later she returned.

"Are you the chemical manures man?"

"No," said Bagshott.

"Or the punnet people?"

"No," said Bagshott again. "Please tell Mr. Race I have come on a small matter of business. I should be glad if he will kindly spare me a few minutes."

She looked at him more dubiously than ever and retired once more. A few minutes later the door at the end of the passage reopened and Race came out, blinking against the sunlight which dazzled him and silhouetted Bagshott against the glare.

"Who are you?" said Race truculently. "I told my housekeeper to tell you I was busy. I can't spare the time to see anybody now."

"I am sorry," said Bagshott politely, "but I'm afraid I shall have to ask you to give me a little of your time." He stepped into the passage as he spoke, and his voice seemed to affect Race unpleasantly.

"Who are you—I can't see in this glare—what's your name?"

"Chief-Inspector Bagshott from Scotland Yard."

Race gasped, clutched at the doorpost, and turned a color which reminded Bagshott of crossing the Channel.

"What's the matter?" asked Bagshott sharply.

"I—I've just been reading the paper," said Race.

"What paper?"

Race held it out in silence. One of the *Morning Star's* young men had been talking to taxi drivers and got a scoop. There were headlines.

THE PUTNEY TRAGEDY
IS IT MURDER?

It has become known that the police are not satisfied that the death of Mr. James Hyde, of Clifton Avenue, Putney, was in fact suicide as at first supposed. Enquiries are being made concerning a man who is said to have been seen leaving the vicinity at the time of the occurrence, and further developments are expected shortly.

"Well?" said Bagshott, handing back the paper. "What about it?"

"My cousin murdered," said Race, ceasing to cling to the doorpost and regaining his natural color. "It's a shock to me, I can tell you. Poor old James! Who could have done it?"

"I was hoping," said Bagshott pointedly, "that you would help me to find that out."

CHAPTER EIGHT
Something on the Drive

Race led the way into his sitting room, shut the door behind them, and offered Bagshott a chair. The chief-inspector sat down with his back to the light, and Race had to face the window.

"I am sure I need not tell you," he said earnestly, "that if there is anything I can do to help you to get to the bottom of this affair I shall be only too glad to do so. Poor old James. I had no idea that it was anything but suicide."

"No?" said Bagshott.

"You didn't tell me, when I saw you at Scotland Yard today, that you'd any doubts about it; but you must have had your suspicions then, hadn't you?"

"Yes," said Bagshott.

"I suppose I ought to have smelt a rat myself, because James was really the last person to commit suicide; not that type, you know. Especially just now when he'd got rid of the business, buried his father if you won't think me unfeeling to put it like that, bought himself a nice house, and settled down to live happily ever after."

He paused for a reply, but Bagshott said nothing. Race fidgeted uneasily and plowed on.

"There was another matter, too, which I might have brought to your notice if, as I say, I'd had any idea that there was anything fishy about it. That's the gun."

"What do you know about the gun?"

"Nothing—absolutely nothing. That's what I was going to say. I mean, I'm pretty sure James didn't own one. He wasn't a gunnish sort of man, if you get me. You see, he never served in either war; he wasn't even in the Home Guard. He told me himself he joined the A.R.P. He never was the sort of bloke to go out for a day's shooting or anything like that, if you get me."

"Yes," said Bagshott.

Small beads of perspiration appeared on Race's temples and he wiped them off, remarking in passing that the day was hot, which was true; but Bagshott was not perspiring.

"So, as I was saying," continued Race, "I suppose I ought to have suspected something, but there, one just doesn't. Especially when it's your own people. I mean, murder is a thing which happens to a stranger, not to people one knows personally. I suppose it was the papers saying it was suicide which misled me. Nairn, too—did Nairn know?"

"Yes," said Bagshott.

"Then I think he ought to have told me. After all, I am the next of kin—"

"Yes," said Bagshott unexpectedly.

Race mopped his face again and definitely wriggled.

"I must say I was very dissatisfied with the way Nairn was dealing with the affair. I told him so. In fact, I gave him a good ticking-off and said that in future I should prefer to be represented by my own solicitor here in Canterbury. There was no sort of a row, of course, I was just firm with him."

"So he told me," said Bagshott.

"Oh, did he? I wonder whether his account would tally with mine."

"I wonder, too."

Race straightened his back which showed a tendency to wilt.

"Actually, I asked him how soon the money would be available, and if I could draw a small sum in advance. There was no harm in that, surely, it was quite a natural question to ask. Not that I'm hard up—don't think that—but I want to put up some more greenhouses, and if I could get them built this autumn they would be ready for use in the early spring. Forcing things, you know, for the early markets. Well, that takes capital, you know; you'd be surprised at the amount of capital there is locked up in even a small concern like this. Well, I freely admit I am under-capitalized—"

"So I heard," said Bagshott.

Race stopped short in mid-career and stared with his mouth open. He shut it with what seemed to be an effort and swallowed once or twice.

"You police seem pretty well informed," he said. "How d'you manage it? Thought reading?"

"No," said the chief-inspector mildly. "We just ask."

"Nosing round pumping the neighbors," snapped Race. "When it's to do with my private affairs I'd be obliged—much obliged—if you'd come and ask me."

"Right, I will. What were you doing on Putney Hill at eleven forty-five on the night of your cousin's murder?"

Race fell back in his chair and gasped, "I didn't—I wasn't there."

"Oh, come," said Bagshott.

"I tell you—"

"I shouldn't, if I were you. You see, we've got a witness."

Race muttered an impious hope regarding the witness.

"Too late," said Bagshott. "We've got his statement. Now, Mr. Race, this isn't doing you any good. What do you suppose the police will think if you deny being there when they know you were?"

Race sat in silence for a few moments.

"Very well," he said at last. "I'll tell you. I didn't say anything before because, if it was suicide, it didn't matter. When I saw that in the paper, I damn nearly fainted." He went on to explain that he was in urgent need of a couple of thousand pounds. His bank manager was getting restive about a small overdraft and there were bills to meet.

"For chemical manures, for one," suggested Bagshott, and Race agreed. He knew a man with capital to invest who had promised to let him have two thousand pounds without fail; they were to meet in London on that Tuesday afternoon and fix it up. "All on a business basis, of course. He was to have a mortgage as security for the loan. Well, he was nearly an hour late at the meeting place, and I got the wind up that he'd been run over or something." Race laughed bitterly. "So far as I'm concerned he might just as well have been. He was full of apologies but he couldn't manage it; he'd been playing the markets and been caught short. He said he'd have to borrow money himself if he wanted to keep out of trouble. I was knocked flat by this. I had to get some money from somewhere pretty quick, you see, the mortgagor was going to foreclose—"

"Another mortgage?"

Well, no. Only one mortgage, but Race wanted to transfer it to his friend, that was all. Quite an ordinary business transaction.

"Go on," said Bagshott.

Race said that he walked about London dismally wondering what he was going to do, and finally decided to approach his cousin. "James didn't like me, I know, but he wasn't a bad old stick and absolutely rolling in money." Race went down to Putney, hoping to find Hyde in a receptive mood after dinner. He reached the house at about half-past nine, and the girl who answered the door said Mr. Hyde was out for the evening.

"Girl?" asked Bagshott.

"She answered the door," said Race. "Girl about eighteen. Why?"

"Nothing," said Bagshott, reflecting that Margaret Baxter had seen everything there was to see that night except the actual murder, and hadn't appreciated the importance of any of it. "Nothing, go on."

Race asked when Mr. Hyde was expected home and was told that he usually returned about eleven o'clock. Race walked up to the Heath and sat on a seat to wait. "It wasn't a cold evening, and anyway I wasn't worrying about the weather." At about twenty to eleven he walked down again to the end of Clifton Avenue and waited about for his cousin to return. "I didn't want him to get indoors and hop off to bed; he wouldn't have liked being hauled out again to listen to a hard-luck story."

The time dragged slowly by as neighboring clocks struck the hour and then the quarter past. Race wondered whether Hyde had come home earlier than usual; he walked along Clifton Avenue and up his cousin's drive far enough to see that there was a light showing through the fanlight over the front door. "So I knew he hadn't gone to bed. Always went round the house last thing at night, locking up and turning lights off. Brought up that way. So I wandered off again and—"

"Just a moment," said Bagshott. "This would be at about twenty or twenty-five minutes past eleven, would it?"

"Twenty-two minutes past. I looked at my watch as I passed under that lamp just beyond his gate. I kept on looking at my watch; you do, you know, when you're waiting for somebody. Keeps good time, this watch," said Race, with a brief return to his usual assertiveness. "I wouldn't carry one that didn't. I always say—"

"Did you see anybody else in the road?"

"A few stray people. A man with a dog turned into one of the houses the same side as James's. Man and woman came along and went into a house opposite, one of those small new ones. Taxi came along, put some people down further along the road. I wished I could take the taxi back to town, I was getting tired. I think that's all."

"Go on," said Bagshott.

"Just before I reached the corner where Clifton Avenue joins Putney Hill, I met my cousin. He was walking fast and I had to speak to him twice before he stopped. Evidently thinking about something else, he looked straight at me and didn't seem to see me—you know how people look when they're thinking of something else. I said, 'Hullo, old chap,' and he took no notice, so then I said, 'Hi, James! I say,' or something like that. He stopped then and said, 'Well? What is it?' quite sharp, for James. He generally had rather a slow voice. I said, 'Could I have a word with you? It's very important. Matter of business.' He said, 'What, at this time of night? Certainly not. In any case, I don't want to have anything to do with you at all. Good night,' and with that he walked off, leaving me stuck there like a blinking pillar box. I mean, why snap my head off? He wasn't very friendly, I know, but he was always polite. Rather old-fashioned like that. Well, I stood staring after him for a minute, and he strode off down the road as though he'd bought it. Well, it wasn't any good chasing him in that mood, so I turned away and walked on. He must have been in a temper about something, because just as I turned into Putney Hill I distinctly heard the front door slam. It was a quiet night, you see."

Bagshott stirred in his chair and a sudden thought struck Race. "I say— wasn't it the door slamming? When was he killed?"

"Tell me this," said Bagshott, ignoring the question, "and please answer carefully. Did anyone pass while you were talking to Mr. Hyde?"

Race considered. "I don't think so," he said slowly. "No, I don't think so, but

I wouldn't like to swear to it. You see, I was pretty well taken up with James; I probably shouldn't have noticed. But I don't think so."

"When you watched your cousin walk away towards his house, was there anyone else in sight?"

"There was one man walking along the other side of the road about thirty yards behind James, I remember that. He came round the corner from the Heath way, down the hill. I didn't notice what he looked like."

"Only one man?"

"Only one, yes."

Bagshott nodded; this was probably the witness Coleman who found the body. If he could confirm Race's evidence, Race was clear. He could not have fired a shot in Hyde's garden from a street corner a hundred yards distant.

"What did you do then?"

"Felt tired. God, I was tired, could hardly drag my legs along. Then I had a stroke of luck. A taxi came down the hill and overtook me; I hailed him and he drove me back to town."

"Where did you go to?"

"The Octagon Tower Hotel, in Kemble Street, just off Drury Lane. I usually stay there when I'm in town."

"How did your cousin look? Worried, or excited, anything like that?"

"Couldn't say how he looked. He passed under the lamp near the corner just before I met him and then he had his back to the light. He was taller than I am, too, not much but a bit; I had to look up against the light, you know. Like you, when you came in here. But I'm darn sure there was something wrong for him to snap me up like that. Walking faster than usual, too."

"When you were in Hyde's front garden for the second time, not when you spoke to the maid, I mean when you looked to see if there was a light in the house, did you see anyone or hear anything?"

"No, I didn't," said Race, and then the implications of the question dawned upon him. "Somebody hidden in the bushes, you mean?" He shuddered violently. "Suppose he'd mistaken me for my cousin!"

Bagshott rose to his feet. "I shall have to ask you to come to headquarters and repeat your statement," he said. "In the meantime, you can think it over, and if there is anything you wish to add to it, you can do so then. I must ask you to remain here or, if you go anywhere else, please inform the police of your intended destination."

Race had cheered up considerably towards the end of his story, since it seemed to be having quite a good reception. Bagshott's last warning, however, swept his self-confidence to the winds once more.

"I hope you'll do your darnedest to find out who did it," he said nervously. "I shan't rest until it's cleared up."

"I am doing my best," said Bagshott. "Good afternoon." He walked out of the house, and Race sat down again suddenly. His knees were trembling.

Bagshott went to Putney and interviewed Coleman, whom he found to be a quiet man with a steady manner and a limp which he brought home from Cassino. Bagshott asked whether Coleman remembered turning into Clifton Avenue from Putney Hill on the night of Hyde's death, and whether there was anyone else in the road.

"There was a small man on the opposite pavement," said Coleman. "He was standing on the edge of the pavement looking up the road after Hyde. I noticed him because he looked irresolute and I wondered whether he'd lost his way. However, he didn't look at me or appear as though he wanted help or advice, so I walked on. I could see Hyde walking ahead of me, of course. To be accurate, I didn't recognize him as Hyde at that moment, he'd got his back to me. But he turned into his own gateway, and I was just saying to myself that that was Hyde going home, when I heard the shot fired. You know the rest."

"Yes, thank you," said Bagshott. "There was nobody else in sight at all?"

"No one."

"Thank you very much," said Bagshott. "Your evidence is proving a great help." He returned to his office, rang up Hambledon, and gave him a summary of the new evidence. "I'm inclined to believe Race's story," he added. "I think he was so frightened that he told the truth for once. Also, it's corroborated by Coleman who, in my opinion, is a thoroughly reliable witness. And, of course, by the taxi driver."

"Yes," said Hambledon thoughtfully, "it sounds true. But Race may have known something about the man in the bushes, for all his display of horror. I still want to be quite sure Race didn't know that Hyde had not made a will, though I've no idea how we could find out. Put it like this. Suppose Race did know there was no will. He stops Hyde and asks him for a loan, or intends to. Hyde refuses, or cuts him short, goes home alone, and is killed. And Race inherits the money. Suppose again, Hyde had said, 'Well, come in, we can at least talk about it,' and two men had walked up the drive together, would Hyde have been shot?"

"Probably not," said Bagshott with a laugh. "Murderers don't like an audience, you know. But you are suggesting that Race and the murderer were working together."

"Race walked up the drive; he told you so. Perhaps he thought he'd better admit it in case someone saw him. He may have spoken to the murderer—Manuel Varsoni, probably—or even posted him there."

"Enquiries can be made as to whether Race and another man were seen together at that time," said Bagshott. "But I doubt any result. Putney has been combed to the scalp for news of Varsoni already."

"You see, my point is this," said Tommy. "The only link so far between Hyde's death and my enquiries after Ribbentrop's money is that confounded revolver of Varsoni's. Hyde doesn't seem to have had the least connection with South America. If Race had, a faint streak of illumination would begin to dawn."

"You mean," said Bagshott in a tired voice, "that Varsoni filled an idle moment between breaking a bank in Argentina and cat-burgling a flat in London by doing a little murder in Putney to oblige a friend?"

"There may be a little more in it than that," admitted Tommy, "but that's the general idea."

"I don't think much of it myself."

"Then produce a better one," said Hambledon justly. "If you find Race has any connection with the old firm in the Argentine, you can always beg my pardon, can't you?"

"I could," said Bagshott coldly, and hung up the receiver.

Several days passed during which Hambledon occupied himself with other matters and members of the police force wore their boots thin trying to get more evidence for Bagshott. Nobody had seen Race with any other person at Putney that night; in fact, except for Coleman, nobody had noticed Race at all. He was not a noticeable man.

No one had seen any man resembling Manuel Varsoni at Chartham, though there was no real reason to suppose he had ever been there. If Race had ever met him, he probably did so in town. No connection could be found between Race and the Argentine, not even a purely business connection like Hyde's, and Race had never owned a passport. His career was fairly easy to trace; he made a practice of buying small businesses which were capable of development, working them up and selling them again. He had been at Chartham nearly five years; it was the first time he had ever lived in the country. The only time he had been in trouble with the police was for an infringement of the blackout regulations in Leeds in 1940; fined ten shillings. He had been married, but his wife was dead and there were no children.

Considerable industry was used in trying to find out where Hyde went in the evenings. He had made some early advances towards a club which Nairn had recommended, but had not yet been elected. The club secretary remembered him from the one visit he paid, but did not know anything about him. The usual particulars had not been supplied. Yes, he had seen in the papers an account of Mr. Hyde's death, most unfortunate. Seemed such a nice fellow, too; quiet old stick—not so old, really. Elderly in manner, perhaps. Not at all the sort of fellow one would expect to be murdered, if it was murder, what?

Hyde had never told anyone where he went in the evenings. If the head-waiter at the D'Artagnan saw the account in the paper, or missed his regular visitor, he did not report it to the police—why should he? They had not advertised for information about Hyde.

Finally, Manuel Varsoni. There were plenty of police notices requesting information about him, and quite innumerable enquiries, all without result. Nobody, it appeared, had known him, housed him, fed him, drunk with him, or wished to attend his funeral. Nobody sent a wreath, not even the New York police. There were no papers on the body and no marks on the clothing, not even laundry marks. Hambledon's own sources of information were no more helpful.

"The wretched fellow is the Invisible Man," complained Tommy.

"Somebody isn't talking, that's all," said Bagshott, and offered a reward. Even this produced no reply.

Ten days after the murder, the milkman visited Hyde's house at Putney at eight in the morning as usual to leave milk for Mrs. Watson, Ellen Patch, and Margaret Baxter. Once past the curve in the drive, he came into view of the gravel sweep before the front door and noticed, to his surprise, a long narrow object on the ground covered with a white sheet. He regarded it with increasing distaste. Of course it couldn't be—it must be sacks of fertilizer for the garden or something like that—but why cover it with a white sheet? It did look so very like a corpse. Couldn't be, of course. Somebody playing a practical joke, trying to frighten him. Probably that Margaret, watching from the window to see him run away. He put down his rack of bottles and marched, unwillingly but firmly, towards the object. The nearer he got, the more like a corpse it looked. The white sheet, which was actually a tablecloth, was held down at the corners by two doorstops, a four-pound weight, and a brick. The morning was damp and foggy and the tablecloth had been there long enough to become clammy with moisture. It lay closely upon the form beneath it, unpleasantly outlining what it had been designed to hide. Pointed nose and dropped chin, one arm flung out with curling fingers at the end, legs asprawl, and one light brown shoe just showing.

The milkman backed away till he reached the front door, keeping his eye on the tablecloth in case the object under it should arise and follow him. He fumbled for the bell, found the button, and kept his thumb on it. He could distinctly hear the electric bell ringing on and on in the silent house.

Presently he tired of this and hammered on the door with the heavy knocker. When it became obvious that this also would produce no result the milkman turned and ran for his life down the drive.

At the end of the road he met a policeman and clutched at his arm.

"Come quick, come on," said the milkman. "There's—there's somethink on the drive."

"Steady on," said the policeman. "What's all this?"

"Somethink unpleasant. On the drive. I think it's dead."

"Whose drive?"

"Where that bloke shot himself. Now there's another of 'em. And I think they're all dead in the 'ouse, I can't get no answer."

"I'll come," said the policeman, and advanced down Clifton Avenue with long strides, the milkman tagging reluctantly along behind.

The constable removed one doorstop and lifted the tablecloth to see what was underneath it; the milkman, irresistibly drawn, peered also and then wished he hadn't. The constable replaced the sheet and the doorstop, rang the front doorbell without result, and tried the doors. They were all locked and the windows were fastened. The milkman looked on, his fingers fluttering round his mouth.

"Do you think as they're all dead?" he asked.

"Gone away, more like. Will you stop here while I go and ring up the—"

"No, I'm 'anged if I will," said the milkman, picking up his bottles and retreating down the drive. "Got me round to see to, 'aven't I? If you wants to ring up, go and do it opposite. There's their maid now, waitin' for the breakfuss milk, look. I'm goin' there now."

"And not a word to anyone, mind," warned the constable. "Understand?"

"Don't want to talk about it. Don't even want to think about it," said the milkman, and went his way.

CHAPTER NINE
Lost Dogs Lose

The duty sergeant at Putney Police Station received a report which startled even him; he in turn disturbed the superintendent in the early stages of his breakfast. He told the sergeant to warn the police doctor and photographer for immediate duty; he himself would be at the station in ten minutes. He then attacked his sausages in the manner of a bulldozer attacking a pile of brickbats.

"You'll ruin your digestion, Wilfred," said his wife.

"It's got to get used to it," he answered sadly. "I've had to."

The object under the tablecloth on Hyde's drive was a tall thin man of foreign appearance; dark, sallow-skinned, with yellowish whites to the black eyes which stared fixedly at the sky. He had been hit in the throat by a bullet which had entered slightly to the left and smashed the spine. The superintendent opened a file of papers he had brought with him, turned the leaves over until he found the one he wanted, and read it through carefully, glancing at the dead man from time to time. He nodded to himself as though something had pleased him.

"Well, Doctor?" he said. "When did this happen?"

"When at last I find time to die myself," said the police doctor, busy with his thermometer, "and when I've climbed wearily up the golden stair and knocked feebly on the golden gate, St. Peter will open it, take one look at me, and say, 'Well, Doctor? When did this happen?' " He tried to move the stiff fingers, lifted one of the legs slightly, read his thermometer, and added, "Seven to nine hours ago, or thereabouts. Seven to ten hours. Say between ten-thirty and one-thirty. I'll get the bullet out at the p.m. Nasty-looking piece of work, isn't he? Know who he is?"

"I think so," said the superintendent. "Don't walk in the bushes, men, keep on the gravel for the present. Thank you, Doctor. Now the photographs, please. Did you say there was nobody at home, Milton?"

"No answer when I rang the bell, sir," answered the constable.

"I don't quite like it," said the superintendent thoughtfully. He examined doors and windows and pointed out a fresh scratch on the paint near the latch of the study window. "Looks as though someone had pushed the latch back with a knife, but it's fastened all right now. Only three women in the house." He paused a moment and made up his mind. "Milton, open that window, get in, and open the front door for me."

"Yes, sir."

The superintendent returned to the body, which was being comprehensively photographed. "When that's finished, cover up the body again and leave it. It is not to be moved."

The front door opened; the superintendent went in and passed swiftly from room to room. There was no one in the house, alive or dead. Three beds had been slept in and left unmade; on the kitchen table was a teapot with the tea leaves still in it, and three used teacups; but there was no sign of any disturbance, let alone of a struggle. The three women had got out of bed, dressed— for there were no clothes lying about—had a cup of tea each, and disappeared.

The superintendent returned to the study, picked up the telephone, and rang up Scotland Yard to speak to Chief-Inspector Bagshott. He was put through to Bagshott's office.

The superintendent introduced himself and said, "There's been another murder in Clifton Avenue, sir, at the same house, number eleven. The body answers the description of another of the Gatello gang, Pietro Gatello."

"One of Varsoni's associates," said Bagshott.

"Yes, sir. He was shot in the throat and the bullet severed the spine. He was found lying on the drive in front of the house when the milkman called at eight this morning. No reply was made to repeated ringing of the bell, so, knowing there were three women in the house, I effected an entrance and searched the place. There was no one there. Three beds had been slept in, and they'd had tea in the kitchen. No signs of any struggle. There were, however, signs that the study window had been forced."

"Found the weapon?"

"It is not near the body. I have not yet searched the bushes."

Bagshott thought for a moment and said, "I'll come along at once. Have you moved the body?"

"No, sir. I left it for you to see, if you wished."

"Good," said Bagshott. "Quite right."

He rang up Hambledon and said, "Putney for murders. There's been another. According to the superintendent, it's another of the Gatello gang, Pietro Gatello this time. Are you coming along? I'll pick you up, shall I?"

"Please," said Tommy, "but why Putney? Do the Gatello gang live there?"

"In Hyde's front garden? I shouldn't think so."

"Are you telling me," said Hambledon, "that there's been another murder on that already blood-boltered drive?"

"I am. What is more, Hyde's three servants have all disappeared. I think we'd better get hold of Nairn, don't you?"

"Unless he's disappeared also, yes. I'll ring him while you're on your way here, shall I? At his private address; he won't be at his office for another hour."

Hambledon rang up Nairn and said, "Have you finished your breakfast? . . . Good. I didn't want to spoil your appetite, but another unpleasant incident has occurred in Hyde's front garden, and the maids have apparently left."

"Good gracious," began Nairn.

"Not that the corpse itself is anything to worry about if he's the man we think he is, but I thought you might wish to do something about the staff."

"They haven't been murdered too, have they?" asked Nairn in an anxious voice.

"No, no, I think not. At least, they haven't found their bodies yet. Bagshott and I are going there at once. Will you come?"

"I'll go straight there. Who did you say had been murdered?"

"I didn't say who, but they seem to think he may have been one of Varsoni's friends."

"But why on Hyde's drive?" persisted Nairn.

"I don't know. Perhaps it'll turn out he wasn't murdered at all; perhaps he went down there and committed suicide out of remorse. I don't know any details. Well, I shall see you there later, then."

Hambledon and Bagshott reached Clifton Avenue to find the scene, except for the presence of the police, exactly as when the milkman first came upon it. The tablecloth had been replaced and, since the wind was getting up, so had the two doorstops, the four-pound weight, and the brick. Tommy surveyed this arrangement with raised eyebrows, and the superintendent explained that it was like that when they first found it.

"Then who covered him up?"

"We don't know yet, sir."

"Where did the tablecloth come from? Out of the house?"

The superintendent looked at one corner of the cloth and then another, and found an inscription in marking ink. "J.C. Hyde."

"If a friend of this man's covered him up, the friend had been in the house," said Bagshott.

"Those three women," began the superintendent, and stopped.

"Perhaps they just ran away," said Hambledon consolingly. "Let's have a look at him."

The tablecloth was removed and the superintendent brought out his file containing descriptions, sent from New York, of other members of the Gatello gang besides Varsoni. "It looks like this one," he said. "There's the scar on the head from a knife cut and the mark of a bullet wound on the left forearm. The rest of the description tallies exactly, and the photograph is like him."

"Yes," said Bagshott. "I agree. This fellow is Pietro Gatello, brother of the gang leader, Angelo Gatello."

"Angelo," murmured Hambledon. "His mother was an optimist, wasn't she? Did anyone hear the shot fired, do you know?"

"The gentleman next door," said the superintendent, "has a statement to make. I asked him if he would make it to you."

"What's his name?" asked Bagshott. "Knight? We'll go and see Mr. Knight."

Mr. Knight said that he was in the habit of working late in order not to be disturbed; he was writing a treatise on Morris dances, their evolution and history. He was in the habit of coming out upon his doorstep for a breath of night air before going up to bed, "to blow the cobwebs away. Last night I stopped work at one-thirty precisely, and opened the front door just in time to hear a scream in a feminine voice. I was curious, gentlemen, I admit it. Of course, there are screams and screams. There is the scream hilarious as well as the scream horrescent; the playful scream and the angry scream; the affected scream and—"

"You heard a scream, anyway," said Hambledon. "We get that. What happened next?"

"I strolled down towards my gate, listening for a repetition, but none came.

I leaned my elbows upon it, admiring the beauty of the night, when suddenly, without warning, there came the sound of a shot. I am not a man of war, gentlemen, I am a writer. I flattened myself against the gatepost. I heard a man's voice utter an exclamation but could not distinguish the words. The next moment I heard the sound of flying footsteps. I leaned cautiously over the gate and observed the figure of a man running at great speed away from me towards Putney Hill."

"Did you see him plainly?" asked Bagshott.

"Oh, quite plainly. Yes. No possible mistake about it."

"Can you describe him?"

"Oh no. Not at all, except that he was rather a small man. You see, the car was in the way."

"Car? What car?"

"The car which was standing by the curb. It was just along here, between my gate and poor Hyde's. It masked the man as he ran, if you understand me."

"Did you recognize the car?"

"No. Besides, there was hardly time to look at it before the two men came out, got in, and drove away."

"Did you see them?"

"Oh yes. Yes indeed. You see, they had to walk towards me to get into the car. There must have been another man in it as well, because the engine started up before they reached it."

"Can you describe these men at all—did you recognize either of them?"

"Recognize—well, that's rather funny. Describe them, yes. One was a slim dark man, at least he seemed dark to me. Not a Negro—I don't mean that—just dark. The other—that's why I laughed just now when you asked me if I recognized them. He was extremely like poor dear Hyde. It quite gave me a turn, at first, though of course I realized at once that it must be one of those chance resemblances which are so misleading. Besides, the light was not really good. I have no doubt that if one saw this man clearly, by daylight, there would be several marked differences. But, in general terms, if you want to know what he was like, he was like Hyde."

Bagshott sighed, and Hambledon asked if Mr. Knight thought either of the two men had seen him.

"No. Oh no. There is some loose ivy there—it hangs down the gatepost— and I looked through the strands."

"Nothing else you can tell us?"

"Nothing, I think. The car just drove away."

"Can you tell us," said Bagshott, "what make of car it was, what shape, color, and so on?"

"I'm afraid I know very little about cars. But I can tell you the number, if that's any help."

Hambledon leaned back in his chair and closed his eyes for a moment, as one engaged in prayer, but Bagshott merely took out his notebook and said, "Please. I should be much obliged. . . . CPJ 182. Thank you. Just one more question, or possibly two. What did you do after you saw these three men leave? Did you go round to Hyde's place?"

"No. No, I waited a few minutes and nothing more happened, so I came indoors and went to bed."

"Having heard a feminine scream," said Hambledon energetically, "and a shot fired, and seen men running away or escaping in a car, it still didn't occur to you to go round next door and find out what had happened to three women all alone?"

"Well, no, it didn't. You see, I didn't know where the scream came from; I didn't locate it. I did know where the shot came from; Hyde's front garden. The armed man might still be there. I have already said, I am not a man of war—"

"No battleship," snapped Hambledon.

"Ha-ha! Very good. No, I'm no battle—"

"Why didn't you telephone to the police?" asked Bagshott.

"I have no telephone," said Mr. Knight simply. "They annoy me. The disturbance—"

"I will tell you this, sir," said Bagshott, rising to his feet. "If any harm has come to those poor women, you cannot hope to escape very severe censure."

"Well-deserved censure," said Hambledon, already on his feet. "I shouldn't like to be in your shoes, sir. I have the honor to wish you good morning."

They stalked out; before the front door closed behind them Hambledon's voice floated back into the room where Mr. Knight still sat gazing vaguely after them. "The spineless, cold-blooded flatfish," it said, and then the door slammed.

"Well, really," said Mr. Knight.

"We got the car number," said Bagshott.

"Probably faked, even if he's got it right."

"And quite a lot of useful information. Simmer down, Hambledon, the creature had its uses."

They returned to Hyde's desecrated garden and found the processes of investigation in full operation by two of Bagshott's detectives. There was nothing more to be done there at the moment beyond telling the superintendent what news they had received next door. The superintendent asked if they would care to come to the police station in case any message had been received from the missing women. "If they did just run away," he said, "they might ring up when they thought they'd run far enough. Oh, here's Mr. Nairn."

Nairn came gingerly up the drive, shied visibly at the sight of Pietro Gatello, and came to an undecided stop near the front door. Hambledon went forward to meet him.

"Never mind the exhibit," he said cheerfully. "He won't bite. Come into the house, will you? I want you to tell us if there's anything missing."

"I shall be here for a time," said Bagshott to the superintendent. "I'll ring up headquarters from here at once and put them on the track of that car. If you get any news of the missing women, ring me up here. I'll let you know when I'm leaving. The body can be removed as soon as Ennis has done with it."

"I've finished with it now, sir," said Detective-Inspector Ennis.

Bagshott followed Hambledon and Nairn into the house and steered them into the study. Nairn cast one unwilling glance out of the window, which gave an uninterrupted view of proceedings outside, and then went to sit down where he could not possibly see out. Bagshott, murmuring apologies about not keeping them a moment, telephoned brief instructions about CPJ 182.

"Well, that's that," he said. "Now, if I get somebody in to test for fingerprints— Ennis!"

"I've done that room, sir," said Ennis. "Numerous prints. They've been photographed."

"Then we can get on," said Bagshott. "I think if you'd open the safe first, Nairn, it would be best. That two hundred and fifty pounds—"

Nairn opened the safe and turned at once to the drawer which had contained the money. Before he opened it Bagshott again tested for fingerprints, but there was only a medley of smears. When the drawer was opened, the money was still there.

"Curious," said Hambledon, "very. What a high-minded burglar."

"I'll just look through the share certificates," said Nairn. "Not that they would be much good to him if we missed them at once and took appropriate action." He drew out the bundle of long envelopes tied together with the traditional red tape; as he did so another envelope slipped out from beneath them and fell to the ground. The three men looked at it in utter silence; Nairn drew back as though he hesitated to touch it.

The envelope had on the outside a printed endorsement of which the blanks had been filled in by hand in almost painfully clear block letters. "The Last Will and Testament of James Clarendon Hyde of Clifton Avenue, Putney, S.W.15; to Alexander Gilchrist Nairn, Executor."

"Dear me," said Hambledon blankly.

"Where did that come from?" said Nairn. "I'm sure it wasn't there before. I should have seen it."

"It's addressed to you," said Bagshott.

Nairn picked it up as though he still disbelieved in it, slit the envelope open, and drew out the contents. Inside was one of those printed will forms which stationers sell and which are called "the lawyers' joy" on account of the employment they give to the profession. There was no ambiguity about this one, however. It simply bequeathed every penny of which James Clarendon Hyde died possessed to Hugh Selkirk, Esq., of Carmen de las Flores, Buenos Aires Province, Argentine, and 27 Avenida de las Rochas, Buenos Aires, Argentina.

"Selkirk?" said Bagshott. "Who's he?"

"Argentina at last," said Hambledon in a tone of deep satisfaction, but Nairn was not appeased.

"Nothing for his servants," he said. "Nothing for the Lost Dogs—when was this made? Friday, March the twenty-ninth, four days before he died. The witnesses are William Forgan, householder, and Archibald Henry Campbell, retired engineer, both of Clerkenwell Road, London." Nairn laid the will down upon Hyde's desk and regarded Bagshott and Hambledon owlishly. "I give it as my considered opinion, gentlemen, that I have never been so surprised in all my life. Unpleasantly surprised. I cannot decide which was the greater shock, to find this will here at all, or to read the contents. So unlike all I knew of Hyde. So entirely foreign to every conception I had formed of his character—" He continued to lament, but Hambledon and Bagshott were not listening.

"Queer it may be," said Bagshott, "but here's a lead at last."

"One of us had better ask the Argentine Legation about this fellow Selkirk, whoever he is, at once," said Hambledon. "I think it'll come better from you, in the first place anyway. Just tell the legation that an Englishman who died recently has left a legacy to one Hugh Selkirk, Esq.—sounds British enough—of all those picturesque addresses. His executor has asked you to make a few preliminary enquiries into the said Hugh Selkirk's bona fides. He hasn't yet, it's true, but he will as soon as he recovers his mental balance. While awaiting the answer, we can interview those two witnesses. They should be interesting."

"I don't believe this will was here when I opened this safe before," said Nairn obstinately. "I should have seen it."

"You weren't looking for it, you know," said Tommy kindly. "You said there wasn't one."

"No. But it wasn't here."

"Will you swear to that?" asked Bagshott.

Nairn hesitated. "Almost. I suppose I could have overlooked it. But I don't believe it."

"Consider the alternative," said Hambledon. "Are you suggesting that somebody broke into this house and opened that safe in order to plant a will in it?"

"We are rather forgetting the intruder," said Bagshott. "Will or no will, that window was forced and something caused the servants to disappear. Would you mind looking through the desk, Nairn, to see if you think anything is missing from there?"

Nairn folded up the will and pushed it back into its envelope as though the sight of it pained him. He passed his hands over his forehead with the gesture of one sweeping away cobwebs, and turned to the desk.

He examined the contents of each drawer carefully and said that he thought one had been disturbed. He could not state definitely that anything was missing, but this drawer was not so tidy as he thought he had left it. There was seven pounds in an envelope in another drawer which was still there; so was Hyde's checkbook, which had not been tampered with. "It seems all right," he said, "but why didn't the burglar take that seven pounds?"

At that moment the telephone rang and Bagshott lifted the receiver. "Yes, Chief-Inspector Bagshott speaking. . . . Oh yes, Superintendent?"

The Putney superintendent reported that he had just received a telephone call from the missing housekeeper, Mrs. Watson. All three women were safe and well; the cook had gone home to her aunt, and Margaret Baxter was with Mrs. Watson at her home at Surbiton for the present. The housekeeper's story was that she was lying awake and thought she heard a noise in the house. It sounded to her like the larder window banging, having been left unfastened, so she got up and went downstairs to shut it. She noticed a light under the study door. Thinking she had inadvertently left it switched on, she opened the door "and saw," said the superintendent, "what she insists was the ghost of Mr. Hyde sitting at his desk. I suggested that she must have been mistaken; what she saw was a burglar going through the drawers for what he could find. But she won't have it. She insists it was Hyde himself, or rather his ghost, since he's dead; she saw him quite plainly in the light of the desk lamp, which was the only one switched on. She gave a loud scream, shut the door again, and rushed upstairs. This awoke the other servants, who opened their doors and came out on the landing to ask what was the matter. She was in the act of telling them when they all heard a shot fired in the front garden, followed by what she calls a yelp in a man's voice. Margaret Baxter made to run into her room and look out of the window, but the other two women held her back for fear, if there were more shooting, she might get hurt. Soon after that they heard a car drive away. Apart from the ghost," added the superintendent sarcastically, "all that corroborates Knight's statement exactly. After that they heard no more. They all three went into the housekeeper's room together for company and stayed there until it began to be daylight. They got dressed, went downstairs to the kitchen and made themselves some tea, and decided to leave at once, as soon as the first workmen's trains started to run. When they came out of the house the first thing they saw was the body of Pietro Gatello. I asked her why she didn't ring up the police and she replied that they were all so frightened they never thought of it. She said that she and the cook pushed Margaret Baxter back into the house before she actually saw the body. I suppose it was masked from the girl's window by those lilac bushes," added the superintendent, "otherwise she'd have seen it before. She's good at seeing things out of windows. The house-keeper and the cook decided to 'cover the thing up,' as she said, to prevent the girl from seeing it. They came out with a kitchen tablecloth and some weights and covered it up. Then they tied a handkerchief over the girl's eyes and led her down the drive. When they got to the gate they all ran. She took Margaret Baxter to Surbiton with her, as I said, because the girl's parents live in Cumberland. They were both rather upset when they got to Surbiton, she says, and really one can't wonder at it. As soon as they had recovered she rang me up. She is anxious about the house being left."

"Curious," said Bagshott. "They seem to have kept their heads about the girl and nothing else."

"Yes," said the superintendent, and laughed. "She said, 'You see, you have to be careful with girls. She might be a mother someday."

"What's that got to do with it?" asked the puzzled Bagshott.

"I wouldn't know, sir. I'm only a father myself."

CHAPTER TEN
You Can't Kill a Ghost

The intruder didn't take the seven pounds," said Hambledon, "nor break open the safe, because Mrs. Watson came in and frightened him before he'd really settled down. Obvious. Look at the timing. She heard a noise, probably the window being opened. She sits up in bed. 'Did I shut the larder window—did I? Didn't I? Did I?' Haven't we all talked to ourselves like that about locking the front door or switching off the bathroom light? She can't be sure. She gets up, puts on dressing gown and slippers, and tiptoes downstairs so as not to awaken the others. While all this is going on, Mr. X climbs in at the window, has a look round, and decides to start on the desk. Perhaps he thought he might find a note of the safe combination—anyway, he sits down at the desk, switches on the reading lamp, and opens that drawer you found disturbed. He is looking through the contents when, to his bone-dissolving horror, the door slowly opens and Mrs. Watson puts her head in. I wonder whether she puts curling pins in at night? Do you happen to know, Nairn? Never mind. She turns even more ghastly-looking than usual, utters a piercing shriek, and rushes away. Mr. X pushes the drawer shut, switches off the light, dives out of the window, and gets clear away, safe but empty-handed. All that trouble for nothing. Poor man, poor man. One can only hope he didn't know there was two hundred and fifty quid in the safe, it would be too cruel. Eh, Bagshott?"

"I agree," said Bagshott. "I mean, I agree with your reconstruction. Of course, the man she saw was the same man whom Knight saw and thought so like Hyde that it gave him quite a turn, if you remember. There must be at least a strong superficial resemblance. If my people can trace CPJ 182, we may be able to drop on him."

"Was he the man who shot that—that thing out there?" asked Nairn, gesturing towards the window.

"Either he, or the little man who ran away," said Hambledon. "And the thing isn't there any longer, they've removed it. What a night our burglar had, first Mrs. Watson inside the house and then a murder just outside. It's enough to make a man turn honest, it is really. I suppose those share certificates are all right, Nairn?"

"Quite. That is," added Nairn sourly, "if I am still capable of checking a list of nineteen items correctly. I am taking the money from both desk and safe, the will, and the share certificates, and lodging them in my strong room. I'll give you a signed statement to that effect, Bagshott. My safes at least do not ingeminate wills."

"Don't take it to heart, Nairn," said Tommy. "I suppose there's no doubt that that is Hyde's signature on that will?"

"I shall submit it to experts for comparison with other examples of his signature in my possession. It looks genuine to me, for what my opinion is worth."

" 'Why restless, why cast down, my soul?' "quoted Hambledon. "Cheer up, do. Consider that you are but mortal. These little things are sent to try us."

"They succeed," said Nairn bitterly.

Hambledon went back to Bagshott's office with him to hear if there was any news of CPJ 182. There was. The car belonged to a garage who let it out on the hire-and-drive-yourself principle. A detective went there at once to make enquiries about those who hired it on the night of the burglary at Clifton Avenue. He was told that three men took it out and the hirer gave his name as Jones, with an address in the Horseferry Road. Since the hirers were not known to the garage, they paid a heavy deposit on the car, which was returned when it came back unharmed. The description of two of them tallied with Knight's; the third was a taller man who did the actual driving. The one who interviewed the garage manager and made the arrangements was a middle-aged man with fair hair turning gray and gray eyes; he was rather stout, not very, but rather. Middle-aged spread, as you might say. A very respectable-looking gentleman. Retired businessman, by the look of him. He was whitish about the jaw as though he'd worn a beard until recently.

"Worn a beard?" said Hambledon sharply.

"Yes, sir," said the detective. "That's what the garage manager said. He wasn't so sunburnt where the beard had been."

"What's the idea, Hambledon?" asked Bagshott.

"Nothing. Only a little theory I was beginning to form, and it's collapsed. Please carry on."

"I asked to see the car," said the detective. "They said it was being cleaned and took me out to a concrete yard at the back where a cleaner was hosing the car down. I asked if the inside had been cleaned and they said, 'Not yet.' I accordingly searched the inside of the car and in one of the cubbyholes in the dashboard I found this note." He handed it over; it was merely a sheet of paper folded up and stuck with a halfpenny stamp in place of a seal. On the outside was penciled, "Kindly hand to C.I.D., London."

Bagshott took the note, opened it with care not to fingerprint it, and spread it out on his desk; Hambledon got up and came to read it over the Chief-Inspector's shoulder.

"The corpse in Hyde's garden was shot by Giuseppe Mantani who lodges at 79 Bignorth Street, Caledonian Road. He is probably in the mood to talk."

It was unsigned, and rather illegible, as though it had been written under difficulties.

"Giuseppe Mantani," said Bagshott to the detective. "Seventy-nine Bignorth Street. Go and get him. Take a man with you and be careful. He is probably armed. To be questioned in connection with the murder of Pietro Gatello at Putney last night."

The detective went out and Hambledon said, "One of the men in the car wrote this on the way back to the garage. That's obvious. But why?"

"Someone who didn't like Giuseppe, I expect," said Bagshott. "Perhaps he'll tell us when he comes. Unless, of course, it's some sort of leg-pull. Giuseppe Mantani is not on that list of names New York sent us."

Seventy-nine Bignorth Road was a grimy narrow-fronted house which had suffered superficial damage by the Luftwaffe and been superficially repaired, giving it a leprous appearance. It had not been painted for some years, and the doorstep was dirty. In one of the ground-floor windows hung a card which said: "Lodgings for Single Men Only."

The door was answered by a brassy-haired woman who evidently considered makeup more important than soap and water. She looked unamiably at the detectives and said, "What d'you want?"

"Giuseppe Mantani live here?" She nodded. "Can I see him, please?"

"Who are you? Police?"

"Yes."

"Perhaps it's as well," said the woman darkly, and opened the door wider. "Second floor back. You can go straight up."

They knocked at the door of the second-floor back room and were answered by a flood of South American Spanish. Since neither of the detectives was a linguist it conveyed nothing to them but a general impression of extreme agitation.

"Open the door!" said the detective-inspector loudly. "Police!"

Dead silence for a moment.

"Thinking that over," murmured the detective-sergeant.

"Pliz to talka some more," said the voice from inside, "or I shoot."

"Don't you dare shoot," roared the detective-inspector, and rattled the door handle. "Unlock this door at once."

"Olla right," said the voice, and there were sounds of furniture being shifted.

"You would almost think," said the detective-sergeant, "that the poor wop was afraid of somebody but not of the police, strange as it may seem."

The key turned in the lock and the door opened a crack, just enough to show the muzzle of a revolver and one rolling dark eye above it.

"Put that gun down," said the detective-inspector sharply.

The door opened wider and revealed a disheveled little man in creased clothes, with a mop of curly dark hair sticking up all over his head like the feathers of an agitated Buff Orpington. Tears were rolling down his face, leaving comparatively clean streaks as they went, and his mouth wobbled uncertainly between anguish and a grin. In his right hand he still held a revolver.

"Pliz, you are *verdaderamente* da poliz?"

"That's right. Are you Giuseppe Mantani? We are taking you to Scotland Yard for questioning in connection with the death of—"

"Shotlan' Yaird?"

"Yes. In connection with the murder of Pietro Gatello at Put—"

"Hush—sh!" hissed the little man, sprang forward and placed a dirty palm right across the Detective-Inspector's mouth before he could dodge it.

"Here, stop that. And give me that gun."

Mantani allowed the revolver to be removed with the indifference of a baby who is tired of its rattle.

"You gotta da automobile?"

"Yes, we—"

"Da automobile not—not passa da bullet, yes?"

"Eh?"

Mantani aimed an imaginary rifle, produced a startling pop with his mouth, and then grinned widely, shrugged his shoulders, and threw out his arms with an air of triumph.

"He means is the car bulletproof," said the detective-sergeant intuitively.

"Oh, ah. Yes," said his superior officer, addressing Giuseppe. "All Scotland Yard cars are bulletproofed, armor-plated, and fitted with anti-submarine devices. Come on!"

They went, but Mantani crossed the pavement in one leap from doorstep to car and made the journey sitting on the floor.

He was then shown into the office where Hambledon and Bagshott waited, and bowed politely from the hips to each of them in turn. Bagshott began it.

"You are Giuseppe Mantani?"

"Para servir, señor," said Giuseppe politely.

"I am making enquiries into the murder of Pietro Gatello at Putney last night, and I must tell you that you can have a solicitor present if you wish and an interpreter. Do you understand?"

Giuseppe grinned and murmured, "Too kind."

"What a phrase!" said Bagshott. "I don't believe he understood a word of it."

"Never mind," said Hambledon immorally. "You've said it."

Bagshott looked horrified, and repeated: "You have a right, if you wish, to be legally represented. Hadn't I better get an interpreter?"

"No, a no," said Giuseppe. "I tella da story, you putta in jail, *muy bien*. I like, *muy mucho.*"

Bagshott blinked and Hambledon laughed. "I should let him get on with it," he said. "He seems easily pleased.

"In connection with the murder of Pietro Gatello—" he began.

"No a no. Notta da murder, *esta da accidente*. I no murder Pietro. What? *Accidente*. I shoot, yes. I shoota da *espectro*. Not Pietro. He is da *hermano"*— Giuseppe struggled for the word—"da brotter of da Boss. Nobody shoot da brotter of da Boss."

"He means that nobody would shoot the Boss's brother on purpose, I suppose," said Bagshott, taking notes. "What was that about a specter? Has he been seeing ghosts too?"

"I tella. We go—Pietro and me—we go see where Manuel keel da man—"

"What was his name?" asked Hambledon.

"Manuel Varsoni."

"No, the man who was killed. What was his name?"

Mantani looked sullen and said, *"No sabe."*

"Oh yes, you do. What was his name?"

After a moment's silence Hambledon repeated doggedly, "What was his name?"

"Selgirk," said Giuseppe unwillingly.

"Selkirk, eh? Well, go on. You and Pietro went to see where Manuel shot Selkirk. Why?"

Giuseppe rolled his eyes round the room for inspiration and got it. He snatched a rosary from his breast pocket, waved it at them, and began, with an air of extreme piety, *"Ave Maria, gratia plena—"*

"You went to Putney to say prayers for his soul? Well, it was a kind thought, anyway," said Bagshott sarcastically. "What happened?"

"I kneela before da door," said Giuseppe passionately. "Pietro go on, I no go on. We not know where *el pobrito* die," he added pathetically. "Then I look up, *y el espectro*, he come." He shuddered violently and covered his face, peeping between his fingers. "I no move, he go. I tella da *Ave* more faster. Alla sodain, one scre-e-eam. I shake. I cry. I get up. I pulla da gun. Da shadow he arriva! I shoot; it is da *espectro*. No! It is Pietro. He rolla da floor. I cry, *'Pietro! Amigo mio!'* He say, 'Gr-r-r.' He die. I run. I run. I tella, señores, it is da *accidente.*"

"No," said Bagshott solemnly. "It is murder. You fired the gun."

"No. No murder. I fire at *el espectro*. No can murder *el espectro*, he too much dead alla ready. Pietro, he getta da bullet I no fire but at *espectro*. Only one dead can die not be dead more times but. *El espectro—*"

"Well, it's an argument," said Hambledon.

"Listen," said Bagshott slowly. "If you were not guilty of murder, why were you so frightened today?"

"Da Boss. He lika Pietro. He ver' annoy. He annoy at me, I notta wanta be! I go. I come here." Giuseppe smiled angelically. "He no come here. I stay." He sat down firmly on a chair and folded his arms. "Da jail, *muy bien*. Da Boss, no. *Vaya*, Boss!"

"Listen," said Hambledon. "This Boss, what's his name?"

Giuseppe shook his head violently. "No name. Justa da Boss."

"Nonsense. He is Pietro's brother."

"He say he is."

"And his name is Angelo Gatello."

"If you know," said Giuseppe nervously, "why you ask? Da Boss no lika da talk. I no lika da die. I no talk. Yes, no?"

"Where does he live?"

"I not know, señor. Truly, I not know. He no tella, I not can say. No."

"I should think that's possibly true," said Hambledon to Bagshott. "Mantani! Why did Varsoni shoot Sel—the man at Putney?"

"I not know, señor. Why not you ask Varsoni?"

"Because he's dead," said Hambledon, watching his face. Giuseppe sprang to his feet and clawed the air.

"Dead? Why he dead? *O mio pobre amigo* Manuel!" Then, with an expression of great cunning, "Who make him dead, señor? You tella me. Da Boss, yes, no?"

"I don't know," said Tommy Hambledon.

Giuseppe sat down again. "I no like. Varsoni, dead. Pietro, dead. Me, I dead too if da Boss— I stay here, yes?"

"Better if da Boss here an' you free, yes, no? Dammit, I've caught it now. Listen. I want Angelo Gatello." Giuseppe nodded. "He wants you." Giuseppe shivered and nodded again. "I think I send you back to Bignorth Street and wait outside. Then, when Angelo Gatello comes for you, I get him. See?"

"No a no, no, no. Oh no, señor. No, no. He come in, you not so fast enough, he giva me da woiks. No, no—"

"He doesn't like being the cheese in the mousetrap," said Bagshott.

"I thought he wouldn't. Mantani! You talk, you stay here. You not talk, you go. Got it?"

"Cruel," said Giuseppe, and large tears rolled down his face.

"Well?" said Hambledon.

"I talk," sobbed Mantani.

"Good. Stop that sniveling. Do you think he might have a cup of coffee, Bagshott?"

The coffee came; Giuseppe sipped it and made a grimace, but drank it off. Hambledon gave him a cigarette and said, "Now then. Why is the Gatello gang after Selkirk?"

"Da money."

"What money?"

"Ours."

"Come on. What money was this?"

"Money what da Germans stole. I not know who da money is to," said Giuseppe, with an air of righteous indignation. "Poor mans dead, yes? In Europa."

"Where was the money?"

"In Argentina. *O mia patria—* "

"Yes, yes. How did you get it?"

"Bumpa da bank," said Giuseppe cheerfully.

"We're getting on," said Hambledon. "Slowly. What happened then?"

"We taka da money *al casa Gatello.*"

"What's this?" asked Bagshott.

"They took the money to Gatello's house. And then?"

"Da Selgirk gang. They come! They climba da roof, they breaka da window, they shoot, they banga da bomb, they cutta da throat," said Giuseppe, with appropriate pantomime and a horrid gurgling noise. "Then they taka da money. Alla da money. They go."

"Where to?"

"New York. We go New York. They go London. We go London. Da Boss, he find Selgirk—"

"Where?"

"But Selgirk, he go. Varsoni, he go. Selgirk, he annoy. Varsoni shoot. Finish."

"Where's the money?"

"I not know. Boss not know. He wanta da money. He annoy for that Varsoni maka dead Selgirk. Boss want him maka talk."

"I see. The Boss was annoyed with Varsoni for shooting Selkirk."

"Now you say Varsoni dead. He only killa Selgirk. Me, I killa Pietro. Ugh!"

"You do seem to be in rather a spot. One more question. Where does Selkirk live?"

"Con los angeles, señor, yes?"

"At Los Angeles?" said Bagshott, looking up from his notes.

"No, no," said Hambledon. "With the angels, naturally. My mistake, Mantani. I meant, where did he live before he died?"

But Giuseppe said he didn't know, and stuck to it till Hambledon gave it up.

"Very well. Not that I believe you, but— You will be charged with the murder of Pietro Gatello and remanded in custody pending further enquiries."

"Perdón?"

"You stay here. Or rather, in jail."

"Muchas gracias. O mil gracias—"

Hambledon just succeeded in fending off the little man before he managed to kiss him. Mantani was removed, still rejoicing.

"Well, we got quite a lot of illumination out of that interview," said Bagshott. "Now you know who's got Ribbentrop's money. Hugh Selkirk."

"Yes. And you know who murdered Hyde, and why. He was mistaken for Selkirk. There only remains to find Selkirk and persuade him to tell us where he's put the money. Apparently we're one up on the Gatello gang in one respect. They think Selkirk's dead, they shot him. We know Selkirk's alive and it's Hyde who's dead. Or—no. It must be. Yes. By the way, I like the argument that it isn't murder to shoot a ghost because it's dead already and can't be more so."

"Selkirk's in a good position," said Bagshott, "to deal with this gang if they think he's dead and he isn't. He and Hyde must be alike for the gang to mistake them for each other."

"Do you believe in ghosts, Bagshott? . . . No. Nor do I. But three people, Mrs. Watson, Knight, and Mantani, saw it, so it must have been there. It therefore follows that the man who broke into Hyde's house at Putney last night was Selkirk. What for?"

"Something to do with the money?"

"Presumably. We must assume that Hyde and Selkirk were allies, they're so much mixed up. Probably relations, on account of the likeness. Besides, there's the will, unless it's forged. Now, if Selkirk was being chased by the Gatello gang for the money, he'll want to park that money somewhere. Where better than 11 Clifton Avenue, Putney?"

"I imagine the Gatello gang are arguing on the same lines," said Bagshott. "Hence their continued interest in Hyde's house. I'll send Ennis and Warren down to look for it. If they can't find it, it isn't there."

"Unless Selkirk took it away last night."

"Yes," said Bagshott. "Mind you, this throws no light on the mysterious appearance of the will. Or on why Hyde left all his money to Selkirk."

"Nairn overlooked it before," said Hambledon. "Must have done. I can't suggest why Hyde did it. It may not be important. May not."

"The next step," said Bagshott, "is to make enquiries about Selkirk at the Argentine Legation, and the next after that is to interview the two witnesses to Hyde's will. Forgan and Campbell, of Clerkenwell Road. We ought to get something out of one or the other."

"No squeeza da banan'," said Hambledon, "squeeza da coconut."

CHAPTER ELEVEN
The Corpse Thinks It Over

Hugh Selkirk's funeral at Putney was attended by Race, Nairn, Hyde's domestic staff, and a few kindly neighbors; Hyde himself walked away before the cortege came out of the house in Clifton Avenue. He had no very clear recollection of returning to the hotel; he went into the sitting room and looked uncertainly about him, as though not quite sure if he had come to the right place. Adam came in as usual upon hearing him enter; James was standing in the middle of the room with his overcoat still on and his hat in his hand. Adam took one look at his stricken face and bowed shoulders and stopped dead in his tracks.

Hyde looked at him after a moment, studied his expression, and said, "You know."

"Yes, sir," said the man, through stiff lips.

"Did he commit suicide?"

"No. I am sure of that."

"Then he was—" began Hyde, and stopped. "Adam, this is a hideous shock to me, what it must be to you—"

"Please don't."

"Very well, I won't. But you know." Hyde walked across the room and put his hands on Adam's shoulders. "Adam, who did it?"

"I don't know exactly which of them did it," said Adam slowly. He drew a long breath and straightened himself. "I think the time has come, sir, for me to tell you a long story. Let me take your coat. Will you have something to drink?"

"I'll have a whisky and soda, and so will you. Bring them both in here and sit with me and tell me all about it."

"Thank you, sir."

Adam brought a tray in, served James with the whisky, poured out another for himself, dropped into a chair, and shed his servant's manner like a loose cloak.

"The story begins, I suppose, in Germany," he said. "One gathers that the Nazi leaders always had doubts about the Party's ultimate success, or perhaps they each thought that quarrels would break out and any one of them might be victimized. So they purchased foreign securities, gathered valuable jewels, and generally got very substantial funds together which they deposited in neutral countries against an emergency. You probably heard about this."

James nodded. "I saw one of the leaflets the R.A.F. used to drop over Germany in the early days. I can't read German, but the man who showed it to me told me what it said. It was headed 'These Are Your Leaders,' and gave a list of their nest eggs."

"I never saw that," said Adam, "but it is perfectly true. Much of this wealth came to the Argentine and was deposited in banks there under various names. In the small country town nearest to where we lived, there was a branch of a well-known Argentine bank; quite a solid building with some good strong rooms in the basement. Here was deposited about the equivalent of seven hundred thousand pounds belonging to Ribbentrop. I say 'belonging' because he sent it there; I suppose he stole it from somebody else in the first place. When Ribbentrop was arrested the money didn't seem to belong to anybody. Ribbentrop's German friends, who had actually put it there, wanted it back, but the manager stalled. He was acting under instructions from the Argentine government, who also wanted it. Finally, there was a gang of local bad men who thought it might as well be theirs. You have seen one of them. Manuel Varsoni."

"Was this the same gang who abducted Mr. Selkirk's father? He told me about that."

"Yes, the same. My—my late employer always kept lines out to inform him of what they were doing. He heard that they were after this stuff and warned the bank manager of it. He—Mr. Selkirk—advised the bank manager not to keep it there but to send it to the head office in Buenos Aires. However, he took no action; he was like that. He would not admit that he could not deal with any situation. So Mr. Selkirk said he'd done all he meant to do; if the bank lost the money it served them right for dealing with Germans."

Adam stopped and sipped his whisky; James gave him a cigarette and lit it for him.

"Thanks very much. Well, one dark night the gang broke into the bank, cut the night watchman's throat, opened the strongroom door, and took Ribbentrop's money away."

"How did they know," said Hyde, "exactly where to find it?"

"Head cashier," said Adam briefly. "He disappeared that night and was afterwards seen in Santiago de Chile in what are called affluent circumstances."

"And Mr. Selkirk had the satisfaction of saying, 'I told you so.' "

"He did more than that. He—we raided the gang's headquarters and took the money away again."

"Well done!" cried James. "Very good indeed. What, you two?"

"We had some other fellows with us. It was rather fun," said Adam with his quiet laugh. "They had a place up in the hills, very remote; it had once been a small monastery, I think. My—Mr. Selkirk waited till some of the gang came into Buenos Aires, throwing money about and enjoying themselves after their fashion, and then we made a little expedition. I can see it now. We picked a moonless night, but the stars were so clear that we could see quite well. We came most of the way by car and finished the journey on horseback, up a twisting track through parched sandy rocks, patches of scrub and cactus thorn. We tied up the horses a mile from the place and walked the rest. Crawled most of it, with gray blankets over us to make us inconspicuous against the earth. Gatello's place was a sprawling collection of buildings surrounded by a wall, standing on a sort of flat shelf in the mountains. They had sentries out; at least, they thought they had. Three of 'em, posted at intervals round the walls. In point of fact, when we arrived they were all three together, squatted round a lantern by the gate, playing *morra*. Do you know it? A childish game, I'll show you sometime. So we went round the other side and over the wall. There were stables and so forth, and then the house. Mr. Selkirk knew the way, he'd been there before. We went in through a window. The house was dirty and ruinous, with battered furniture sprawled about. There was only one place where they'd keep the money, an ironbound wooden chest, very old, in the Gatellos' bedroom upstairs. Pietro Gatello was there in bed, very sound asleep; he'd been drinking. Angelo was away in Buenos Aires. We left men posted outside the door and on the stairs; Mr. Selkirk and I went in." Adam paused for a drink, and James Hyde, flushed and eager, leaned forward and said, "The room—what was it like? How could you see? Electric torches? You were armed, of course?"

"The room? A long low room with whitewashed walls, very grimy, one or two native rugs hung on them. Wooden floor, two untidy beds, and over them a small statue of the Virgin with a little lamp burning before it. Bright enough to light the room when you came in out of the dark. The chest was between the beds and it was locked. We made rather a noise trying the hasp, and Pietro left off snoring and sat up. So I tapped him on the head with the butt of my revolver, took the key from round his neck, and opened the chest in comfort. Sure enough, the loot was there, in a sort of canvas bag with red woolen tassels on it and a leather strap studded with brass. Mr. Selkirk took the bag and we went out. So far so good. We collected the two men we'd posted—another was by the wall and the fourth with the horses—and tiptoed down the stairs. We could hear men snoring in the other rooms as we passed—"

"How many? Men, I mean."

"Oh, six or eight. Then, in the passage at the bottom, we bumped into a man who happened to be about. Mr. Selkirk half choked him and we took him with us as far as the wall. You see, we didn't want to wake 'em all up. Funny little fellow called Giuseppe Mantani. He didn't give any trouble. It was uncanny, how quiet it was. We tied him up, gagged him, and left him lying while we got over the wall and clear away to the horses. No trouble at all."

"But," said James, "wasn't Angelo furious—"

"Fairly gibbering. Of course, the party at the house, and the sentries, made up a lovely tale of wrath and violence to appease him. We heard all about it later. We smashed in through the roof, I understand, firing with both hands and yelling like demons, dozens of us—"

("They climba da roof," said Giuseppe to Hambledon, "they breaka da window, they shoot, they banga da bomb, they cutta da throat—")

"I imagine," went on Adam, "that they did some smashing up themselves, to manufacture evidence. They are all terrified of Angelo, even Pietro, his brother."

"What happened then?"

"We got back to the cars and drove like blazes. We only stopped at Carmen de las Flores long enough to pack a suitcase and change our clothes and then went on to Buenos Aires and took the first plane for New York. They knew it was us, you see. Pietro saw us, so did Mantani. In fact, Mr. Selkirk wanted them to know it was he who'd done it. Part of the payment for his father's life."

James drew a long breath; he felt as though he had been violently swimming

in tempestuous seas. This was life; real men did these things and laughed as
they did them.

"What happened then?"

"They got after us in New York, so we came on to London."

"And where's the money now?"

"As a matter of fact," said Adam with a twinkle in his brown eyes, "you're
sitting on it."

James sprang to his feet and looked at his comfortable armchair as though it
had bitten him.

"In there?"

"Tucked in among the springs."

James looked at the chair for a moment longer. "Well," he said, "I think
I shall continue to sit on it," and did so. He spoke with a certain grimness
of tone, at which Adam nodded his head almost imperceptibly and continued his story.

"I ought to explain that the whole scheme was definitely planned from the
outset. As soon, that is, as Mr. Selkirk heard the Gatello gang were after
Ribbentrop's hoard. The gang killed Mr. Selkirk, Sr., and my master was deter-
mined to make them pay for it. He would not kill them himself; he said he was
neither a murderer nor an executioner. But they had committed, and were continually committing, crimes which would bring them under the law in any country but the Argentine. There, they had friends; they had money; people were
afraid of them. It was impossible to get anyone to give evidence against the
Gatello gang. In England it would be different. Here, if they robbed, beat up, or
murdered any citizen—or even each other—the police would get them and
they would be tried and punished. The difficulty was to get them to England.
That is why, when we took Ribbentrop's loot away from them, we came to
England, hoping they would follow. They did."

"I see," said James. "After that, the idea was to keep them hanging about till
they destroyed themselves or each other."

"With a little assistance from us. One childishly simple plan was to inform
two members of the gang that each was betraying the other. They always are,
anyway, so they'd believe it at once, if backed up by a little proof of some kind.
Then one would probably murder the other, or try to, and the police could deal
with the survivor, and so on."

"I see," said James again. "Er—where did I come in?"

For the first time Adam looked a trifle embarrassed. "I feel we owe you an
apology and so did Mr. Selkirk. It came about like this. He saw you one evening
at the D'Artagnan and noticed the likeness; he came home and told me about
it. 'There's a man who could impersonate me if he cared to try,' he said. Then

he made friends with you and—and liked you. I want to make that quite plain. He was not pretending to like you because he thought you might be useful. He was not that sort. I hope you believe me, because that is true."

"I do believe you," said James in a low tone. "I can't think what he saw in me, but I believe it all the same."

Adam smiled faintly. "Then things got rather hot. The gang found out where we lived and haunted the place. It cut Mr. Selkirk off from his other friends— we have other friends in London—he could not go to see them because some of the gang would follow him. Mr. Selkirk met you quite openly, and no doubt the gang knew you quite well by sight. You came here with him more than once. No danger for you; you had no connection with Argentina. His idea was that they should see you and him come in here together, and apparently you go away again, as had happened before. He was going to your house at Putney for the night, to throw them off the scent, and then start operations against them when they had lost sight of him. You were to stay here for a day or two, and no doubt some of the servants here would report that Mr. Selkirk was still in residence, though he'd shaved off his beard. Then I was to give you a message that he'd been unexpectedly called away and would see you later. You would have returned to your own house, and all would have been well."

"What went wrong?"

"I don't know. Evidently they were not deceived; they knew it was he who went to Putney that night, not you. They would know if they saw him close to; you are not doubles. We hoped that removing the beard would fox them; it didn't, obviously. By the way, I was to give them a chance of seeing you plainly so that they would know you weren't he. No need, they knew that at once."

There was a short pause which James broke by saying, "And what do we do now?"

"I suggest," said Adam, "that you return to your house at Putney and explain that there was a mistake in identity and how it came about. Put all your cards on the table, in fact. Then the police can get on with finding the murderer and you can take up your own life again."

James got up; Adam made as though to rise also but Hyde pressed his shoulder and said, "No, sit still. I want to think for a minute." He walked up and down the room, his head bent and his hands in his pockets. If his breath came fast sometimes as he thought, if he turned cold about the heart or his knees felt a little weak, at least he did not show it. By degrees his jaw came forward and his step was more assured. He stopped.

"No," he said decidedly. "No, I'm damned if I will."

Adam looked at him. "Have you considered—" he began.

"Of course I've considered. What d'you suppose I've been doing? And I admit quite frankly that there's a lot I don't like the look of at all. But I've also considered this. Your master was my friend. I think there's quite good reason to believe he was my cousin also; we can go into that later. He has been murdered by this gang of dagoes. Am I to sit down under that? He had a plan he meant to carry out. Are they going to get away with it after all? Adam, can't we carry on with it? You and I? I'm no good without you. I'll try not to let you down——"

"Stop, please," said Adam. "I can't listen to that. Of course you won't let me down, as you call it. You looked so like him as you walked about; he used to 'quarterdeck' like that when he was thinking. But I don't believe you realize the risks you run. Frankly, we are not very likely to be alive in a month's time, either of us."

"Well?" said James. "Tennyson's old-fashioned, I know, but 'we die, does it matter when?' To hear people talk, you'd think that by avoiding risks we could live forever. Besides, you forget, I'm dead already; the police say so. What a fool I should look, walking in again and saying, 'No, I'm not.' What's more, I loathe that house at Putney and I never want to see it again. Especially after this," he added, as though to himself, and Adam nodded. "Finally, there's my housekeeper. What a relief to be quit of her! Also, when I told Selkirk I wanted adventure, it was quite true, you know. Well, here it is."

The two men looked at each other.

"But suppose you're killed," began Adam doubtfully.

"Selkirk's dead, isn't he?" said Hyde harshly, and bit his lip.

"I give in," said Adam. "When you say it like that, there's no answer. Very well, come in with me and we'll down these fellows—or not, as the case may be. We'll have a run for our money, anyway."

"That's the way to talk," said James. "By the way, talking about money, what did Selkirk mean to do with it ultimately?"

"Send it anonymously to the Chancellor of the Exchequer. That will have to wait till we've finished with the Gatellos, though, because there is sure to be a mention of it in the papers, and once they know it's finally out of their reach they'll just pack up and go home. That was what Varsoni came here the other night for, of course, to look for the money."

"And saw me? But if, as you said, he knew me by sight before, why was he so frightened?"

"Because you look as though you've shaved off a beard. Hyde had no beard to shave. Varsoni knew he'd killed Selkirk, and these people are horribly superstitious. He thought you were a ghost, no doubt. You've finished off one of them already, haven't you?"

"Inadvertently," said Hyde.

"But effectively, and by the right method. He was destroyed by his own lawless act."

"Well, yes. Anyway, it's a start. What do we do next? Go on living here, I suppose?"

"Why not?" said Adam. "It's very comfortable. Besides, they know where to find us, here. You see, to attain our object, two things are necessary. To keep the gang where we can find them, and to remain alive. We could go away and lose them easily enough, no doubt, but that won't do."

"About the money," said Hyde diffidently. "Ours, I mean. This must be a very expensive place to live in, and I can't even draw a check."

"Oh, that's all right. Mr. Selkirk was a very wealthy man and I have authority to draw checks for him. That's all arranged."

"Good. Now about the gang. How many of them are there?"

"Seven, now Varsoni's dead. There's Angelo Gatello and Pietro, his brother. Ramon Jacaro—that means Ramon the bully; most of their names are nick-names. Pacorro Pagote—*pagote* is a slang word meaning the poor innocent who's always left to take the can back. The scapegoat, if you like. Giuseppe Mantani, Cesar Mariposa, though why he thinks he's like a butterfly I can't imagine. He's the fat one. Tadeo el Caballero—Gentleman Teddy, I suppose."

"Is he?" asked James. "A gentleman, I mean."

"No. Oh no. He likes having a bath when he can get one, that's all, and the others think that's rather pansy. He told me once, with the air of one apologizing for a weakness, that he got into the habit when he was in hospital for a time."

"And you know where they all live?"

"Oh yes. I'll give you their addresses whenever you want them. Angelo and Pietro live in a fairly decent hotel; they are quite presentable in appearance. The others are in lodgings and cheap boardinghouses. They can all speak English of a sort."

There was a long pause while both men pursued their own trains of thought. James broke it by saying, "Reverting to my own affairs for a moment—"

"Yes?"

"I'm dead, aren't I? And buried—by the way! Why didn't my staff know Selkirk wasn't me?"

"I don't know," said Adam grimly, "but I can guess."

James shuddered and went on hastily. "What I was going to say was that I haven't made a will. I've died intestate, so that repulsive little squirt, my cousin Walter Race, will come into every penny. I don't want that to happen."

"You don't seem to like him."

"I don't. Double-dealing, dishonest little weasel. I always loathed him ever since we were small boys. His sister wasn't so bad, but she's dead."

"Something will have to be done," said Adam thoughtfully. "If you made a will leaving everything to Hugh Selkirk, you would get it yourself. That could be arranged. Would that do?"

"Leave it to myself, eh? Yes, but what about the date?"

"It will have to be antedated, of course. Any date before last Tuesday will do. One day last week."

"But the witnesses," objected James. "They date their signatures. I know, I've been a witness to a will."

"I'll find some witnesses," said Adam, "who can be relied on to make a mistake in the date and stick to it."

"Isn't that a felony?" said James doubtfully.

"Why? It's your own money, you're not stealing it."

James laughed. "You have a refreshing directness of thought, Adam. I buy one of those will forms, do I?"

"No, I do. Something might crop up, and it's as well to be careful. Too late tonight, and tomorrow's Sunday. I'll get one on Monday morning."

"When it's written and signed, what do we do? I mean, I can't just post it to Nairn—"

"Have you got a safe?" James nodded. "The most natural course would be to plant it in there, I think. Let 'em find it. Have you got your safe key with you, or—"

"No key. It's a figure combination lock. But—"

"Well, that's all right. You write the will; we'll get it witnessed. Then we'll just slip into your house one quiet night and put it in the safe. It'll be a little practice for you."

James looked a little apprehensive and then cheered up. "After all, it can't be a felony to break and enter your own house," he said.

"You're markedly averse to felony," smiled Adam.

"Well, you see," apologized James, "I'm not accustomed to it—yet."

CHAPTER TWELVE
G.P.O. in Paradise

James Hyde made his will in the simplest terms possible, writing it out with his own hand and using the big green fountain pen he always carried. "It will help to convince Nairn," he said, "if I write with this pen. He knows it so well. He calls it Robespierre."

"Eh?" said Adam. "Oh, I've got it. The 'sea-green incorruptible.' "

"Yes. It's a gold nib," said James simply. "Now, what?"

"Now we go and see two friends of ours. Their names are Forgan and Campbell. Forgan keeps a model shop in the Clerkenwell Road, but I think we'll start by going to South Kensington."

Adam took Hyde for an extensive but rapid tour of London by underground, bus, and taxi in turns. They went into shops by one entrance and out by another; sometimes they loitered and sometimes hurried. When at last they alighted at Aldersgate Street Station, the only passengers to do so, Adam hustled James out of sight before the train pulled out.

"That's all right," he said. "We've lost them."

"Have we been followed all this way?" asked James.

"Not quite. The last time I actually saw our friends was at Baker Street; I think they went to Pinner by mistake. I'm sorry to have taken you for such a trip, but I didn't want to lead them to Forgan. We can go straight ahead now."

Forgan's shop at once appealed strongly to the indestructible small boy in James Hyde. While Adam explained what was wanted of the modelmakers, Hyde listened with only half of his attention, his eyes roaming round the shop.

"The only point of importance is the date," said Adam. "Friday, March the twenty-ninth, will do quite well."

"Friday, March the twenty-ninth," repeated Forgan, and Campbell nodded. "It is simple. If we are asked, we shall remember. How well do we know this gentleman?"

"Not too well, just as a customer. He is a retired businessman who lives at Putney. He is a bachelor. I think that's all you need know when you are asked."

"He has been in here," said Forgan gravely, "perhaps a dozen times in the last four months. We were shocked to read in the paper of his tragic death."

"That's right, that'll do nicely."

They signed, not on the shop counter in full view of the public passing the open door, but at a desk in the workshop behind.

"Thank you very much," said Hyde shyly. "It is very good of you to do this for a stranger."

"From what Adam has told us," said Campbell, "you won't be a stranger very long."

"I should like to come here often," said Hyde, "and inflict myself upon you for hours. But I think that would be unwise at the moment."

"Wait till we have killed off these vermin," said Forgan, "and you shall come every day and stay as long as you please."

"In the meantime," said Campbell, "no doubt we shall meet elsewhere. And have lots of fun," he added savagely. "Rat-hunting, you know."

"Before that actually begins," said Adam, "I should be glad if you'd drive a car for us one night, Campbell."

"Certainly," said the redhaired man. "When? Tonight?"

"Not tonight, there'll be a moon; it's only just past the full. Thursday will do, I think; she won't be rising till nearly three in the morning and we should be home by then. Mr. Hyde wants to pay a visit to his house at Putney; actually, to put this will in his safe. He thought it might cause comment if he just posted it."

"Suggesting a branch of the G.P.O. in Paradise? I expect he's right. All the best people leave their wills in their safes, no doubt," said Campbell.

"Have you got your latchkey?" asked Forgan.

"No," said Hyde. "Er—he had it, of course."

"Of course," echoed Forgan, "of course," and his wide mouth shut like a trap.

"But there's an easy window to the study," said James. "The catch is loose. I meant to have it replaced."

"You'll make a burglar yet," laughed Campbell. "Under Adam's tuition, naturally. Where do we get a car? I take it we'd better not use our own, or do we?"

"Certainly not," said Adam, "it might be noticed. We'll hire one to drive ourselves. We'll see to that; I'll let you know the details later. By the way," he added suddenly, "have you seen anything of a man just over six feet tall, fair hair cut very short, square face with deep lines across his forehead and round his mouth, nose broken at some time in the past. He speaks with a slight German accent. I don't know how he is dressed now and I don't know where he lives."

"No," said Forgan thoughtfully, and Campbell said: "No, we haven't seen him yet, but we'll look out for him. Why?"

"His name is Hommelhoff, Konrad Hommelhoff. He is one of the Germans in Buenos Aires who were trying to get Ribbentrop's money from our bank manager before the Gatellos got it. I may be mistaken, but I thought I saw him yesterday in Piccadilly Circus. He didn't see me; at least, I don't think he did."

"Is it your idea," said Forgan, "that he has come here after the Gatellos?"

"Yes. But I may be wrong and perhaps it was just somebody who looked like him. I didn't like to examine him closely."

"He wouldn't know us, would he?" said Campbell. "We left Argentina long before all this business started."

"You did, of course, but somebody might have told him about you. Quite likely there's nothing in it; I just thought I'd better mention it."

On Thursday evening James Hyde went to a garage and hired a car, explaining that he and his friends were going to spend the evening with some more friends at Kingston and might be late. His name, he said, was Jones; he gave an address in the Horseferry Road and paid the necessary deposit without hesitation. Then the three men got into the car and drove away. Campbell said that Mr. Hyde was definitely a useful man for occasions like this as he did look so very respectable; a remark which startled James, who felt that he had gone a long way in the last ten days. No one had ever congratulated him upon looking respectable before.

They drove up Putney Hill, turned into Clifton Avenue, and went along it to the far end, where Campbell turned the car round. The road sloped down towards Putney Hill; they were able to coast the last fifty yards and arrive in silence at a point just short of Hyde's gateway. Adam got out; Hyde, with clammy hands and a feeling that his collar was two sizes too small, followed him, and Adam closed the door quietly.

Hyde led the way, walking in rubber-soled shoes on the grass verge until he reached the gravel sweep in front of the house. He looked round to see if Adam was following, and a ray of light from the street lamp outside found a gap in the shrubbery and fell full upon his face. Six feet away, just within the screen of bushes, a small tubby man with a mop of black curly hair saw the face and recognized it, or thought he did. He was so petrified by terror that he did not move or breathe; he shut his eyes tight and silently petitioned his neglected saints. He neither saw nor heard Adam following Hyde towards the study window.

Pietro Gatello, intent upon deciding once for all whether or not the Ribbentrop treasure had been deposited in that house, was working upon the study window. He also knew about the loose catch; he had discovered it during a previous reconnaissance. He knew, too, that there were only three women in the house and was not anxious on that account. He had dealt with dames before. He slipped a thin-bladed knife between the sashes and pressed the catch back; before pushing up the window he glanced over his shoulder and saw, dimly but unmistakably, two men coming across the gravel towards him. He did not recognize them; his first thought was that they were probably police, keeping a routine eye upon the scene of a murder. He melted into the lilac bushes without a sound.

Hyde and Adam reached the window and Adam shone a tiny pencil of light upon the catch. "It's not latched," he murmured.

"Careless," whispered Hyde indignantly. "Very careless. Surprised at Mrs. Watson." He pushed up the window cautiously, but in spite of his care it bumped in the slides as it went up and James muttered, "Oh dear," in an exasperated whisper.

"Never mind," said Adam. "Get on, quick. Perhaps no one heard it."

The two men stepped over the low sill and slipped between the drawn curtains. The next moment a faint glimmer of light told the interested Pietro, hushed among the lilacs, that the newcomers had switched on a light. A shaded light. It was, in fact, the desk light with the beam directed towards the floor. Hyde turned at once to the safe and opened it. He looked at the contents and said, "Somebody's been here already. It isn't quite as I left it."

"Police, I expect," said Adam. "Or your lawyer, on their instructions. Push the will into the middle somewhere; they may think they overlooked it before."

Hyde did so and closed the safe again. He then turned to his desk, saying, "Just one moment, something I want," and pulled open a drawer. He was rummaging among the papers in it when, to his speechless horror, the door opened and Mrs. Watson put her head in. Master and housekeeper stared dreadfully at each other for a moment—Adam was outside the circle of light—then the woman uttered an appalling scream and fled, shutting the door behind her.

In the meantime Pietro Gatello had decided that these intruders were not the police. He didn't know much about the English police, but he had always heard that they were quite ridiculously noble-minded and never thought for a moment of entering a house without ringing the bell. These must be burglars. Was he, a Gatello, to sit like an owl in a bush while two strangers went off with the loot under his nose? Several times, no. He began to edge cautiously round the bushes towards Giuseppe Mantani, who, by the way, ought to have warned him that there was someone coming. Appropriate reprisal for neglect of duty must be applied to Mantani later. At the moment, however, they would join forces outside the window, fall upon the men as they emerged, silence them, and take from them whatever it was which they had secured. He sidled round the edge of the gravel and paused to listen to a faint muttering ahead.

"St. Christopher, pray for me. Blessed St. Anthony, pray for me. Blessed St. Joseph, pray for me. Oh most blessed St.—"

Pietro grinned to himself; Giuseppe had the wind up, the poor fool, he—

A loud shriek hit the silence, a high, wavering scream; it came from the house. Pietro froze in his tracks and Giuseppe even stopped praying. There was the sound of a shutting door and the dim light disappeared in the study window. A moment later there was a faint bump as someone kicked the paneling in the act of stepping over the window sill. Pietro moved; it was now or never. He advanced upon Giuseppe, stretched out his hand to touch him—

Hyde was out upon the gravel and pausing for Adam to join him. His heart was still racing from the shock of that awful scream, but he was mainly conscious of a desire to laugh. Mrs. Watson's face—

There was a bright flash in the shadows ahead and a sharp crack. Immediately a torch was switched on, plainly showing a man rolling on the ground and, more dimly, another man bending over him. A cry followed, the same cry which Hyde's housekeeper had correctly described as a yelp. "Pietro," it said, and then a gabbled phrase. The torch went out again and flying footsteps retreated down the drive, out of the gate and along the road, till they died away in the distance.

Adam ran forward with Hyde at his heels and shone his tiny torch momentarily upon the face of the man upon the ground, who chose that moment to die.

"Pietro Gatello," said Adam calmly. "Now I wonder what he was doing here?"

Campbell, waiting in the car outside, intelligently started his engine. When Hyde and Adam came out of the drive he moved slowly to meet them; the moment they were in the drove rapidly away. Not even Adam noticed the earnest sheeplike face of Mr. Knight, anxiously peering at them through a skein of ivy at the next gateway.

When they were well away and none had blown whistles at them or shouted "Stop!" Campbell relaxed comfortably and tilted his head towards the back seats.

"What set Mantani off like that?" he asked. "Did you pot at him?"

"Oh, was that Mantani?" said Adam in an interested voice. "I didn't see him well enough to recognize him. No, he did the potting. Pietro Gatello. He's dead."

"Mantani shot Pietro?" said Campbell incredulously. "What the devil made him do that?"

"No idea. Angelo will be annoyed, won't he? No, the whole business was a complete surprise to me; I didn't know they were there. They must have been sitting in the bushes watching us."

"Do you mean to say," said the horrified James, "that those two men were in the garden behind us all the time?"

"Well, they didn't follow you in," said Campbell.

Hyde remembered Selkirk's simile of diving into danger as into an ice-cold river, and finding it exhilarating after the first shock. It seemed, however, that he had been up to his neck in it without knowing it. He drew a long breath.

"Who screamed?" asked Campbell. Hyde told him, and added, "I never managed to alarm her before; I suppose she took me for my ghost."

"I hope so," said Campbell, "because then nobody will believe her. You're very quiet, Adam."

"I was thinking," said Adam. "I think a little note to Scotland Yard is indicated, then they can collect Giuseppe Mantani. It will give us one less to deal with."

"Sound idea," said Campbell. "Got anything to write on?"

James produced a half sheet of paper and wrote at Adam's dictation the message which sent Bagshott's man to 79 Bignorth Street.

"I haven't an envelope," said Hyde.

"Fold it over, stick it down with a stamp, and write, 'Kindly hand to C.I.D., London' on the outside. We'll leave it in the car; somebody will find it. The sooner the better for Giuseppe."

Hyde took the next day easily after a late breakfast. One does not take to murder and sudden death after the age of fifty with the resilience of nineteen; it needs a little time to become acclimatized. He said as much to Adam, with an air of apology.

"Indeed, sir," said the perfect manservant, "a certain degree of reaction was to be expected. If I may say so, sir, you display it less than I should have thought likely, under the circumstances."

"Must you talk to me like that, Adam, 'under the circumstances'?"

"Yes, sir. Definitely. Living as we are in a hotel, with servants likely to enter at any moment to perform their duties, even the most momentary relaxation has its dangers."

"Of course you're right. Well, what's the next move?"

"May I suggest that you should join a night club? It would be a natural course for a single gentleman like yourself to take. This hotel is not well provided with evening amusements, however innocent."

"You're pulling my leg, you know," said James comfortably, but Adam did not smile.

"The night club I had in mind," he said, "is called the Red Macaw, and is situated in Soho. There is music, dancing, and cheerful company available."

"Really, Adam! I—"

"They also serve an extremely good dinner at a moderate cost. The premises consist of the first floor of a block of buildings in Marjorie Street, a turning off Soho Square. The ground floor is composed of a row of shops; the stair leading up to the Red Macaw has a private door between two of these shops. The second floor—that is, the one above the club and served by the same stair"—Adam paused and allowed a faint smile to rise to the surface—"is the headquarters of the Gatello gang."

A week earlier James would have leapt to his feet and said "Ha!" but he had learned restraint since the night when Selkirk died. He merely raised his eyebrows and said, "Really. How long have you known that?"

"My master, sir, became informed of it not long ago. Actually, he never visited the place, but I became a member and have been there more than once. The manager is quite a friend of mine, sir. I was able to put him in the way of obtaining some vodka, which is, I understand, in short supply. I am, therefore, in a position to introduce you, sir, if you agree."

"Do I take it," said Hyde, "that you expect any definite outcome from a visit to the Red Macaw, or is it in the nature of a reconnaissance?"

"Only reconnaissance. I had no particular plan in mind. I thought you might find it interesting and helpful to see for yourself, sir, at least the environs of the locale."

"We will inspect the environs of the locale," said James. "When do we go? Tonight, or tomorrow?"

"Tomorrow night would perhaps be better, sir."

"By the way, how much risk do you consider is involved in walking about London with these fellows after our blood? Are certain situations safer than others, or do we expect a knife in the ribs at any moment? I am thinking," said James, anxious not to appear nervous, "of your remark that if we are to succeed we must remain alive. It's obviously true. Are there any steps we can take without—er—impairing our efficiency?"

"A very sensible question, sir, if I may say so. One thing to be remembered is that these men go in terror of the police. They will go to any lengths rather than be arrested. They will arrange an accident if they can—one of them tried to push Mr. Selkirk off the platform in front of an underground train—but they won't, I think, attack us in the street. They might be caught. They only got Mr. Selkirk because he was alone in an unfrequented spot. Provided we avoid secluded spots and decline invitations to enter strange houses, we have a fair chance. Tomorrow night, for example, we shall be in populous streets or in a rather noisy club. We will take a taxi to Soho Square."

James nodded. "That's good enough. Thank you, Adam."

They left the hotel separately the following night, met at the corner of Argyle Place, and picked up a taxi which took them to Soho Square.

"It's that street over there," said Adam. James turned to cross the road and collided awkwardly with a small man who was in the act of overtaking them. Hyde apologized with his usual courtesy, but the small man grabbed him by the arm and hung on like a bull terrier.

"James! Great Scott, James in the flesh! James, old chap, I can't tell you—"

Hyde always had disliked his cousin Race, but at this moment he could willingly have murdered him.

"I beg your pardon, sir," he said stiffly. "A mistake in identity, I imagine."

"Come off it," said Race vulgarly. "Look here, James, this won't do. Do you know you're supposed to have been murdered?"

Hyde and Adam exchanged glances over Race's head while he babbled on.

"Of course, if you're merely having a week or two out on the tiles it's no business of mine—do you good—wish you luck—but this murder business is too much. Do you know the police suspect me of having a hand in it?"

Race's voice was squeaky with excitement and several passersby caught the word "murder." They slowed down and came back; or stopped, pretending to light cigarettes or admire the view. In another moment a crowd would begin to form. Adam touched Hyde on the arm and jerked his head in the direction of the Red Macaw. Hyde nodded.

"Look here, sir," he said to Race. "We can't have a scene on the pavement. You will come with me to my club and we'll put a stop to this nonsense."

Race hesitated. The face and form were those of James Hyde, but the firm tones and assured manners were quite strange. His gentle malleable cousin never spoke like this.

"Well, really," he began, and drew back, but Hyde took a firm grip of his elbow. Obviously, it would never do to have Race trotting off to the police with this story, they might inconveniently believe it.

"Come along," he said firmly. "It's only just over there."

"I'll go on ahead," said Adam, "and engage a table. I shall want a word with the manager—"

He went ahead rapidly, leaving Hyde and his captive to follow. Race came unwillingly; one minute talking of curious coincidences and extraordinary likenesses, and the next moment calling him "James" and imploring him to come to the police and put things right. Hyde barely answered; he was wondering what sum Race would take to hold his tongue and, possibly, go abroad for a long visit. Or it might be just possible to convince him that he was wrong and that to go to the police with a cock-and-bull story like that would only serve to increase their suspicion. A private word with Adam would be a help.

He found the door, between a chemist's and a shoe shop, which opened upon a stair leading up to the Red Macaw. He was so absorbed in thought that he did not notice a small group of men about the door. As he approached, two of them turned in and went up the stairs ahead of Hyde and Race; the other three fell in behind.

The stairs were dark and twisted steeply round a well. Halfway up, the two men leading stopped so abruptly that Hyde almost cannoned into them; at the same moment the three behind closed up, and a smooth voice murmured into Hyde's ear.

"You will not stop at the Red Macaw, no. You will not cry out or struggle. Very peaceably you walk on upstairs. I think so, yes?"

Something hard and round was pressed into Hyde's ribs, and his heart seemed to leap up into his throat and settle down again into the wrong place. Race began, "Now, what is all this—" But the silky voice cut him short.

"Complete silence, please," it said. "I am short-tempered, me. I do not like the arguments."

The procession started up the stairs; at the top of the first flight was a landing with a pair of double doors in it. They had glass panels set in them; as the cortege passed by Hyde saw Adam just inside, waiting for him, and their eyes met. The party went on up the stairs towards the second floor.

CHAPTER THIRTEEN
The Precious Pair

Bagshott put a routine enquiry to the Argentine Legation on the subject of Hugh Selkirk, Esq., of Carmen de las Flores, Buenos Aires Province, Argentine, and 27 Avenida de las Rochas, Buenos Aires. Was the gentleman known in the Argentine; was his name, as quoted, fully correct; were these his present addresses at which letters could reach him; and was Mr. Selkirk in the Argentine at present? If not, where was he?

"They probably know his London address," said Hambledon. "Well, shall we now go and call on the two witnesses?"

Mr. Forgan's establishment in the Clerkenwell Road was a small shop with one window and a door in its narrow frontage. The window contained, on the left, a very fine Gauge O scale model of the L.M.S. Company's 2-6-0 type locomotive; a small ticket leaning against it said, "Steam. Reconditioned. A Bargain." Behind it were several more railway engines of various types and sizes from clockwork tank locos to a model of the Royal Scot rather the worse for wear, and some assorted rolling stock. On the right were waterline models of warships; one or two toy yachts, Bermuda rigged; and several power-driven models, from steam launches to the humble toc-toc. In the middle of the window was a tray full of spare parts for miniature locomotives and tiny ships' fittings. Above all these, high up in the window, hung a large wooden model of a barque, fully rigged but without sails. It was such a model as one sees hanging as votive offerings in churches on the maritime coasts of Europe, beautifully built and with great wealth of detail. It was dusty and out of order; the broken mizzen topmast hung tangled in the rigging, and the poop rails were missing on the portside, but it was still lovely. Tommy Hambledon flattened his nose against the window and said, "Look at that. Somebody's pride and joy, you know."

"I wish I were a small boy again," said Bagshott. "Look at that signal gantry. Oh, at the back there! There's an old brass model of a beam engine. I wonder if it works."

On the door was painted, "William Forgan. Models, antique and modern. Repairs executed." Hambledon and Bagshott detached themselves regretfully from the window and went inside. The shop was divided across by a wooden screen; from behind this there came the sound of machinery in motion.

The front half of the shop contained a counter with a small area of clear floor space in front of it; the rest of the room was taken up with show cases, cabinets, and cupboards, all crammed with odd fittings and spare parts of every conceivable description. Behind the counter stood a tall thin man with red hair and a sallow complexion, an unusual mixture. "Been in the tropics," thought Bagshott.

"Can I get you something?"

"Are you Mr. Forgan?" asked Bagshott.

"Mr. Forgan is busy at the moment, but if you wanted something I expect I could find it," said the redhaired man cheerfully.

"I'm extremely sorry to interrupt Mr. Forgan, but what I really wanted was some information. I am Chief-Inspector Bagshott—here's my card—are you by any chance Mr. Campbell?"

"I am," said Campbell. "What's Forgan been doing? Selling passenger-hauling miniature locos on the black market? You could, you know. I'll call him." He disappeared behind the partition; after a moment the sound of mechanized industry ceased and Campbell returned, bringing a short stout man with him whom he introduced as "my partner, the head of the firm, Mr. William Forgan."

Forgan showed the same tropical sallowness of skin as his partner, but had dark wiry hair with a thin patch on the top and beady brown eyes at once intelligent and wary.

Bagshott shook hands with him and apologized for coming at an inconvenient time, but Forgan said that there was no need to apologize as Bagshott's time must be more valuable than his own. "We are honored by receiving a visit from a chief-inspector," he added without a smile.

"We are also rather alarmed," said Campbell.

"What I wanted to ask you," said Bagshott, "was about a will which you witnessed recently for a Mr. James Clarendon Hyde."

"The poor man who was killed," said Campbell. "We read about it in the paper."

"Very sad," said Forgan. "Yes, we witnessed his signature to a document he said was his will. It was on one of those printed will forms; I saw the top of it above the blotting paper. He covered up what he had actually written, while we signed."

"He actually did sign it," said Bagshott, "in the presence of both of you at once?"

"Certainly," said Forgan. "In fact, he signed it on this counter, standing on the side where you are, and Campbell and I stood this side watching him. Then he turned it round and we signed."

"I see," said Bagshott. "When was this?"

Forgan and Campbell looked at each other. "It was five or six days before we saw his death in the paper, and that was ten days ago, wasn't it, Campbell?"

"I kept the cutting," said Campbell, opening a drawer. "In fact, all the cuttings I saw; we were interested, naturally. There seems to be something slightly mysterious about his death, doesn't there?"

"One or two of the attendant circumstances are rather obscure," said Bagshott. Hambledon, modest in the background, suppressed a grin.

"Here's the cutting," said Campbell, "dated April the third. 'Last night,' so he died on the second. It was sometime during the previous week."

"Not Thursday," said Forgan. "We are shut on Thursday afternoons—"

"I remember," said his partner. "It was Friday, because Mr. Hyde passed the rent collector in the doorway as he went out. She always calls on Fridays."

Forgan glanced at the calendar behind him. "It was Friday, the twenty-ninth, then."

"Thank you," said Bagshott, and made an unnecessary note. Friday, March the twenty-ninth, was the date on the will.

"Forgive me if I'm indiscreet," said Campbell, "but is there something funny about that will?"

"It appears to be quite in order," said Bagshott correctly.

"Consider myself snubbed," said Campbell cheerfully. "I only wondered, because I should have thought a solicitor would be making these enquiries, not a big shot from Scotland Yard."

Hambledon again suppressed a smile; Bagshott was not having it all his own way by any means.

"I am really sorry," said the chief-inspector amiably, "to appear so mysterious, but I'm afraid it can't be helped under the circumstances."

"The obscure circumstances," laughed Campbell, and became serious at once. "Not that there's anything amusing about poor Mr. Hyde's death. We were, both of us, extremely sorry to hear of it."

"Did you know him well?" asked Bagshott, and Forgan answered this time.

"Yes and no. He had been in this shop quite a lot over a period of—what, three months, Campbell?"

"Quite that," said Campbell.

"But he never talked about himself or his affairs. I put him down as a retired businessman looking for a hobby. He told us his name the third or fourth time he came in, and mentioned once that he lived at Putney. He took more interest in the way things were made than in finished models; once or twice latterly he came round behind the screen to watch me working on the lathe."

"Did he buy much?"

Forgan shrugged his shoulders. "Clockwork toys, the sort you give to small children. I asked him once if they were for his own nursery and he said no, he was an old bachelor, and muttered something about children's hospitals."

"Could you describe Mr. Hyde?"

Forgan gave a description of a man very like what Hyde must have been in life, and Campbell added corroborative details.

Bagshott straightened up and thanked them, put his notebook away, and looked round the shop. "Fascinating business, this," he said. "Made me wish I was a small boy again, just to look at it."

Forgan smiled. "You don't have to be a small boy to find models fascinating, quite the contrary. Most of our customers are men like Mr. Hyde, running models for a hobby. You'd be surprised the money some of them spend on it."

"I daresay," said Bagshott, and bent to examine a tiny model galleon in a glass case. "You've been doing this for a long time, I suppose."

"Eight years next month," said Forgan. "I started it when I came home from the Argentine."

Neither Hambledon nor Bagshott showed the faintest trace of anything beyond polite interest.

"I thought when I first saw you," said Bagshott with a laugh, "that you'd lived in a hot climate at some time in your life. Was Mr. Campbell out there too?"

"Yes," said Campbell. "We were on the same ranch. He was the engineer and I was the storekeeper. We had a lot of time on our hands and we got bored—right out in the back blocks, you know, eighteen hours' traveling from the nearest civilization. So we started making models to pass the time. I made a galleon from a construction set—I blush every time I think of it, now. Forgan made a model refrigerating plant, and it worked, didn't it, Bill?"

"It did," said Forgan. "I still wonder why. However, we improved with practice."

"We made up our minds," said Campbell, "that when we retired we'd start a place like this. And we did. It wasn't very like this"—he waved his hand round the shop—"eight years ago, but as Forgan says, we improved with practice."

"Talking about the Argentine," said Bagshott, "does the name of Hugh Selkirk convey anything to you?"

"Heard of him," said Forgan. "Never met him. Millionaire, or thereabouts.

Got a big cattle ranch somewhere, forget where. Got a big steam yacht, ocean-going, the—the *Naomi?*"

"*Niobe?*" suggested Campbell.

"Something like that. Well-known man. Why?"

"I heard something about him in connection with another matter," said Bagshott, "and when you mentioned the Argentine I remembered the name, that's all. Well, I really mustn't waste any more of your time. I am very much obliged to you," and so forth. The partners returned equivalent courtesies, and Bagshott left, followed by Hambledon beaming amiably upon everyone within reach.

"Well?" said Bagshott. "What did you make of that?"

"Anyone would have thought that they were expecting us," said Hambledon slowly. "I did, myself. Innocent people, confronted with a chief-inspector from Scotland Yard, say to themselves, 'Gosh, what's this for?' They exude query marks from every hair, especially their eyebrows. Those two didn't. They said to themselves, 'Well, here it comes,' and girded themselves for battle. They won, too, didn't they? I particularly enjoyed the moment when Red Hair asked you why you'd come yourself instead of sending a solicitor."

"Anything else?"

"Only that this isn't the first time that precious pair have been in an awkward spot. Notice the natural way they backed each other up? They fell into it with the oiled click of a crosstalk act in its third season."

"What I really meant to ask," said Bagshott patiently, "was whether you had gained any fresh light from that interview."

"Not a dazzling amount. The Argentine keeps cropping up now, doesn't it? When Hyde wants to make a will benefiting a British resident of the Argentine he gets two British ex-residents of the Argentine to witness it. Is that coincidence?"

"Coupled with the fact that he was murdered by a native of the Argentine, I should say not," said Bagshott.

"Of course we don't yet know whether Hyde's signature was genuine," said Hambledon. "Have you heard from Nairn about it?"

"Not yet. I'll ring him up when we get back to the office and see if there's any news."

"Nor do we know whether Forgan and Campbell were telling the truth when they said they came from the Argentine. It may have been a leg-pull."

"If it was, they know a lot more about this case than they admit," said Bagshott. "We didn't mention the place first. I've got a man who was born and brought up there; I'll turn him onto them."

"You might put a constable on to ask the rent collector whether she remembers passing Hyde in the doorway when she called on Friday, March the twenty-ninth."

"Of course I shall. I'll ask the Argentine Legation about Forgan and Campbell, too. Well, here we are; I'll ring Nairn up."

Nairn said that he had taken the will himself, in person, to one of the foremost calligraphic experts in the country. His opinion was that not only was it undoubtedly Hyde's signature, but that it was written with the same pen he habitually used. It had an unusually thin and flexible nib, producing a marked differentiation between the up- and downstrokes. This in itself would make Mr. Hyde's signature a difficult one to counterfeit with success, and in this instance the expert had no doubt that the signature was genuine.

"I remember the pen," added Nairn. "It was unusually large for a fountain pen, and dark green in color. He always carried it."

"I don't remember seeing it among the things we found in his pockets," said Bagshott.

"Now you mention it, no. It wasn't there, nor in his desk."

"Perhaps he lost it, or took it somewhere to be repaired. I don't suppose it's important." Bagshott went on to tell Nairn about the interview with the two witnesses. "I can't say they impressed us very favorably, and Hambledon says they're wrong 'uns, but this story seems all right. I'm checking it in every way I can think of, and we'll see."

The Argentine Legation replied at once to the enquiry about Hugh Selkirk, Esq. He was not only known in Argentina, but very well known. He was still a British subject but was a very wealthy and highly respected figure in Argentine society. He had an immense cattle ranch at Carmen de las Flores, where he had a country mansion famous for its hospitality. He also bred and trained race horses. Twenty-seven Avenida de las Rochas, Buenos Aires, was his town house. Letters sent to either of these addresses would certainly reach him. As to whether Mr. Selkirk was in the Argentine at the moment, the Legation regretted they could not say. Mr. Selkirk was a great traveler and was frequently absent from home for considerable periods. An enquiry upon this point should be made, if considered advisable, to his Buenos Aires address. His man of business there invariably dealt with all correspondence during Mr. Selkirk's absences from home.

As regarded the subsequent enquiry about William Forgan, engineer, and Archibald Henry Campbell, storekeeper, who were presumed to have left the Argentine in or about June or July 1938, a request for information had been sent through to the appropriate department in Buenos Aires. Any such information, as and when forthcoming, would be transmitted at once. They had the honor to remain, etc.

Bagshott handed this letter to Hambledon, who read it with raised eyebrows.

"Sounds all right," he said. "Hugh Selkirk seems to be a well-known and long-established character."

"Yes," said Bagshott. "I'll send this letter to Nairn; it is for him to write to Buenos Aires about the legacy. He's the executor. He'll let us know what answer he gets. Evidently the legation don't know Selkirk is in London, but the news of a legacy may produce him."

"I hope so," said Tommy. "I should like to know why Hyde disinherited the poor Lost Dogs for the benefit of a man who is apparently rolling in money already."

"Even before he looted six hundred and seventy-five thousand pounds of Nazi money from the Gatello gang, if Mantani was telling the truth."

Hambledon nodded. "One of the odd things about this case is that there's too much money in it. Unlike my bank balance. You know, I've known a lot of victims in my time, Bagshott, and not one of them has ever left me a brass farthing. Cruel, as Mantani would say, and rightly. I think I shall go home; it is Saturday afternoon, and I hope nobody murders anybody else before Monday at earliest, though you can't trust these fellows to respect an Englishman's weekend. No moral decency. No sense of sanctity. Try not to ring me up before Monday, won't you? Good-bye."

At nine-thirty that night Hambledon was comfortable in an armchair with *The Times*'s Saturday crossword puzzle to occupy his mind until bedtime. He yawned and decided to make it an early night. "A bad-tempered organ," in six letters, second letter *p.* Spleen, of course. Twenty six across— The telephone rang, and Tommy nearly decided not to answer it; curiosity rather than duty uplifted him from his chair. After all, it might be something pleasant.

"Hambledon speaking."

"Bagshott here," said the voice at the other end. "I thought—"

"Look here, Bagshott, I did hope—"

"I thought you'd be interested to hear that—"

"I'm not interested in anything but the—"

"Race has been murdered," said the chief-inspector in a loud firm voice.

"Race! Why?"

"I don't know. In a flat in Marjorie Street, Soho. And Ramon Jacaro is there in custody, though he doesn't know it yet. He's another of the Gatello gang, in case you've forgotten. Of course, if you don't want to turn out again tonight I can always give you full partic—"

"Are you going there at once? . . . Good, pick me up on the way, will you?"

"I received an anonymous telephone call," said Bagshott, when Hambledon entered the police car. "It wasn't a hoax; I sent a patrol car there at once to see.

The man who telephoned to me said he thought I should like to know that a Mr. Walter Race, cousin to the late Mr. James Hyde, had been murdered by the Gatello gang. He thought I was interested in Mr. Race. One Ramon Jacaro, understood to be wanted by the American police, was also on the premises in a state of unconsciousness which looked like being prolonged. He then wished me happy hunting, and rang off."

"The Gatello gang," said Hambledon, "appears to be diminishing. Varsoni and Pietro Gatello, dead. Mantani and Ramon Jacaro in custody. How many more are there?"

"I don't know. Perhaps the Jacaro will tell us when he wakes up. He can't run away; there is a constable standing over him. Here we are. There is a local inspector at the door. All well, Inspector?"

"Yes, sir. Shall I lead the way? It's on the second floor."

The first-floor landing had showy glass doors leading from it into a large room full of lights, laughter, and the music of a dance band. Hambledon asked, in passing, what it was.

"It's a night club, sir. Respectable, as they go. It's called the Red Macaw."

CHAPTER FOURTEEN
At the Red Macaw

Hyde and his cousin Race, firmly shepherded by the Gatello gang, passed the door of the Red Macaw and proceeded up the next flight of stairs. The floor above was arranged as a self-contained flat. The door at the head of the stairs led into a short passage; other doors opened off this, and there was one across the end. The prisoners were pushed along this passage and through the last door into a large room which did not appear to have been visited by any housemaid for months. Dust lay thick upon the shabby furniture scarred by cigarette burns and ringed with the imprints of wet glasses. The fireplace overflowed with cigarette ends, cigar butts, screws of paper, old corks, and miscellaneous debris. There was a heap of empty bottles in one corner of the room, incompletely masked by an elderly couch with the stuffing emerging at salient points. The place smelt of stale wine, tobacco smoke, hair oil, and unopened windows.

James looked about him with an expression of contempt.

"You like my little home, yes?" said the man who had spoken on the stairs. "We are private here. All soundproofed, yes. We are not overheard here; it is convenient."

Hyde looked at him and was immediately reminded of the man whom he had seen, for one unforgettable moment by the light of Adam's torch, dying on the drive of the house in Clifton Avenue. This man was bigger and stouter, but the resemblance was strong; presumably this was Angelo Gatello. Thinking of Pietro Gatello reminded him of Selkirk, who had also died on that drive at this man's orders; Hyde's jaw came forward and his expression hardened.

"I've seen cleaner pigsties," he said deliberately, and Race gasped.

"Ah," said Angelo Gatello, and nodded once or twice. "Just a moment, then we enjoy ourselves, yes? Ramon, guard these men; if they move shoot at once." He spoke in English, no doubt in order that Hyde and Race should understand; the Argentine grinned and leveled a heavy revolver. Gatello left the room with one of the other men, leaving the rest standing by the door and the prisoners in the middle of the room.

"What is all this?" babbled Race in a horrified whisper. "Who are these men?"

"Gangsters," said Hyde, "only gangsters." At the back of his mind he felt a growing surprise at the things he heard himself saying; not at all the sort of things he would have expected himself to say. They seemed to come into his mind from outside, as though someone were prompting him. The sort of things Selkirk might have said. . . .

"But why bring me here?" persisted Race.

"You tacked yourself onto me. That's why."

"But—who are you, then?"

"Don't you know?" asked Hyde sarcastically.

"I thought you were my cousin James Hyde, but now I'm not so sure. You look exactly like him, but you're quite different, somehow. Besides, I thought James Hyde was dead."

"I think he's dead too," said Hyde softly. "I think I'm somebody else—tonight, at least."

"Oh, it's all mad," Race burst out, "mad and horrible. Can't you get me out of this?"

Angelo Gatello came back, and Race edged behind Hyde to keep as far from him as possible.

"Ramon! Search these men for guns."

"Good evening, Ramon Jacaro," said Hyde. The man scowled but did not answer; he ran his hands over Hyde and then Race while Angelo Gatello held a revolver at their heads.

"No arms, eh?" said Gatello. "Little helpless lambs. "You," he added to Hyde, "you remember my brother Pietro, yes?"

"Quite well," said Hyde. "He wore yellow shoes. Do you remember William Selkirk? He was an old man in bad health. You dragged him round the countryside to extort money. He died, do you remember?"

"Where is the money that was stolen from me?"

"Ah yes, that money. You're interested in money, aren't you, Gatello? Varsoni came to look for it, didn't he? I think Pietro was looking for it too, at Putney, wasn't he? It doesn't seem very healthy money, somehow. Are you going on looking for it, Gatello?"

"No," said Gatello. "You are going to give it to me."

Hyde laughed. "I don't carry it about with me, you know."

"Who are you?" asked Gatello suddenly, and Race looked up in surprise.

"The Wizard of Oz," said Hyde. "Didn't you know?"

Gatello turned on Race. "Who is this man?"

"I—I don't know."

"I think you do. I think you're going to tell me. Ramon! Take this fellow"—he pointed at Hyde—"into the office and keep him there till I send for him."

"Don't leave me!" shrieked Race. "Don't—"

Hyde was hustled out of the room and down the passage to a small room next to the entrance door. It was simply furnished with one office chair and a table littered with materials for writing, a battered typewriter thick with dust, and a pile of old newspapers. Jacaro pushed Hyde into the room, prodding him with the muzzle of his outsize revolver. The Argentine shut the door, took the chair, put it with its back to the door, and sat down on it. As there was nowhere else to sit, Hyde sat on the table, which rocked ominously but did not fall. James thought it would be safer to sit well in the middle; he put his hands behind him to lift himself back and felt something hard under the litter. He slipped his fingers under and secured it; it was a heavy round ruler. He sat still and waited. Ramon Jacaro sat on the chair, knees crossed, revolver resting on his knees but pointed at Hyde, and stared unwinkingly at him.

"You remind me," said Hyde, at the end of five minutes' silence, "of a pet toad I had when I was a boy."

Ramon's lip lifted like a dog's; just at that moment there came the sound of a raised voice shouting something, followed by a sharp crack. It might almost have been a stick breaking, or the tap of a hammer upon metal, but Hyde recognized it at once as a shot. He listened intently and heard the sound of a door opened and shut somewhere in the passage. Ramon Jacaro was plainly interested; he got up and drew the chair back from the door, glanced momentarily at Hyde sitting placidly on the table, and then opened the door and looked out.

Hyde leapt at him and struck with all his strength and the heavy ruler. It caught the Argentine just behind the ear; he sagged at the knees and slid slowly to the floor. James looked at him for a moment, but he did not move. Hyde stepped over him into the passage, seeing no one; opened the entrance door quietly and shut it silently, and walked down the stairs. His knees were becoming unstrung.

Through the glass doors of the Red Macaw he saw Adam watching the landing with a drawn look upon his face which gave place to incredulous relief. Hyde walked in, saying, "I am so sorry to have kept you waiting; some tiresome business," for the benefit of the doorkeeper.

"It is of no account," said Adam, "since you have come. I was afraid you might be prevented." He led the way to a table.

"So was I," said Hyde, with a nervous cackle very unlike his usual quiet laugh, and he sat down with an almost audible thump.

"Cocktails," said Adam to the attendant waiter. "Two Red Macaws, please."

Hyde tried to say, "Excellent idea," but did not seem to have enough breath, so he nodded instead and wondered why the table was quivering. Then he realized that one of his knees was against the table leg. He removed the knee and the table became still. Adam sat opposite to him, watching him with a half-smile, and neither spoke until the cocktails came in frosted glasses with a gay macaw painted on them. Hyde picked his up and drank half of it at a gulp.

"We will have dinner at once, please," said Adam to the waiter.

"Very swish glasses, these," said James.

"Very pretty," agreed Adam.

Hyde sipped again and said, "That's better, that's warming. I think I was a little cold." He sat up and drew a long breath; his pulses were steadying and his knees appeared to be under better control. Adam did not answer, and Hyde looked about the room. It was a big place; masked girders across the ceiling showed that several rooms had been thrown into one, and windows at the far end proved that it ran the whole depth of the building. Tables were set on a carpeted strip by the door and along both sides; the middle of the floor was polished for dancing and several couples were dreamily enjoying themselves upon it. Walls and ceiling were silvered, with frosted glass panels repeating the red-macaw motif on the cocktail glasses. At the far end a raised dais enthroned a colored dance band with grinning mouths and somber eyes; one of them was a crooner.

Hyde looked up. One of the supporting girders ran right across the ceiling two thirds of the way down the room. That, he reckoned, would carry the party wall of the filthy sitting room where he had left Race. The soup arrived and diverted his thoughts, but a moment or two later he glanced up again. The dance band began another tune; beneath the saxophones and drums quiet voices would be inaudible at a yard's range.

"What are you watching for?" asked Adam, leaning forward.

"A stain on the ceiling," said James, "but I expect the floor is packed with sawdust or something like that. Soundproofing, you know. You couldn't hear the band at all, up there. Did you hear a shot fired?"

"No," said Adam. "Did you fire it?"

"No. I wasn't even in the same room. I think they shot Race, poor devil. He was an objectionable little beast, but he didn't quite deserve that."

The waiter removed the soup plates, brought the fish, and offered potatoes and sauce.

"Extremely good service they give here," said Hyde.

"Yes, quite good. How did you get away?"

"Ramon Jacaro was told off to mind me in a little room they called the office. His attention was distracted by the shot, so I hit him on the head and came away. There didn't seem to be anything I could usefully do to help Race; there were four of them there besides Jacaro. By the way, I hit him with a ruler and left it on the floor. I expect it's got my fingerprints on it; does it matter?"

"Is he dead?" asked Adam.

"I don't know, I didn't wait to see. 'The pace was too good to enquire,' " quoted Hyde. "I shouldn't think so, really."

"The United States Federal police want him," said Adam, "for a murder down near the Mexican border."

"I should hate to deprive them of him," said Hyde, and the manager strolled up to be introduced and talk about wines.

Hyde was sitting with his back to the glass doors which gave upon the landing; towards the end of the dinner he saw Adam look past his shoulder in that direction with an interested expression. James repressed an impulse to turn round.

"What is it?" he asked.

"Three—no, four of them going downstairs. They seem to be clearing out; they are carrying suitcases. All except Angelo, who had suitcases carried for him."

"Beneath his dignity, eh? He only carries a gun," murmured James. "Four of them, did you say? Was Jacaro one of them?"

"No. Angelo Gatello, Pacorro Pagote, fat Mariposa, and El Caballero. I wonder where Giuseppe Mantani is. Did you see him? A short fat man with lots of curly hair, quite young, about twenty-two, and very emotional. He weeps on the smallest provocation."

"I didn't notice anyone like that; nobody wept for me so far as I saw. He may have been in one of the other rooms. Do you suppose I slaughtered Jacaro?"

"I think I'll go up and see. You sit tight and go on with the cheese; nobody will notice if I slip out. Order benedictine if the waiter comes round. I shan't be long." Adam rose to his feet and moved away. There were always people walking about among the tables, looking for a seat or getting up to dance; Adam's movements were not at all conspicuous.

Hyde sat still and watched the dancers for what seemed to him an intolerably long time. The waiter came and brought benedictines, but James left his untouched. He felt as though it would choke him. What was happening to Adam?

Someone brushed past his shoulder, and Adam sat down again.

"Race is dead, you were quite right," he said. "Shot through the head. Well, that's a big stick waiting for Angelo if we put it into the hands of the police. I don't think Jacaro is dead, though I'm sure he won't wake up yet awhile. I telephoned to Scotland Yard, by the way. I didn't tell them who I was, needless to say."

"Only that if they call at the above address they will meet with information of interest to them, I suppose?"

"Words to that effect. Would you like to wait and see what happens?"

"Very much, it might be interesting. Unless you think we'd better clear out before they come?"

"I think we shall do better to stay," said Adam. "They might ask if any patrons had left hastily. We might leave this table for some other customers, though, and get chairs over there. We might even dance, if your knees have quite recovered. Do you dance?"

"I think I'd rather like to. This is an evening, isn't it?" said James with a schoolboy grin. "I used to tell myself stories about just this sort of thing. D'Artagnan, and all that." He sobered down suddenly as the mention of D'Artagnan reminded him of the place where he had met Selkirk, and added hastily, "How does one acquire a partner? Just go and ask somebody?"

"Not quite," said Adam. "There are dance hostesses. I'll see to it."

Hyde thought it better to start with a slow foxtrot. He was so busy conducting his partner without collisions, not stepping on her feet, and trying to remember an art he never knew well, that he almost missed the sight of a group of men crossing the landing outside the glass doors on their way upstairs. Some of them were in plainclothes and some in the familiar blue uniform of the police. He paused momentarily in his exercises, and the girl asked him if he were tired.

"Tired? No, rather not. Not unless you are. It must be quite exhausting dancing with a performing bear like me. Would you rather sit down? It really isn't fair to expect you—"

"Oh, nonsense," said his partner cheerfully. "I'm enjoying it, I am really. One can tell you're out of practice, of course, but you're so gentle and careful that it doesn't matter a bit. It's when people try to be dashing and don't know how that it's so devastating."

"So you don't think I'm the dashing sort, eh?" said James, rather devastated himself.

"You're much too nice," said the girl with quick tact, and immediately had another relapse. "I think you're a dear old thing, I do really."

James thought this over. A dear old thing, but not dashing. Very deflating, and his steps dragged perceptibly. Then it occurred to him to wonder what she would say if he told her he had just broken his way out of a den of gangsters, himself armed only with a ruler, and left a murdered man behind him. He began to laugh.

"What's the joke?"

"Nothing. Only a story I was told the other day."

"Tell me."

James was definitely not of those who have a supply of stories ready on tap. He floundered mentally, and his dancing deteriorated.

"Better mind what you're doing," said his partner severely. "Never mind the story, you can tell me that later."

Hyde rested, with a sigh of relief, while Adam gave an exhibition of how the tango should be danced. Half an hour or so passed, till at last the glass doors were pushed open and three men came in. There was a small bar near the entrance, little more than a serving hatch; the men sat on stools in front of it and the manager in person rushed to attend to them. A sort of awed hush fell upon the assembly, and a few people gathered up coats and handbags and left.

Adam caught a passing waiter. "Who are those men, do you know?"

"They say," said the waiter, "that the tall one is Chief-Inspector Bagshott from Scotland Yard, and the younger man nearest the door is Detective-Inspector Ennis. I don't know who the third man is. Nor what they've come for," he added in a worried voice, and passed on his way.

"Bagshott," said Adam in Hyde's ear, "is the man I spoke to on the telephone."

"The third man can't be a policeman," said Hyde. "He's not tall enough. See him looking round? He doesn't look as though he'd miss much, does he?"

At that moment a man came up to a girl who was just in front of Hyde and said, "Do you see that fellow who's just come in? Not the tall one, the short broad-shouldered one with fair hair. That's Tommy Hambledon."

"Tommy Hambledon?" said the girl. "Who's he?"

"British Intelligence," said the man in an awed voice. "What the devil brings him here? If I had a pain in my conscience, I'd flee, by gosh I would."

"The others are Scotland Yard men, I heard somebody say so," said the girl.

"Something's very much up, I wonder what. Scotland Yard's bad enough, but Thomas Elphinstone Hambledon! Phew!"

Hyde and Adam glanced casually at each other and went on sitting still. In Hyde's case this was a matter of necessity; he felt that if he stood up his legs would not support him.

"Are these cocktails unusually strong?" he asked after a few minutes.

"Not more so than usual," said Adam. "They aren't a teetotal drink. Why?"

"I feel rather as though they were affecting my legs," said James. "I have a sense of noncooperation. Do you think it's the cocktails?"

"It might be," said Adam, and laughed. "Wait a bit, perhaps the effect will pass off."

Hambledon and the two Special Branch men at the bar finished their drinks and went out; James stretched out his legs in front of him and looked at them with curiosity.

"I feel better now," he said simply, and again Adam laughed.

"You aren't the only one," he said. "Notice how the place is cheering up?"

"Laughter and babble break out afresh," said James. "Very gay, very enlivening. Do you think we might go home soon without causing remark? I think I'm tired."

When they reached the hotel Hyde sank with a sigh of relief into his favorite chair, the same which had treasure hidden between the springs. He smiled rather sheepishly at Adam and said that it was nice to be home again.

"Yes, sir. I trust the evening's entertainment came up to your expectation?"

"Oh, can it, Adam. Dear me, where did I pick up that phrase? Do you suppose that fellow whom I hit will die?"

"No loss if he does; it will save the cost of trial and execution. You might apply for a rebate of your income tax on the ground of having effected a saving in public expenditure."

"But weren't the C.I.D. looking for whoever did it? By the way, what about that ruler?"

"I wiped it clean and put it back on the table. As for the C.I.D., I hope they will think that one of Jacaro's pals did it and left him there to take the blame for Race's murder. I admit that I spoke on the telephone with just that trace of a foreign accent which I thought artistically correct. It might help."

"Anyway," said Hyde, "they've got Jacaro, alive or dead. One more missing from the clan Gatello. What happens next?"

"I think," said Adam slowly, "that Race's murder is a nuisance, in a way. Scotland Yard is now in full cry after the Gatello gang, and if we want to poke our noses in, too, we shall have to be careful. And quick."

"I can't think why Gatello shot him. Surely it was a very stupid thing to do?"

"Gatello gets into blind rages. Besides, Race knew too much. They meant to dispose of you too, of course, after you'd told them where the money was.

Then they'd collect the money and return to the Argentine. Quite simple."

"But two bodies," objected Hyde.

"Oh, they'd leave them in the flat. They must have paid three months' rent in advance or they wouldn't have got it, and it was nobody's business to go up there."

James turned rather green.

"I expect Race was tiresome," continued Adam, "so Gatello shot him. Then they came to look for you and you weren't there; so disconcerting. They cleared out, bag and baggage, and left one man outside somewhere to keep watch on the place. If the police hadn't arrived they would have returned later and collected Jacaro."

"If you hadn't rung up the police," said Hyde, "the scheme would probably have worked."

"Yes. By the way, I was giving you another five minutes and then coming up to look for you. I didn't want to if it could be avoided, because it would almost certainly have meant a shooting match, and then the Metropolitan Police would have been looking for me instead of for the Gatello gang. The thought alarms me. Your way out was much better."

James glowed with pride but only said: "I merely saw a chance, and took it."

"That's all anyone ever does. What I was going to say was this. If we're going on with this, we'd better act quickly, or the police will bag the birds first."

Hyde sat up. " 'If we're going on with this'? What d'you mean?"

"Actually, the job's done, isn't it? Mr. Selkirk's idea was to let them get into mischief and destroy themselves, wasn't it? They've done it now. They've murdered Race, and your evidence will hang them. I don't know whether the C.I.D. can prove they murdered Mr. Selkirk, too, but it doesn't really matter; they can only be hung once. A line to the police telling them where the Gatello gang are to be found, and that will be that."

"I see," said James, and leaned back in his chair. "Have we got any coffee readily available, Adam, without too much trouble?"

"Of course," said Adam, and turned to the door. "I'll get some at once."

"I want to think this over," murmured Hyde.

CHAPTER FIFTEEN
The Anxious Butterfly

When Hambledon and Bagshott came to the flat above the Red Macaw, the police inspector who had greeted them at the entrance led them first into the small room on the right which now contained, in addition to a table, a chair, and a telephone, one unconscious man. He was lying upon the floor with a cushion under his head; the inspector said that they had found him in a heap across the doorway and that they had straightened him out in the course of examination. He had been hit on the head.

"Doctor here yet?" asked Bagshott.

"Not yet, sir. He'll be here in a moment, I expect."

"This fellow doesn't look too bad to me," said the chief-inspector. "Watch him carefully if he shows signs of coming round, he may be dangerous."

"This gun was under him, sir, when we turned him over," said the inspector, and indicated a large revolver lying on the table.

"What a cannon," said Hambledon. "Where's the other man?"

"In the room at the end of the passage."

"Don't leave this man unwatched for a moment, Inspector."

"Very good, sir."

In the large room at the end of the passage Race was lying across the hearthrug with his head in the fender among a litter of cigarette ends and similar debris. He had knocked over a chair in falling and that, in turn, had upset a table with a bottle on it which had broken, and a pool of red wine had soaked into the floor. Race had a small hole in the middle of his forehead and had obviously died at once.

"Yes, that's Race all right," said Hambledon, bending over him.

"There must have been a considerable crash when he went over," said Bagshott, "besides the report of the gun. You would think somebody would have heard something."

"Not with that band playing downstairs," said Hambledon. "Incidentally, I don't hear the band."

"Perhaps it isn't playing," said Bagshott, and sent a constable to find out. The man came back and said that they had just started another tune, but no sound of it came into the flat above.

"The floors must have been soundproofed," said Tommy. "Well, I should do that if I lived over a nightclub."

The police doctor arrived, followed by the official photographer, the finger-print expert, and Detective-Inspector Ennis. The room filled with busy men and Hambledon said that he was only in the way. "I'd like to interview the man Jacaro," he said, "as soon as he can talk. I suppose it is Jacaro?"

"I've got his particulars," said Bagshott; "I'll look him over and make sure. I'd like him in the cells first, though. I think we'll have him removed at once. See to it, Inspector, will you? In the meantime, Hambledon, what about having a look at the night club downstairs? Ennis, I think you'd better come too."

"Good idea," said Hambledon. "We might even get a drink to take the taste of this room out of our throats. What's in these other rooms?"

"Very little, sir," said the inspector. "One's a kitchen, one's a bathroom, though I don't think they worried the bath very often, it's thick with dust. The third's a bedroom with two beds in it and nothing else. Doesn't look as though it was used much."

"They didn't really live here, then. Perhaps the owners of this property will be able to help us," said Bagshott. "I'll get onto them early tomorrow. Their tenants may have given some other address. I don't think we need stay up here, Hambledon, so if you really want a drink we'll go down. The attendant at the door of that nightclub might be able to tell us something."

The doorkeeper at the Red Macaw said he was sorry but he hadn't noticed anything out of the ordinary. There were a lot of dagoes who habitually passed the door on their way to and from the flat above, but he knew nothing about them and didn't want to know them. So long as they didn't attempt to enter the club he wasn't interested. Patrons were coming in and going out all the evening; he was sorry, but it was quite impossible to say who came or went at any particular time. As they could see, the gentlemen's cloakrooms were through another door on the landing outside the actual club premises; members were passing through the club's outer door all the time and no one could be expected to remember them all. He was, after all, only human.

"Oh, quite, quite," said Bagshott soothingly. "I don't expect impossibilities. Did you by chance happen to see any one or more of your members going upstairs or coming down?"

The doorkeeper said he had not. His business was merely to keep an eye on people actually passing through his door; particularly, of course, those coming in. Where they went when they went out was no business of his, and he was much too busy to concern himself over what didn't matter to him.

Bagshott, who had not really hoped much, was not much disappointed. He and Hambledon, accompanied by Ennis, paid a short but refreshing visit to the bar and looked about them. The place was a nightclub like any other nightclub, all chromium plating and frosted glass with red macaws decoratively represented in all the obvious places, and none of the people present was of any immediate interest to the police so far as they knew.

They finished their drinks and went out again; if anyone there sighed with relief to see them go, the emotion was not obvious. Detective-Inspector Ennis returned to the flat; Hambledon said that if Jacaro had regained consciousness he would go and talk to him, if not it didn't matter as tomorrow was also a day. He yawned.

"We'll drive round by the police station and see," said Bagshott. "Cold water has a very reviving effect, especially on those who aren't used to it."

At the police station they were told that the prisoner had indeed recovered consciousness. No, he had given no trouble so far, merely asked where he was. Yes, the superintendent had checked over the description supplied of a man named Ramon Jacaro, wanted for murder in America, and in his opinion this was the man.

Bagshott said that he and Mr. Hambledon would interview the man in his cell and it would be a convenience if a shorthand writer was available—oh, good. Let the said constable attend, and they would begin at once.

Jacaro was a bigger man than is usual with his race, with heavy features and a sullen expression. He did not look much the worse for his adventure except that he winced slightly when he turned his head. Hambledon pulled a chair forward and began.

"Your name?"

"George Washington. What's yours?"

"That will do," said Hambledon sharply. "You are detained here upon a charge of being concerned in the murder of Walter Race in the flat where you were found this evening. You will be tried in the English courts and if you are found guilty you will be hanged. If you are acquitted you will be handed over to the police of the United States of America. Now then!"

"Seems like it don't matter what I say, then, don't it?"

"Insolence won't help you. What is your name?"

The man stared at Hambledon for a long minute, but Tommy had met this sort of thing before. The Argentine was the first to look away.

"Find out," he said.

"I have. You are Ramon Jacaro."

The man stared again, with astonishment this time.

"You come from the Argentine," said Hambledon, pursuing his advantage. "You were implicated in a bank robbery there. You are wanted by the American police for a murder down near the Mexican border. You were probably involved in the murder of another man at Putney on Tuesday, April the second, this year. Now there is this other murder tonight. I think you are in rather a tight corner, Jacaro. Don't you?"

Jacaro nodded.

"Now. What happened at the flat tonight?"

"I don't know a thing about any murder. Nobody was bumped off while I was there."

"Listen, Jacaro. In that flat tonight a man was shot dead. When the police got there, all your friends had gone, leaving you behind. You were lying on the floor, and," added Tommy significantly, "somebody rang up the police."

"Who done that?"

"Chief-Inspector Bagshott, here, took the call, I believe."

"Somebody rang up," said Bagshott, "saying that they were speaking from the telephone in that flat. That was in the room you were found in. Some man, he didn't give a name. He said that Walter Race had been shot dead and that Ramon Jacaro had been knocked out. He added that the American federal police wanted you, if we didn't. We can't check up on the call because it's an automatic exchange, but we went round to the flat at once and it was all quite true."

"And who else could have known about it except your friends?" added Hambledon, driving the point home.

"Framed," said the Argentine. "Framed." He rose slowly to his feet.

"Sit down," said Hambledon sharply.

Jacaro looked at him as though he had forgotten that Hambledon was there and was surprised to see him. He sat down again and said: "What you want to know, huh?"

"Who was in the flat tonight?"

"Angelo Gatello. Pacorro Pagote. Tadeo el Caballero. Cesar Mariposa. That's all."

"How many more of you are there?"

"Only Giuseppe Mantani, and he's gone. Don't know where. He's skipped, I reckon. Got the wind up."

Neither Hambledon nor Bagshott enlightened him as to what had happened to Mantani.

"Varsoni's dead, of course," said Hambledon thoughtfully, "and so is Pietro Gatello."

Jacaro grunted, and Hambledon asked again what had happened that night.

"There was two men the Boss wanted brought in. They come to that Red Macaw joint below us. We got 'em on the stairs and persuaded 'em to come on up."

"Who were they?"

Jacaro hesitated. "One of 'em I never seen before. Little weaselly guy. Don't know if the Boss knowed him."

"And the other?"

"One of the Selkirk gang," said Jacaro undecidedly.

"Not Selkirk himself?"

"No. He's dead. Varsoni gave him his, down at Putney."

"You're sure?" persisted Hambledon.

"Course I'm sure," said Jacaro, but there was an undertone of doubt in his voice. "Had this guy right in front of me tonight as near as you are. He was very like that guy Selkirk, but it wasn't him. Brother, I reckon."

"Oh. Well, we'll pass that for the present. You got these two men up to the flat. What happened then?"

"The Selkirk guy started actin' tough and the Boss says, 'Take him out while I talk to this other guy.' So him and me goes and sits in the office. Where the telephone was."

"What did the Boss want to talk to the other guy about?"

"When we come out of the room," said Jacaro, "the Boss was sayin': 'Now you tell me who that man is.' "

"So the Boss wasn't sure."

Jacaro shrugged and asked for a cigarette, which Bagshott gave him.

"You and this man went and sat in the office," prompted Hambledon.

"I call that to mind quite plain," said the Argentine. "He sat on the table and me in the chair by the door. After that I can't remember nothin'. I woke up here. Reckon the roof must have fell on me; I don't pass out that easy."

"The murdered man's name was Race," said Bagshott. "Walter Race."

"It don't mean a thing to me, mister. Never heard the name nor seen the guy before."

Hambledon nodded. It seemed to him possible that Race had been deceived by the likeness between Selkirk and Hyde and had pushed himself into the group, with fatal results.

"You know where all these people live? Gatello, Pagote, and the other two?"

Jacaro hesitated, and Bagshott said: "Does Gatello speak English well?"

"Yeah. Why?"

"I was thinking of that telephone call," said Bagshott. "Whoever it was spoke quite good English. Just a trace of foreign accent, but quite good."

"I don't know where Gatello lives," said Jacaro.

"And the others?"

"They don't speak good English."

"I see," said Hambledon. "If it was one of your gang who rang up the police, it must have been Gatello."

"You've got it, mister. But I ain't so sure it was Gatello."

"Who else could it have been?"

"I don't know. Look, I don't feel so good. I'll think it over. I can't talk no more tonight." Indeed, the man's face was gray with pain and his head was throbbing almost visibly.

"Whoever clouted you," said Hambledon, "certainly made a job of it. What do you think, Chief-Inspector?"

"I agree," said Bagshott, rising. "We'll call it off for tonight."

Jacaro rolled onto the bed and covered his face from the light as Hambledon and Bagshott rose to go.

"By the way," said Tommy, turning in the doorway, "where does Selkirk live?" But Jacaro remained silent under his blanket.

"I think a doctor had better see that man," said Bagshott when he met the superintendent in the outer office. "I don't quite like the look of him."

"He certainly had a nasty crack on the head," said the superintendent. "I saw it myself when he was brought in."

Bagshott was informed next day that Jacaro was unconscious when the doctor saw him and had been removed to hospital. A depressed fracture of the skull. An operation would be performed as soon as possible, but the patient had a high temperature and was not what the doctor regarded as a particularly good case.

Police investigation proceeded throughout Sunday and Monday. The flat gave up its few secrets, which were not particularly helpful except for a nice collection of fingerprints to compare with those sent from New York. One of the gang used Jasmine Hair Oil; judging by the prints on the bottle, that was Tadeo el Caballero. One of them drew cats with human heads on odd bits of paper which were found screwed up in the fireplace. The drawings were spirited but unrefined; Detective-Inspector Ennis looked askance at the adventures of this South American Pasht.

"Insanitary minds, these fellows have," he said, and used a large book as a paperweight.

The only things in the whole flat on which anyone had used a duster for weeks were the telephone and a heavy ebony ruler beside it. These were conspicuously clean.

"Our friend who telephoned to me," said Bagshott thoughtfully.

"Yes, sir," said Ennis. "And the ruler might possibly have been what was used on Jacaro. No marks on it, but there wouldn't be. Hard stuff, ebony."

"All the marks appear on the skull," agreed Bagshott. "Leave a man in the flat by the telephone for a couple of days, Ennis. I don't really suppose any of them will be idiot enough to ring up there, but it's just worth trying. Put that feller on who can speak Spanish; it'll be a change for him from watching Forgan and Campbell in the Clerkenwell Road. Put someone else on there."

The detective-sergeant really preferred the Clerkenwell Road to a scruffy flat in Soho, but policemen soon learn to be philosophers or cease to be policemen. He took some textbooks with him, cleared a space on the littered table in Gatello's office, and put in some useful hours working for his examination for inspector. Just before eight on Monday night the telephone rang. The sergeant lifted the receiver and said, *"Que es?"*

"Cesar," said a cautious voice at the other end.

The sergeant smiled to himself and continued to speak Spanish. "What's the matter, Cesar?"

"Who are you?"

"No names over the telephone, you ass. You know me all right. What d'you want?"

"I am anxious. I am frightened."

"What about?"

"The newspapers," breathed Mariposa. "Have you seen the papers?"

"A lot of rubbish," said the sergeant confidently.

"No, no."

"Yes, yes."

"I want to see the Boss," said Mariposa plaintively. "He told me to wait here, but I am not happy."

"I'll tell him when he comes in," said the sergeant. "Where are you?"

"No names over the telephone," said Cesar reproachfully. "You reminded me just now."

"Quite right, so I did. Look here, you give me your telephone number and then I shall know where you are and no names mentioned."

Mariposa gave it.

"O.K.," said the sergeant, making a note in the margin of a geography book. "O.K. You go and sit somewhere quiet and dream of chile con carne, you'll be all right." He rang off and immediately handed on the news to Scotland Yard, who in their turn rang up Bagshott.

Chief-Inspector Bagshott had a wife, though Mrs. Bagshott sometimes said she didn't feel as though she had a husband. There was a semidetached male who was about the house at odd times, if you called that a husband. This night, Monday, April 15, was their wedding anniversary and there was a party. Mrs. Bagshott told the chief-inspector that he was to be there, whatever happened, and if anybody murdered anybody between the hours of seven-thirty and eleven someone else could go and sweep up the pieces.

"Very well, dear," said Bagshott meekly.

Accordingly, when Scotland Yard rang him up at a quarter past eight to tell him that Mariposa had been located in a hotel off Euston Road, Bagshott gave orders for the place to be watched and a car to call for him at eleven that night. It did not sound as though Mariposa was going to run away. Bagshott rang up Hambledon, arranged to pick him up, and turned from the telephone to meet an awful look from his wife.

"It's all right, dear," he said before she could speak. "I've put it off."

"You'd better," she said in pretended menace, and slipped her arm through his. It is not undiluted fun, being the wife of a policeman, even if he is a chief-inspector.

Bagshott and Hambledon stopped the police car short of the hotel entrance and walked towards it; a plainclothes man reported that Mariposa was still inside. The hotel was an ugly flat-fronted building of several stories above lockup shops on the ground floor. The entrance hall was large and pretentious, with oilcloth-covered stairs running up at the back. When the three men entered everything was quiet and even sleepy: one resident reading a letter and the porter yawning in his chair. As though Bagshott's arrival had been a signal, tumult immediately broke out upstairs: doors opened and slammed, voices cried out indignantly, and the sound of pattering footsteps was heard. The porter, who had got up to ask the visitors' business, broke off in the middle of his question and listened; a door labeled "Office" opened and a large man came out and ran upstairs. People, nearly all men, arrived through every doorway at once; it was like the enchanted palace at the moment when somebody kisses the Sleeping Beauty.

"What's going on here?" asked Bagshott.

"I couldn't say, sir, I'm sure," said the porter, but a voice from upstairs supplied the answer. "Murder!" it cried. "Murder!"

"Oh, not another one," said Hambledon irritably, and took the stairs three at a time with Bagshott at his elbow. Numerous other persons were also rushing up; the only one who was coming down was a middle-aged man holding a handkerchief to his face and coughing as though he would choke. Bagshott noticed automatically that this man was wearing a gaudy dressing gown of foreign appearance; his face was largely obscured by the handkerchief, but what could be seen of it was scarlet and his eyes were streaming tears.

The passage at the head of the stairs was full of people who were packed most closely, as bees round their queen, about a door halfway along the corridor. Bagshott, announcing his official status in a loud voice above the tumult, plowed his way through till he reached the storm center, a door half open upon a lighted bedroom.

"He is dead," said a man in the doorway. "Quite dead. He was shot, I heard it. I lodge next door."

"I'll take your evidence later," said Bagshott, and pushed into the room with Hambledon following behind. Against the wall behind the door was a bed, and upon it the body of a very fat man grotesquely perched in the attitude the Moslem assumes at prayer. His face was deeply sunk into the pillow, and it was quite plain that he was not even attempting to breathe.

In the middle of the room stood the large man who had come out of the room labeled "Office" downstairs. He was fixedly regarding the unpleasant object on the bed when Bagshott walked in and announced himself.

"Glad to see you. Save me sending for you. My name's Quint and I am the manager of this hotel."

"Mr. Quint," said Bagshott in acknowledgment. "What's happened here, do you know?"

"No. Only just got here. Was in my office. Heard a hullabaloo upstairs and came up. About fifty-seven people told me there was a murder in here. Came in, pushed out about six people. Saw man obviously dead, so didn't touch."

"What's his name?"

"Mariposa. Cesar Mariposa from the Argentine."

"Really," said Bagshott in a surprised voice. "He gave that name?"

"Certainly," said Mr. Quint. "Without hesitation. Besides, it was on his passport. Quiet inoffensive fellow. Never gave any trouble. Till now."

"Somebody said he'd been shot," said Hambledon. "He looks as though he might have been stifled."

"Mr. Quint," began Bagshott.

"Samuel Quint. Don't know if my parents had a strong sense of humor or none at all."

Bagshott smiled politely. "Would you please ring up"—he gave a number—"tell them what's happened and ask them to send a police surgeon here instantly. Say I'm here, Chief-Inspector Bagshott."

Quint turned towards the door as Hambledon was saying: "I suppose we mustn't touch him till your doctor comes." Before he had finished speaking the figure on the bed relaxed perceptibly, sagged, and suddenly rolled to the floor with a heavy thud.

"Dear me," said Tommy, "how very cooperative. He might almost have heard us."

Quint uttered a strangled sound and hastily left the room.

CHAPTER SIXTEEN
Candles for Mariposa

"If this man has been shot," said the Chief-Inspector, on his knees beside the body of Cesar Mariposa, "all I can say is that I don't see where. I should say from his color that he died of heart failure. The doctor will tell us, of course."

"Look here," said Tommy Hambledon, and moved the bedclothes very slightly with a careful finger. "Here's a gun, and," sniffing at it, "it has been very recently fired."

Bagshott got up and looked at it. "That must have been underneath him as he lay on the bed. Curious." He picked up the revolver carefully with his handkerchief and looked down the barrel at the light. "Quite right. Still smoke in the barrel. That's because he lay on it as soon as it was fired. Why did he fire off a revolver, and at what, and then immediately die a natural death? I suppose there was only one shot?" He went to the door and opened it upon the patient crowd outside. "One of you gentlemen said he lodged next door, I think—ah, you, sir. Just a moment."

The man pushed forward eagerly. "My name is Timol Rassool and I am a—"

"Yes, yes. I'll take your statement in proper form presently, if you don't mind. At the moment—come inside for a minute, will you? Thanks. Now if I shut the door—that's right. Now, you live next door?"

"In that room," said Rassool, pointing.

"And you heard a shot fired?"

"Yes. You see, I am—"

"Only one shot?"

"Yes. Only one."

"You're sure?"

"Absolutely. I was in my room alone, studying. It was quite quiet. The shot was so loud it startled me. I cried out with an exclamation aloud. I listened. I heard other doors opening and much speech. I put my books down and came into the passage also. There was growing concourse of people, all masculine, and very much question-asking. I also—"

"Just a moment. Can you estimate how long it was between your hearing the shot fired and your coming out in the passage?"

"While one might count forty, I should estimate. It is not so easy."

"No," said Bagshott, "I realize that. About half a minute, shall we say? And there were already people in the passage when you looked out? . . . Yes, I see. Now tell me, how much can you hear through these party walls between the rooms? Can you hear talking in the next room, for example?"

"Not generally. Only the raised or excited voice or the loud and raucous laugh. Not refined speech, and in any case, never words themselves."

"I see. Did you hear any sound from this room suggesting that this man Mariposa had a visitor?"

"No, sir."

"Nor the door opening and shutting?"

"No, sir. So many doors open and shut, no man could distinguish between them."

"Yes, quite. That was absolutely all you heard, just this one shot and then silence?"

"Only the coughing after, but I think I may make the mistake."

"Coughing," said Bagshott, and thought of a middle-aged gentleman with a handkerchief to his face who had passed them on the stairs.

"There was coughing I estimated to be within this apartment, but when I opened my door there was one member of the concourse without who coughed severely. I assume the mistake and him to happen to be passing at the moment."

"When you got out in the passage, was this door open?"

"No, sir. It was young Mr. S. Jenkins in room forty-nine who opened the door and switched on the light."

"Switched on the light! What, in here?" Rassool nodded. "Do you mean to say it was perfectly dark in here?"

"Completely obfuscated. Mr. S. Jenkins will corroborate."

"Yes, I'll see Mr. S. Jenkins presently. Well, thank you very much, Mr. Rassool, that was most helpful. I shall have to trouble you to repeat your statement formally later on when it can be taken down in writing. For the present, I think that's all."

"I shall be honored to make my statement at any time convenient, sir," said Rassool, and bowed himself out.

Bagshott looked at Hambledon, and said: "Well? What d'you make of that?"

"It seems," said Tommy slowly, "as though this poor devil fired at something he saw in the dark and immediately died of—of fright, Bagshott? Did he really see something in the dark or was the light switched out, the instant the shot was fired, by someone who immediately left the room? The coughing gentleman in the strike-me-blind dressing gown who passed us on the stairs and dived into that bathroom on the half landing?"

"Was that where he went?" said Bagshott. "Somebody else must have noticed that dressing gown; we shall probably pick him up."

"You didn't order your constable to keep watch at the front door and not let anyone go out, did you?"

"Of course not, on the strength of a hysterical yowl of murder from someone unknown. This may be a case of natural death."

"Oh, quite," said Hambledon. "I don't know Mariposa's habits, but suppose he'd got hold of some black-market hootch. He drinks it and thereafter sees in the dark a pale blue warthog wearing a striped shirt and a crown of live lizards, and carrying a brass vase filled with lilies. He fires at it, and rightly, and immediately dies. The coughing gentleman was merely passing on his way to the bathroom to get himself some water. Pass, friend, all's well. What the devil's that?"

"What?"

"That parcel thing on the table by the door. Let's look before we touch it. Top and halfway down the sides covered with red cartridge paper, and the lower half displaying the naked ends of what look like candles. Fat yellow carriage candles. Didn't know you could get them these days. Oh, ah, and here's the origin of the curious smell I noticed when we first came in. I thought it was just—never mind." Hambledon indicated an ashtray on the same table. On it, and lying over the edge upon the table, was a trail of ash, the shape and size of thick string. "Looks like burnt fuse," said Hambledon, and touched it lightly with his finger. "It is fuse, it's still sticky. Smells of tar, too. Now, why burn fuse, Bagshott?"

"Not to light the candles, anyway," said Bagshott. "It's nowhere near them. But it may have been what Mariposa saw in the dark. There's where the bullet went, in the wall there. Yes, he fired in the general direction of this table."

"If there was anybody standing near the door," said Tommy, "he had a pretty close call. He probably felt the wind of the bullet."

"Why red paper?" said Bagshott, looking at the candles. "They wrap explosives in red paper, don't they?"

Hambledon agreed, and at that moment the door opened to admit the doctor and the local superintendent of police. Bagshott went into conference with the superintendent while the doctor was about his business, and Hambledon made a rapid and efficient search of the dead man's possessions. The doctor reported that the man had certainly not been shot, and that only a post-mortem would tell accurately how he had died. Hambledon said that nothing of interest presented itself in any prominence, and Bagshott said that the superintendent would make all the necessary arrangements for official investigation. The candles should be treated with particular interest and then sent to his office.

"Is that all?" said Hambledon. "Then I'm going home."

On the way downstairs—the crowd in the passage having given it up and gone to bed—Hambledon said: "Excuse me a moment," and turned into the bathroom on the half landing. He was hardly inside the door before he called Bagshott.

"What is it?" said the chief-inspector.

"Hanging up behind the door, look. That's the fatal dressing gown, surely. Tiger lilies and blue bananas, there cannot be another. What did the gentleman walk out from here in, Bagshott? If in his usual clothes, why was he wearing a dressing gown? This is bedtime, not breakfast time."

The police doctor reported next day that Cesar Mariposa's heart was in an advanced state of fatty degeneration, and this alone was the cause of his death. There was no sign of violence on the body and no trace of poison in the intestines. Death from natural causes, in short; that is, if a heart in that condition could justly be called natural.

Bagshott asked whether such a sudden death could be attributed to any immediate cause, such as a severe fright or an attack of indigestion after eating.

"If you ever develop a heart like that, Chief-Inspector," said the doctor, "don't get frights and don't overeat; both will be bad for you. But you'll die anyway."

"I see," began Bagshott, but the doctor interrupted him.

"You said something about a heavy meal. Actually, this man had had nothing to eat for at least twelve hours and probably longer. He'd been drinking water, but that was all."

"Oh, really," said Bagshott, and rang up Hambledon to tell him the news.

"Natural death, eh?" said Tommy. "Well, it looked like it to us, didn't it? But I'd still like to know why he fired that shot. Of course it may just have been that he felt ill and couldn't reach the bell. Perhaps that's how they habitually summon their servants in Argentina; one shot for the butler, two for the chauffeur, and the whole contents of the magazine for the cook. I don't know, I've never been there. But why light the fuse? In order that the smell should remind him of happy far-off boyhood days when they used to blow up presidents once a month before breakfast? Do you believe that, Bagshott? No, I was afraid you wouldn't. Nor do I. I say, I wish you'd turn any resources the Special Branch may have to spare to finding out where those candles were purchased and by whom. Of course, he may have bought them himself in order to soothe the outraged feelings of his patron saint. I should think Mariposa's patron saint would take a bit of soothing, though I always understood one bought the right sort of candle for the job inside the church itself. Incidentally—don't interrupt, Bagshott—incidentally, his having gone without food all day rather bears out this suggestion. He was fasting in atonement for his sins. Did anything fresh transpire from your enquiries at his hotel this morning?"

"Not a great deal. He wouldn't admit the housemaid yesterday morning when she wanted to do his room. The door was locked and he called to her, without opening it, that he wasn't feeling well and didn't want to be disturbed. Yet when Mr. S. Jenkins went to the door just after the shooting, it wasn't locked. Rassool was right, by the way, the room was in darkness till Jenkins put his hand round the doorpost and switched on the light."

"Nobody missed Mariposa at mealtimes, I suppose," said Tommy.

"No. No reason why they should; the boarders had their meals in or out, just as they liked, without notice. The housemaid didn't report Mariposa's telling her he wasn't well; she just thought he was sleeping off a binge. He was in the hotel for all the meals on Sunday, which reminds me that there was a Sunday paper in his room with an account in it of Race's murder."

"I always think," said Tommy Hambledon, "that the most amusing part of murder must be reading about it in the papers next day. The police are in possession of clues from which the arrest of the miscreant may shortly be expected; he is said to be a dark man wearing a felt hat and a fawn-colored raincoat."

"Or a short man who isn't wearing a gaudy dressing gown," said Bagshott, and rang off.

The constable who was given the task of finding out where the candles were bought was quite cheerful about it. Carriage candles used to be obtainable from shops which sold harness and saddlery, and there are not so many of these in London as there were even twenty years ago. On the last occasion when he was directed to trace a purchase, it was a common type of mousetrap with a stain of green ink underneath it, and the number of shops in London who sell mouse-traps is nearly astronomical.

The first shop at which he enquired had similar carriage candles in stock— old stock, dating from before the last war—but no one had bought any of them since 1926. The next two shops had none and had received no enquiry for any for years. The fourth shop had none either, but had been asked for some as recently as last Monday.

"Indeed," said the constable, and asked for a description of the intending customer. He received the usual word picture of a middle-aged man with nothing remarkable about him except a slight pallor about the jaw suggestive of his having recently parted with a beard. The pallor was barely noticeable now because Adam was an artist; such traces would naturally become much less marked at the end of a fortnight.

The fifth shop denied both candles and any enquiry for them, but the proprietor of the sixth shop said: "Dear me, yes. On Monday morning, just before we closed for the lunch hour, a gentleman drove up in a taxi and asked for carriage candles. I remember it well; I don't think I've sold such a thing over the counter for thirty years. In fact, I have only two customers left who buy them now, and both are post orders, one from Connemara and the other from the Isle of Skye. Dear me, yes."

"You were able to supply him, then?"

"Yes, yes. A two-pound packet, he bought."

"Might I see a similar packet, if you have one?"

After some excavation in the recesses of the shop a similar packet was produced in its original wrapping of brown paper, which completely covered the candles and had a white label stuck across the end announcing the contents. The constable bought it. Asked for a description of the customer, the proprietor recited the formula now so tiresomely familiar to Bagshott. He had not noticed anything suggestive of a retired beard, but he did say that the candle buyer wore a hat with a brim rather wider than is usual in London. "I said to myself: 'You bought that hat somewhere abroad, my dear sir.' Dear me, yes. That is what I said."

"The gentleman came in a taxi, I think you said?"

"Yes, yes. And drove away in it again. It waited outside for him. Of course, it would wait outside, I should be very surprised—dear me, what foolish things one says—I only meant that the taxi remained just outside the door where I could see it all the time."

"And this was at about a quarter to one—ten minutes to—on Monday of this week?"

"That is right, yes. About five or ten minutes to one, last Monday."

Official enquiry among taxi drivers for one who had driven a gentleman to this particular shop at that time, and waited while he made a purchase, produced an immediate response. One taxi driver reported that a fare—whom he described in the usual terms, including both hat and jaw—asked him to drive to saddlers' shops one after another till he found what he wanted. After which they drove direct to a certain large hotel just off the top of Regent Street—the taxi driver gave its name—where the fare paid him off and went inside.

Hyde, hurried and excited, had been careless and made a mistake at last.

Bagshott rang up Hambledon and said: "I think I may have located Selkirk for you."

"Where is he?"

Bagshott repeated the evidence, adding: "Of course, he may only have gone there to meet somebody. Lunch time, you know."

"Oh, quite. Still, I'm going there at once. Are you coming?"

"Naturally. You can pick me up this time, it's your turn."

They walked into the hotel and asked for the manager. While they waited Hambledon looked about him and remarked that it was obvious that Selkirk was really a millionaire or he could not live there. "The only thing that puzzles me is where they find enough millionaires to keep the place going."

"It is mysterious," agreed Bagshott. "But we don't know that Selkirk is a paying resident, do we? He may be the headwaiter, or not live here at all, as I suggested just now. I shall start by asking to look at the list of residents, of course, but probably that will only be a polite method of opening the conversation."

They were standing together in a room with the door open. As they waited, a thin dark man came along the passage and glanced in through the doorway as he passed. He showed no sign of interest in the two men who stood there.

Presently the manager came, apologizing for having kept them waiting. So many duties—staff shortage—half-trained servants—one wants as many eyes as there are in a peacock's tail to keep order everywhere at once. . . .

Bagshott said that they would not detain him from his affairs a moment longer than was unavoidable, and asked to see the list of residents. The manager raised his eyebrows, said: "Certainly, Chief-Inspector," in a pained voice, and went to fetch it. Outside the door he was seized upon by a voluble lady wearing several splendid emeralds who told him a long story about a dripping tap.

"I wonder if that's the lady Varsoni was trying to burgle when he broke his neck," said Hambledon in a low voice.

"Serve her right if he'd succeeded," said Bagshott crossly. "I loathe women who wear showy jewelry at four in the afternoon."

The manager detached himself with the skill of long practice and went away. He returned with a large and heavy book which he laid upon a table and opened at the most recent arrivals. Bagshott ran his finger up the column of names, turned back one page—another—and stopped with his finger against an entry.

"Hugh Selkirk, British subject, of Carmen de las Flores, Buenos Aires Province, Argentina, and 27 Avenida de las Rochas, Buenos Aires. Arrived Saturday, March 9, 1946.

"Robert Adam, manservant, British subject, of the same addresses. Arrived the same day.

"Suite D2."

"Positively no deception, ladies and gentlemen," murmured Hambledon.

"Do you know if Mr. Selkirk is in the hotel at the moment?" asked Bagshott.

"I will make enquiries," said the manager, starting towards the door.

"No, don't do that. We'll go straight up, I think. Where's the lift? And are there stairs too? On the fourth floor, yes, but I think I'll walk up. Hambledon, will you take the lift and wait for me at the top?"

"I'll wait at the bottom, I think, since there are two lifts. Carry on, Bagshott, we shall meet on the fourth floor."

"Oh, really," said the manager, exhibiting agitation. He met Hambledon's unsympathetic eye and subsided.

Tommy gave the chief-inspector time to walk up four flights of stairs and then allowed himself to be taken up in the lift by the manager in person. Bagshott was waiting at the top.

"Where is this suite?"

"This way, gentlemen, this way," said the manager, and scuttled down the corridor before them in a manner which reminded Hambledon of the White Rabbit.

" 'Oh dear, oh dear, I shall be late,' " quoted Tommy in a whisper.

"What's that?" said Bagshott.

"Only he hasn't got any white gloves."

Bagshott, who was not an Alice addict, looked at him severely, and the manager stopped at an ornate door.

"This is it, gentlemen," he said, and knocked.

There was no answer and he knocked again. Bagshott put him aside, opened the door, and walked in. They entered a large and comfortable sitting room with fresh flowers in a bowl on the table, a newspaper thrown down in a chair, and an open book face downwards on a settee. There was even the stub end of a cigarette just smoldering its last in an ashtray, but there was no one there.

Hambledon crossed the room to a second door which opened upon a passage leading to two bedrooms, a bathroom, and a small kitchen no larger than a cupboard, still fragrant with the smell of coffee.

"They've gone," said Bagshott. The manager looked relieved and Hambledon laughed.

"Very able people, these," he said. "I take it, from your pleased expression, that they don't owe you any money."

"I was more worried about a possible scandal," said the manager frankly.

"Is there another staircase down from this floor?"

"The service stairs. Also the service lift."

"Show me," said Bagshott.

At the bottom of the stairs there was a large hall, and in it a table where an elderly woman was counting table napkins.

"How long have you been standing there doing that?" asked Bagshott.

"Half an hour or more," she answered.

"Did you see two gentlemen come down by the stairs or the lift within that time? Less, within the last quarter of an hour? Residents, I mean. One was a—"

"I did see two gentlemen come through, yes, sir. They went straight on towards the luggage entrance."

"Carrying any luggage?"

"One of them was carrying a pigskin bag, like. One of them soft things with two 'andles and a zip fastener all along it. I noticed it because I—"

"Initials on it?"

"I—I think so. Can't say what they were. I didn't notice, like."

"Were these the only two who passed you recently?" asked Hambledon. "Can you describe them?"

She did, not very well, but recognizably enough for the manager.

"That would be Mr. Selkirk and his servant Adam," he said. "The residents do not as a rule come down here unless they wish to speak personally to the luggage porter."

"I wonder if Selkirk had anything to say to him," said Hambledon.

But the luggage porter said that the two gentlemen had merely nodded to him in passing and walked out.

"Walked out," repeated Tommy. "I should like to know what made them walk out just then. Did they see and recognize us, or did somebody give them warning?"

"Nobody could," said Bagshott. "We didn't waste any time after seeing Selkirk's name in the register."

"No. Then, to quote the poet, 'it wasn't the words that startled the birds, but the horrible dooble ongtong.' You and me, Bagshott."

"Looks like it," said the chief-inspector.

CHAPTER SEVENTEEN
The Coughing Man

"I gather," said Adam, "that you don't much care for my suggestion of sending the Gatello gang's various addresses to the police."

"No," said Hyde slowly. "Does it satisfy you?"

"No. Not really. Why don't you like it?"

"Too impersonal, I think. Too accidental, as it were. We didn't arrange that affair tonight, it just happened, at—at their will, not ours. I want—I'm not sure what I want—"

"You want to put them in a tight corner, beat them over the head, and say: 'That's what you get for killing Hugh Selkirk.' "

"Something like that," said James, nodding. "I don't want misfortunes just to fall naturally upon them. I want to hurl misfortunes upon them and for them to know why."

"I agree. So do I. Well, if we're going to act we must act quickly, before either the police get them or they make a bolt for it. There will be notices out tomorrow, I expect, stuck up on police notice boards all over the country. 'Wanted, for Murder, Angelo Gatello, Pacorro Pagote,' and the rest."

"Yes. The only one I've really acted upon so far," said James wistfully, "was Ramon Jacaro tonight, and I didn't wait to tell him why. Besides, it was self-defense, not attack."

"Very well. Now, what will happen is probably this. The police will get these men in time. Angelo Gatello will be hung for the murder of Race; Pagote and El Caballero have capital charges against them in the Argentine. They and Mariposa will turn King's Evidence, of course, and get off with a term of imprisonment here. I suggest we deal first with Mariposa."

"He's the fat one, is he?" Adam nodded, and James continued: "He wasn't doing much in the flat tonight so far as I saw. By the way, you suggested my giving evidence. I don't want to give evidence; it means the whole story coming out, and I'd rather it didn't. At least, not yet. Not till we've disposed of the money, anyway."

"I agree. Well, Mariposa lives in a hotel just off the Euston Road. It's a biggish place, though rather third-rate. The sort of place where colored students live, and anyone else who can't afford anything better. Men, almost entirely. Actually it's something between a hotel and a boardinghouse. My idea, in general terms, is to go there and terrify Mariposa into running to the police for safety. 'I'll tell you all about everything if only you'll protect me,' that sort of thing."

"But the police," said Hyde, "will want to know who has terrified him."

"Yes, but if we make it fantastic enough they won't believe him."

Adam and Hyde talked far into the night.

When the Gatello gang divided after the affair above the Red Macaw, Cesar Mariposa returned to his room. Gatello told him to go home and keep quiet until further instructions reached him, and as there seemed no alternative he obeyed, but he was not happy. London oppressed him; there were too many policemen and too many law-abiding citizens in the place. Nowhere to bolt to if things got hot and Gatello did not communicate with him. No raffish friends to console him with red wine and an evening spent in gambling. No one in whom to confide his anxieties except Pacorro and Tadeo, and he had been told to keep away from them for a day or two. Gatello had scattered his force singly about London with the idea that they would be less easily traced by the police, and Mariposa was lonely and frightened. All this shooting—he had a feeling that London would disapprove of too much shooting. It seemed so out of place here, but one could not argue with Gatello. It was no use; besides, it wasn't safe. Gatello's temper was getting worse, if possible.

The day after Race's murder was Sunday. Mariposa went down for his meals but did not enjoy them because he fancied his fellow feeders were staring at him; he spent the rest of the time sitting miserably in his bedroom wishing he were back in his native Buenos Aires, in the Boca where he belonged. There, if a gentleman was in a little trouble, there were dozens of places where he could go; rabbit warrens of tenement houses divided by familiar alleys, short cuts and alternative routes with many hideouts and ways of escape. He ached for the hot sun and the dust, the taste of harsh red wine and the smell of garlic and spiced cooking.

After the evening meal, a sketchy affair on Sunday nights, Mariposa drifted wearily across the dining room and picked up, in passing, a Sunday paper someone had abandoned. The Argentine did not read English with any ease, but it would be an occupation to puzzle out some of it.

He threw himself on his bed, lit a cigarette, and turned the paper back to the first page. The next instant he was sitting upright on the edge of the bed and his heels were drumming on the floor. There were the headlines: "Murder in Soho. Man Found Shot in Flat above Night Club. Killed While the Dance Band Played. . . ."

Gatello said that nobody would go there for weeks. He was wrong. The police had walked in at once.

Mariposa struggled on down the column, gathering the gist of it. The dead man's name was Walter Race, a something-or-other from a place called Chartham, wherever that was. Ramon Jacaro—he'd wondered what had become of Jacaro. Cesar had asked Gatello and had been told not to argue— Jacaro had been arrested and was now in hospital. Presumably the police had beaten him up; nothing remarkable in that, of course. If Jacaro had talked, the police might come at any moment.

Mariposa leapt from the bed and went to the door to make sure he had locked it. He had; he took the key out. No, better not do that, the police would get the master key from the housemaid and open it. Leave the key in the lock; nobody can put another key in when there's one there already. There was no bolt.

The Argentine spent a sleepless night, starting at every step in the passage outside and peering in the dark from the window at every sound of approaching traffic. Once he saw a policeman come along the pavement, pause, and look about him. Mariposa's heart thumped so hard that it almost choked him, but the constable walked on.

The housemaid whose duty it was to attend to that room found herself locked out in the morning. The gentleman told her to go away, he didn't want to be disturbed, he wasn't well.

"Out on the razzle, I expect," she said to her assistant. "Nasty fat creature. I 'ope 'is 'ead aches. One room less to do, that's one blessing." She promptly forgot him; there was enough work already without worrying about trifles. For Mariposa, the day passed somehow and Gatello did not come. Cesar dared not go down to a meal; by the evening he was sick with hunger. It occurred to him that there might be a letter for him in the rack in the hall; he made a hurried dash downstairs during dinner when no one was about. There was no letter and he retreated again. A little later he made a telephone call but received neither satisfaction nor comfort.

By eleven o'clock that night he had fallen asleep from weariness, a light uneasy sleep, lying on the outside of his bed fully clothed. He was awakened by the sound of the key turning in the lock; he sat up to see the door slowly opening. Somebody came in, closed the door again, and switched on the lights.

Mariposa sat up, dazzled by the sudden glare. Either Gatello or the police— his eyes cleared and he shrank back.

"Selgirk," he said.

"Fat hog," said James Hyde dispassionately.

"I locka da door," said Mariposa stupidly.

"So what? Locked doors won't keep me out, Mariposa."

"Who are you?"

"You called me Selkirk just now," said Hyde.

"You no can be Hugh Selgirk, he dead. Too, you no looka da same."

"People do look different after they're dead. You will, in a minute."

Mariposa wrung his hands. "I no keel you," he whimpered. "Mercy! 'Ave mercy, most excellent señor—"

"Why? Did you have mercy on William Selkirk when he asked for water and you poured it on the ground? Men with his complaint suffer from thirst, you know. Well, you'll be thirsty enough in hell."

Mariposa uttered a low howl and groveled on the floor. He was a disgusting sight and Hyde sickened at it.

"Your gang killed his son, too. You'd have done it yourself if you'd had the chance. See this, Mariposa? Look up, you lump of fat pork."

Mariposa looked up and saw his visitor holding a parcel wrapped in red paper. The wrapping did not completely cover its contents, which showed for a couple of inches at the bottom: round tubular objects about two inches thick, and yellow in color.

"Know what that is, Mariposa? Gelignite. It explodes."

Hyde glanced round him. There was a table near the door; he put his parcel on it and produced from another pocket what looked like a length of thick black string.

"Fuse," explained Hyde.

Mariposa scrambled frenziedly on the bed and hid his face in the bedclothes; he could not get behind the bed since it stood against the wall. He did not scream; he gasped noisily for breath and his fat body jerked with every gasp.

"The light hurts your eyes," said James politely, and switched it out. "Now we light the fuse—"

There was the flare of a match in the dark and a spluttering sound as the fuse took fire. The match was blown out, and a dull red spark glowed in its place.

Mariposa thrust his head under the pillow and encountered something he had forgotten, his revolver. He snatched it out and fired once. The bullet whistled past Hyde's head; he gasped and received a full dose of the fumes from the smoldering fuse. He began to cough violently and uncontrollably, and the sound masked any small noises from the bed. He heard, however, a shrill scream from the room on one side of Mariposa's, and a cry of surprise in a man's voice from the other side. That shot had awakened the adjacent sleepers; in a moment the corridor would fill with people and here he was helpless with coughing. He blundered against the door and felt a dressing gown hanging behind it.

The next moment doors opened all along the corridor and people leapt from their rooms in various stages of disarray. Among them was a middle-aged gentleman with fair hair turning gray, who coughed as though he had the croup. He was scarlet in the face and tears ran from his eyes. Apart from this he was in no way remarkable among a crowd of men in dressing gowns or coats hastily hurled on over pajamas, or simply in unmitigated pajamas. The lady who had screamed opened her door a modest slit and peeped out; the first object she saw was a medical student from Seringapatam in green-and-orange stripes. She withdrew again and Hyde heard the key turn in the lock.

"You have a cough," said the medical student, addressing Hyde, who nodded and gasped something about getting a drink. Holding a handkerchief to his face, he slipped away through the crowd, now giving tongue with questions and suggestions, and made his way downstairs against the stream of people coming up. There was a door labeled "Bathroom" on the half landing; Hyde turned into it and found himself a drink of water and some fresh air at the open window. Having regained control of his glottis and pharynx, he hung up the dressing gown behind the door and walked quietly down the stairs into the hall. Adam had somehow managed to render himself inconspicuous among all the commotion. Hyde caught his eye and walked straight out into the street, where Adam overtook him a moment later.

"We can get a bus in Euston Road," he said, and Hyde nodded. "You weren't hurt, were you?"

"No," said James. "Oh no. I had a bad fit of coughing, that's all." He chuckled. "It was rather funny; I'll tell you when we get home."

They went into the hotel by separate entrances as usual. The staff entrance was in a side street, so no one could tell that they had been together. When Hyde reached their sitting room Adam was already there.

"I was getting anxious," he said. "Somebody shouted 'Murder' and I was afraid you might be the victim."

"No, that was a rush of imagination on somebody's part. It all went off quite nicely, and Mariposa was suitably terrified. Then, when I put the light out and lit the fuse, he fired a gun at me in the dark. I gasped, I suppose, and inhaled a lungful of fumes. I thought I was going to choke to death, so I grabbed his dressing gown and mingled with the crowd in the corridor. They were giving tongue, weren't they? I retired to a bathroom till I felt better, left the dressing gown there, and came away."

"Did you see two men who went upstairs just after the row started?"

"Two men? I thought there were about fifty, but perhaps I was seeing double. Which two men d'you mean?"

"Two who came into the Red Macaw the other night. Hambledon of British Intelligence, and Chief-Inspector Bagshott of Scotland Yard."

"Great Scott, no. At least, I didn't recognize them. In fact, my eyes were streaming so much that I shouldn't have recognized you if you'd come up. Blurred shapes are all I saw."

"But they saw you, no doubt."

"They saw a segment of scarlet face peeping from behind a handkerchief, that's all. I was weeping into it," said Hyde. "But what brought them there at that moment?"

"I haven't the least idea. They walked into the hall just as the uproar began and dashed straight upstairs."

"They'd find Mariposa in the right mood to talk," said Hyde. "He was so overcome that he was mooing like a calf. When he points at those candles and says: 'Look. Gelignite,' they'll think he's out of his mind."

Adam fidgeted about the room. "I don't like the prompt way they turned up," he said. "Two minutes earlier, and they'd have walked in on you."

"Yes. Very awkward. But there's nothing criminal in playing a practical joke on a man. If I'd just laughed lightly and walked out they couldn't have stopped me, could they?"

"Hambledon would," said Adam decidedly. "I've heard stories about him. Well, it didn't happen, so it's all right. You managed to open the door without trouble?"

"Oh yes. The key came out through the keyhole, as you said, and I turned it easily. Here are your pliers, by the way. Queer-looking things, what are they for?"

"They're dental forceps."

"I thought they reminded me of something unpleasant. If I'd waved them at Mariposa he might have passed out altogether."

Next morning, when the papers came, their satisfaction was roughly swept away.

"Dead?" said Hyde. "I don't believe it. He wasn't dead when I left the room. Dammit, he fired a gun at me."

"He must have died very soon afterwards," said Adam anxiously. "Not that I mind that, but we don't want those two on our tracks for murder."

"But I didn't murder him. It doesn't even say he was murdered; it says he died under mysterious circumstances."

"I suppose he didn't shoot himself?"

"The bullet whistled past my ear, I heard it. That's what made me gasp."

"I don't like it," said Adam.

"They can't trace us," said Hyde, "can they?"

"I shouldn't think so, but one can't be sure. The police are excessively capable and Hambledon's worse. I don't like the way he keeps on turning up. Anyway, I think I'll pack your small kit bag, just in case, and if I see the slightest signs of anyone looking for us here we can walk out at once. The service stairs are just along the corridor."

Two days later the early editions of the evening papers published a three-line paragraph saying that the Argentine subject, Cesar Mariposa, whose death had been a matter for official enquiry, had died from natural causes.

"There," said James. "Just coincidence, that's all. I'm glad that's settled."

"So am I," said Adam. "It might have been awkward."

They spent the afternoon arranging a future plan of attack upon the three remaining members of the gang, Angelo Gatello, Pacorro Pagote, and Tadeo el Caballero. At about four o'clock Hyde lit a cigarette and remarked that it seemed to be his last. Adam, saying that he would go down to the smoking room and get some more, left the room, and James began the *Times's* crossword puzzle.

Five minutes later Adam came back with a rush. "Get your hat and coat, quick. They're here and we're leaving."

"They?" said Hyde, throwing down the paper. "Do you mean—"

"Hambledon and Bagshott. In the small waiting room. And the porter's looking for the manager."

James leapt to his feet and ran into his bedroom. A minute later the two residents of Suite D2 were walking decorously along the corridor towards the service lifts.

"Down the stairs," murmured Adam. "I want to be out of sight."

They ran down the four flights of stairs, passed through a large hall where an elderly woman was counting table napkins, and out through the luggage entrance, nodding casually to the luggage porter as they went. Once out in the street, Adam led the way, turning left and right through once aristocratic squares till they came out in Picadilly.

"Where are we going?" asked Hyde.

"Forgan's place for a start. After that, we'll see."

"But we've left all that money behind."

"We'll do something about that presently. This bus will do."

They came to the model shop in the Clerkenwell Road and dived in like rabbits into their native burrow.

"We're on the run," said Adam. "Can you take us in?"

"Police or Gatello?" asked Forgan.

"Police."

"Then the answer's no, I'm afraid; they've got a plainclothes man watching the shop. He's just over there—no, he isn't. He's gone, probably to telephone Scotland Yard."

"Oh dear," said James, and put down his kit bag on the counter.

"Come round behind the screen," said Forgan. "No need to stand in full view of the street."

"I was hoping," said Adam, "that we could stay here for a few hours while we found somewhere else to go."

"My house is yours," said Forgan with sudden passion, "and everything in it, as you know. But it isn't a refuge from the police. Gatello—I wish it were only Gatello."

"I know," said Adam. "I—"

"Would it be a good idea," said James diffidently, "to leave London for a few days? Just till things settle down?"

Adam thought it would be an excellent idea, but Forgan said that the police would trace them wherever they went.

"Not if we turned into somebody else. I am James Hyde from Yeovil, where I've lived all my life and everybody knows me. You, Adam, are a business friend of mine and we're having a week's holiday in one of the hotels there, looking up old friends. Is that a silly idea?"

"But they think you're dead," said Adam. "They saw it in the papers. They would have been interested, wouldn't they? Murder of a fellow townsman?"

"That was another man of the same name, of course. When they see me," said James simply, "they'll know it wasn't true, won't they?"

"I think you've hit on it," said Forgan, and James added that it would be rather restful to spend even two or three days not being chased about by inquisitive police or vengeful Argentines.

"You are quite right," said Adam. "We'll go to Yeovil at once."

"Go by the back door," said Forgan. "Through the scullery there and across the yard into the lane at the back. The gate isn't locked."

"I'll just get my kit bag," said James, and made a move towards the front of the shop. Forgan glanced up in a mirror fitted at an angle above his head which gave him a view of the shop over the partition.

"Heavens, no. Look who's looking in the window! That chief-inspector and his pal—run!"

Adam seized Hyde by the arm and they bolted out through the back of the house just as the shop bell rang. Forgan paused to shut the door after them before he went forward to attend to the customers—if they were customers. It was immediately made plain that they were not.

Hambledon leaned his hands on the counter and said: "Mr. Selkirk is here.

Can I speak to him, please? At once."

Forgan raised his eyebrows and said: "Mr. Selkirk? There is no Mr. Selkirk here."

"Nonsense. He came in here less than ten minutes ago."

"Oh no," said Forgan.

"It is no use your denying it. I must see him at once, please."

"But I do deny it," said Forgan firmly. "I tell you, there is no Mr. Selkirk here. In fact, there's no one but me in the house at all; even Campbell is out at the moment."

"Since you persist in your denial," said Bagshott, "I shall search the premises."

"Forgive my even appearing to question the doings of a chief-inspector," said Forgan, "but have you got a search warrant?"

"I have; here it is," said Bagshott, and produced it. Hambledon had foreseen that it might be necessary.

Forgan read it carefully and handed it back. "Thank you; all in order, I see. I am flattered that my poor house should be considered of such importance. Please carry on. The stairs are on the left, through that door."

CHAPTER EIGHTEEN
The Ghost Goes Home

Forgan's house was tall and narrow, three floors above the shop with two rooms on each floor. The front room on the first floor was a sitting room, the back one a storeroom full of materials for modelmaking, unfinished and broken models and miscellaneous items of all kinds. Above this were two bedrooms in obviously masculine occupation and above that again two attics, only partly furnished and evidently unused. It did not take long to search the place; Hambledon and Bagshott returned downstairs and found the door which led out to the yard.

"I had no idea," said Bagshott, "that there was any way out at the back of these premises."

The yard was narrow and three-parts covered in by a lean-to roof along one wall giving shelter to a small Ford van, inconspicuously shabby. The yard gate was not bolted on the inside, as Hambledon pointed out. He opened it and looked into a narrow lane which ran behind it.

"What a rabbit warren our London is," said Tommy. "Well, that's the way they went. Now I think we'll go back and talk to Mr. Forgan."

Mr. Forgan was serving a small boy with six dozen small brass rail stanchions for a ship model, and some discussion was proceeding about the size. Hambledon noticed that the kit bag had been moved off the counter to a shelf at the back, and said so to Bagshott.

"Looks like the one the linen maid at the hotel described Selkirk as carrying. I don't see any initials."

"He's turned it round, that's all. If it's the same one," said Bagshott. "There are plenty of those things about."

The small boy went out and Forgan turned courteously to his visitors.

"I fear your search was unsuccessful," he said.

"You knew it would be," said Bagshott.

"Yes. I even said so, didn't I?"

"Why didn't you tell us that Hugh Selkirk and his servant had gone out through the yard?"

"I never lie to the police," said Forgan earnestly, and Hambledon bit his lip.

"Do you deny that two men came into this shop and went out through the back?" said Bagshott.

"No, of course I don't. Why should I?"

"Who were they?"

"Two customers."

"Their names?"

"I haven't the slightest idea," said Forgan, without hesitation. "It is not usual, in business, to ask the names of cash customers. I don't even know the name of that schoolboy who has just gone out, though he has been here once a week for months past. When he gets his pocket money, no doubt. He is building a—"

"Why did Selkirk and his servant go out through the back of the shop?"

"You do keep on about a Mr. Selkirk," complained Forgan. "Who is he, anyway?"

"Listen, Forgan," said Bagshott. "Once before, when I was in here, I asked you if you knew Hugh Selkirk in the Argentine, and you denied it. I have been in communication with the Argentine Legation, and they tell me that both you and Campbell worked on the Selkirk estate at Carmen de las Flores. Do you still say you don't know him?"

"Oh, that Selkirk," said Forgan. "I thought you meant the old chap, his father. I never met him."

"So you do know Hugh Selkirk."

"Of course I do. I worked for him. Are you sure you said 'Hugh'?"

Bagshott was by no means sure, so he let that pass. "Do you still insist that it was not Hugh Selkirk who went through this shop half an hour ago?"

"Certainly," said Forgan steadily.

"Do your customers usually go out that way?"

"Not as a rule, but why shouldn't they if they want to? I don't mind. Perhaps it was the nearest way to wherever they wanted to go. I didn't ask."

"Who does that kit bag belong to?"

"One of my customers."

"Why is it here?"

"My dear Chief-Inspector," said Forgan with an exasperated laugh, "because he left it here. He didn't want it with him and he asked me to keep it for him for a few days."

"Do you know his name, or is he one of your cash customers?"

"His name is Hubert Scott," said Forgan blandly. "The bag has his initials on it, look."

He put the bag on the counter, turned to show the initials H.S. on the side. Bagshott tilted his head to look along the bag against the light; the surface shone perfectly clean.

"I'll bet you gave it a rub with a duster while we were upstairs," he said.

"Very likely I may have done," agreed Forgan. "Habit, you know. Always got a duster in your hand when you keep a shop. Especially in London."

Hambledon turned abruptly away and looked into a showcase at the other side of the shop. His shoulders were shaking with suppressed laughter. Bagshott, who was not at all amused, saw that it was no use going on.

"I must warn you, Forgan, that it is a serious matter to mislead the police when enquiries are being made."

"I'm sure it must be," said Forgan. "A wicked thing to do. Antisocial. But do tell me, what has this poor Mr. Selkirk who you thought came through here—what has he done?"

"I am not here to answer questions," said Bagshott, whose temper was getting the better of him at last. He turned to go out, and Hambledon crossed the shop to join him.

"If I ever see my customer again," said Forgan, rushing round the shop to open the door for them, "I'll tell him the police want to interview him, shall I?"

"I'll take the kit bag with me for examination," snapped Bagshott, and took it off the counter.

"My customer's bag? Certainly not!"

"It is within our powers," said Bagshott. "I will give you a receipt for it, which you can show your customer if necessary." He gave Hambledon the bag to hold while he wrote out a receipt and handed it to Forgan, who took it without a word. "If the bag contains nothing of interest in connection with this case, it will be returned to you in a matter of hours. Good afternoon."

The chief-inspector walked out of the shop, closely followed by Hambledon. Several doors up the road Tommy turned suddenly into the entrance of a shop, which happened to be a jeweler's, and gazed earnestly into a showcase full of secondhand trinkets. Bagshott looked at him and noticed with surprise that his face was red and that there were tears in his eyes.

"What on earth's the matter?" asked the chief-inspector. "Aren't you well?"

"I'm—I'm all right," said Hambledon. He laid hold of the corner post of the window and leaned against the glass.

"For heaven's sake," said Bagshott, "what is it? Just a minute, I'll call a taxi if there's one about."

"You'd better," gasped Tommy. "Then at least I can laugh in comfort. Forgan—that man'll be the death of me. Oh, what a pain I've got!"

"Oh," said Bagshott in a relieved voice, "you're just amused, are you?"

"Oh, don't," said Tommy, and laughed until he cried. "Antisocial, I call it." He doubled up, holding himself, and Bagshott took him home in a taxi.

"I'm sorry," apologized Hambledon. "It—it was suppressing it all that time. I got the most awful pain, I did really. I don't think Forgan's a good man to interview, do you?"

The bag contained merely such things as a man would need for the weekend; they were all practically new and unmarked, and there were no letters or papers of any kind. There were, however, a nice set of fingerprints on the case of the shaving brush which coincided with a set on the glass doors of the kitchen cupboard in Selkirk's flat. Bagshott sighed with relief.

"I knew we weren't barking up the wrong tree," he said, "but it's nice to be able to prove it. The assistant commissioner will be pleased; he likes things tidy. Hubert Scott, indeed!"

"Going to send it back to Forgan?" asked Tommy.

"No. If Selkirk wants his bag he can come and ask for it. By the way, about the Gatello gang. I had enquiries made from the owners of that flat of theirs above the Red Macaw and it appears that Angelo Gatello, under another name, took it and paid three months' rent in advance. He was then staying at a hotel in Paddington temporarily; he was only there a week."

"What name did he give?"

Bagshott laughed. "He has a nerve, that fellow. What do you think? La Guardia. The flat owners were duly impressed."

A few days later the police were informed that there had been a theft from the hotel where Selkirk had lived; one armchair taken away by fraud. When it emerged in the course of enquiry that the armchair had been removed from Suite D2, recently occupied by Hugh Selkirk, the local police looked at each other.

"It seems trivial," said the superintendent. "But—"

"This Selkirk case, whatever it is," said the inspector who was dealing with the chair mystery.

"Yes, quite. A security matter, I understand."

"Indeed," said the inspector, and the affair was brought to the attention of Chief-Inspector Bagshott.

"An armchair?" he said. "It was all hotel furniture, wasn't it? I mean, it wasn't an odd chair belonging to Selkirk?"

"No, sir. It was a padded armchair upholstered in gray velvet, and was part of the suite of furniture in the sitting room. The hotel people say that the loss of it spoils the suite."

"How was the trick worked?"

"The system is this. The hotel has a pad of order forms with their official heading, interleaved with counterfoils. Whenever there is a job to be done in the hotel—furniture repaired, sash line replaced, and so forth—the order is written out on this pad and the top copy given to the tradesman concerned. When he comes to do the job, he brings this order with him as his credential, and hands it in. It goes through the office and is compared with the counterfoil as a check on whether the work has actually been done or not. The same system is used for the removal of residents' heavy baggage from the luggage hall when they leave the hotel."

"I see," said Bagshott. "Carry on."

"On this occasion, two men with a light van came to the luggage entrance and handed in a chit on the correct form authorizing the Zee-Dee Furnishing Company to remove one armchair from Suite D2 for repair. The luggage porter looked at it and it seemed to be all in order; also, there was the name, 'Zee-Dee Furnishing Company,' on the van. So he sent these two men, with a page boy to guide them, up to Suite D2 in the service lift, and they removed this chair quite openly, put it in the van, and drove away. When the order went through the office it was found that there was no corresponding counterfoil. Enquiries were made and it was established that no order had ever been given for any chair from Suite D2 to be repaired. Further, when they came to look up the Zee-Dee Furnishing Company in the telephone directory and the London directory, there was no trace of any such firm."

"Really," said the chief-inspector, and drew patterns on his blotting paper. "Of course, furniture is still in desperately short supply, especially good non-utility stuff. On the face of it, this might be a black-market stunt to get hold of some, though you'd think they would take more than one chair."

"I thought of that, sir. If that had been the case, one would expect complaints from other hotels who've been robbed in the same way."

"Aren't there any?"

"Not so far, sir."

"And seeing that that was Selkirk's flat," said Bagshott thoughtfully, and stopped. "I was going to say that anything queer which happens is apt to be a lot queerer if it has a connection with Selkirk. I'll look into the matter."

He rang up Hambledon and told him about the theft.

"A chair?" said Tommy. "What sort of a chair?"

"A large padded armchair with coiled springs and horsehair stuffing, covered with plain gray velvet. Oak knob feet," said Bagshott, reading from the hotel's description. "Besides, we saw it; it must have been the one with the newspaper lying in it."

There was such a long silence at the other end of the line that Bagshott said: "Are you there?"

"No," said Hambledon in a choked voice. "Evidently not. At least, not all. Only partly."

"What are you talking about?"

"Me. You asked if I was all there, or so I gathered. The reply is in the negative. I am not. Do you realize that we stood there with our hands in our pockets and looked at it?"

"Looked at what?"

"Three million dollars."

Bagshott whistled. "I told my police to search Selkirk's belongings," he said. "It didn't occur to me to tell them to tear the hotel furniture to pieces too."

"Next time I get a line on a house which Selkirk has inhabited," said Tommy, "I will have all the wallpapers steamed off to see if there are negotiable securities pasted on behind. I will have the furniture dissected by a gang of veterinary surgeons and the bath water analyzed by Sir Bernard Spilsbury. Then I'll have the house pulled down and every brick broken in case it's hollow. After that—"

"At this moment," interrupted Bagshott, "would you like to come to the hotel with me? I'll pick you up at once."

"The trouble with me," said Hambledon as they drove up Regent Street, "is that I haven't got enough imagination. Or too much, I'm not sure which. I concluded without question that a man of Selkirk's type, with the Gatello gang after him, would put the loot in a safe-deposit, not keep it on the premises in a piece of furniture that didn't belong to him."

"That clears up the Varsoni mystery, anyway," said the chief-inspector. "He knew it was there."

"Varsoni. The fellow who broke his neck going after the widow's emeralds— of course. He wasn't after the emeralds. . . . Where is the widow's flat? I'll bet you my next quarter's salary that it's directly under Selkirk's."

"I'm not taking," said Bagshott. "I'm sure of it."

"Why didn't somebody report that Selkirk lived next above—or next door, or whatever it is?"

"We weren't looking for Selkirk then. At least, not intensively."

"Weren't we?" said Hambledon dreamily. "I feel as though I'd been looking for Selkirk for years. I dreamt the other night that I chased him through a gateway with two stone lions on the posts, and when I came back the stone lions had gone, so I knew they were Selkirk in disguise, and you said I ought to have known because hippogriff was the anagram of Hugh Selkirk. Well, here we are. I don't think I like this hotel."

They interviewed the manager and passed on, leaving him uncomforted, to the luggage porter who had admitted the two furniture removers and the page boy who had taken them upstairs. There emerged a fairly clear picture of a rather shabby Ford van with the name "Zee-Dee Furnishing Company" on a long narrow board on each side, and two undistinguished men in caps who came with it.

"Ford van," said Hambledon. "I suppose it's asking too much to expect you to have noticed the number?"

The porter said, with apologies, that it was, but the page boy said brightly that he couldn't remember it all but he knew it had two sevens in it.

"You're sure?"

"Yes sir. Quite sure."

"What makes you so certain?"

"Well, it's—it's a little bit of a superstition, like. If I has anythin' to do with a car with two sevens in the number, I'm goin' to have a good day with tips. Silly, I know, but it always works, sir."

"I see. Bagshott, have you the number of that Ford van we saw in a back yard the other day?"

Bagshott looked up the number of Forgan's van in his notebook and said there were no sevens in it at all.

"Oh. Well, we can't expect to have it handed to us on a gold-mounted salver. About those two men, what were they like?"

One was older than the other and the younger man was taller than the older, who had a red scar down one cheek, the left—yes, the left side. A long scar, like a healed cut. The younger man had one finger bandaged on his right hand; he had referred casually to it, saying that no matter what he was doing he always seemed to be hitting it. The older man had gray hair, and they were both dressed in rather shabby clothes and wore aprons. Caps, too, but of course they took those off when they went upstairs. Also their boots looked too big for them, as removal men's boots generally do.

"What color was the younger man's hair?"

"Sort of brown," said the page boy, and the porter said it was nothing notice-able. He would know them again if he saw them, having been trained to re-member faces, but they looked just like any other removal men to him.

"When they went into the flat," said Hambledon, "they knew which chair to take?"

"Oh yes," said the page boy. "The big armchair, they said they'd been told to fetch. There is only the one big chair in them suites; there's a settee and some smaller ones besides."

"They brought the chair down—"

"In the lift," said the boy.

"Just put it in the van and drove away, is that all? Did they seem in a hurry?"

"No," said the porter. "They brought sheets of sacking and that matting stuff movers use, and wrapped up the chair before they put it in the van. Then they both lit cigarettes, and the older man asked me if there was anywhere 'andy where they could 'ave a glass of beer before they went off. I said, well, there was the Crown & Sceptre, but they wouldn't be open for another 'alf-'our yet, and this man looks up at our big clock 'ere and says he supposes they'll 'ave to go dry, then. So they says, 'So long, mate,' and gets in the van and drives off. No, they weren't in no 'urry."

Hambledon and Bagshott returned thoughtfully to their car.

"You were thinking," said the chief-inspector, "that the younger man's hair might have been red, but it could have been faked to look brown. Gray hair's easy. Flour."

"There's nothing easier to fake," said Bagshott, "than a nice scar for people to remember."

"A bandaged finger is easier still, especially when you call attention to it."

"The name, you noticed, was on a board along the side of the van, not painted on the side itself. Easily removable."

"And the number plate with the two sevens in it more easily removable still," said Hambledon. "I think the doings of that blest pair of sirens is worth looking into. Much as I hesitate to expose you to further—"

"You can talk to them this time," said Bagshott hastily. "The man I had watching the shop that morning will be able to tell us whether they were there or not between the hours of ten and twelve. If they were at home all the morn-ing," he added, cheering up slightly, "we needn't bother to go."

But the watcher reported that on the morning in question the shop remained shut until nearly one o'clock.

"Did you actually see them return to the house?"

"Yes, sir. They drove the van to the shop door in the main street."

"Did they take anything out of the van?"

"Yes, sir. A large package wrapped in sacking."

"Oh, I can't believe it," said Hambledon, "it's too easy. Are you sure this was the same day?"

The detective-sergeant turned over the pages of his notebook and verified that it was.

"I don't, of course, suppose for a moment that the chair is still on the premises," said Bagshott, "but they'll have to answer some rather awkward questions. Shall we go now?"

"By all means," said Tommy, "though it is written that it is better to travel hopefully than to arrive. But don't let me discourage you."

CHAPTER NINETEEN
Mention Toledo

Forgan and Campbell were both in the shop when Chief-Inspector Bagshott and Tommy Hambledon entered. Bagshott addressed the partners in his most official manner.

"In connection with a larceny alleged to have been committed on the morning of Tuesday in this week, I have to ask both of you to account for your actions between the hours of nine and twelve noon on that day."

"Tuesday morning?" said Forgan. "We were here as usual, weren't we, Campbell?"

"Surely," said Campbell. "I think we were."

"That's your story, is it?" said Bagshott. "You were both here on these premises between the hours I mentioned?"

"Yes," said Campbell, with a dawning doubt in his voice, but Forgan interrupted him.

"No, we weren't. We were out that morning, don't you remember?"

"So we were," said Campbell, and shuffled his feet.

"What were you doing?"

"As a matter of fact, we were doing a job of furniture removing," said Forgan unwillingly.

"Oh, were you? What furniture did you remove, where from, and where did you take it?"

"Look here," said Forgan truculently, "if we are to be accused of a larceny, whatever that is, I think you must say plainly what we're accused of instead of trying to bounce us into inculpating ourselves. Inculpate, is that the right word, Campbell?"

"Inculpate," said Campbell, nodding slowly, "is, I think, the correct word under the circumstances."

Bagshott drew a long breath and started again. "In connection with the removal by fraud of an armchair from the Westerley Hotel on the morning of Tuesday in this—"

"Campbell," said Forgan sternly, "have you unlawfully removed an armchair?"

"No," said Campbell. "Have you?"

"Not for years, and then it wasn't an armchair. Do you remember that morning in the Buen Rato in Buenos Aires"—Forgan ran on so quickly that Bagshott could not interrupt—"when I removed a chair just when Diego el Diablo was going to sit on it? You might justly call that unlawful removal; he sat down on the alleged marble floor and was he wild, or—"

"He threw a knife at you," said Campbell, corroborating.

"And missed," said Forgan triumphantly.

Bagshott repressed, "What a pity," with such difficulty that he actually spluttered, and Campbell offered to get him a glass of water. Hambledon thought it both kind and timely to intervene.

"I think, if I may say so," he began in his mildest tones, "that you two gentlemen are not treating this matter with the seriousness it deserves."

"I am terribly sorry," said Forgan instantly, "but it really does strike us as rather farcical. We are modelmakers, not furniture removers, you know. And we already have an armchair each and one extra for a visitor."

"No doubt. All the same, I am afraid that it is necessary for you to account for your actions on the morning of Tuesday last."

"May we know your name?" asked Forgan politely.

"Hambledon."

"And your—forgive us our ignorance of what is doubtless well known—your official status?"

"I am an official of the Intelligence Branch of the Foreign Office."

"It must be a very important armchair," said Campbell.

"It is," said Tommy simply; then his tone hardened. "And now, gentlemen, may we have a plain—and truthful—account of your doings on Tuesday morning?"

"We went to the house of a customer to bring away a piece of furniture for repair," said Forgan. "This sort of thing isn't really in our line, but we thought it might prove interesting and the old gentleman is a valued customer. So we took it on."

"May we see this piece of furniture, please?"

"Certainly," said Forgan. "If you will come upstairs I'll show it to you. I said, show it, it's not unpacked yet." He led the way to the back room on the first floor, with Bagshott close at his heels; Hambledon, after a moment's hesitation, followed more slowly.

"That's it," said Forgan, indicating a package about four feet square and nearly three feet thick wrapped in sacking and tied with rough string.

"It doesn't look much like a chair," said Tommy.

"It isn't," said Forgan.

"Undo it, please," said Bagshott, and helped to cut the string with his own knife.

"So thorough, the police," murmured Forgan, and ripped off some of the wrappings. The object inside was a little like a cupboard except that it had a keyboard like that of a piano, but shorter, and a queer bent pedal near the floor in front.

"What is it?" asked Hambledon.

"It is an organ, a genuine 'Father Smith' organ. I suppose you might call it the grandfather of the familiar harmonium beloved of chapels. It is a genuine antique," said Forgan, warming to his subject, "a real collector's piece, but it is slightly out of order, and our customer—"

"Thank you," said Bagshott, red behind the ears. "Now I'm afraid I must look through your house again."

"Certainly," said Forgan cheerfully. "That is—your search warrant is doubtless still valid?"

"It is."

"Very well, gentlemen. Carry on."

He retired downstairs and left them to their search, which was thorough on Bagshott's part. "There may be a communicating door to the next house," he said.

"You're wasting your time," said Hambledon, and followed him about, idly humming a tune which reminded the chief-inspector vaguely of his childhood till he caught the words.

"William O'Forgan
With his little organ—"

Bagshott finished his tour in a hurry and went down to the shop.

"Mr. Forgan, can you produce any independent evidence to show that that musical instrument upstairs actually is the same package which you brought here on Tuesday shortly before 1 P.M.?"

"I think so," said Forgan sweetly. "Yes, I think so. The organ was rather awkward for two to handle, so we called a man to help us. He was one of two young men who are always loitering about here—not the one who's on duty at the moment, the other one. He most kindly helped us to carry it in."

One of Bagshott's two detectives, of course. Hambledon clutched at his sense of propriety and missed; he burst into a roar of laughter. Forgan smiled politely, as one who has inadvertently amused the company without quite knowing how, and even the chief-inspector looked a trifle sheepish.

"Now I'll have a look at the van," he said coldly, and went out through the back of the shop with the others trailing after him. The van's number plate was still as Bagshott had originally noted it; the name, William Forgan, was not painted on the sides of the van itself but on long narrow boards fastened on with screws. Bagshott walked closer and examined them.

"May I use your telephone?" he asked suddenly.

"Certainly," said Forgan. "It's in the shop."

"I'm going to ring up for somebody to come and take those boards off."

"Oh, but why bother to ring up?" asked Campbell cheerfully. "I'll take them off for you; it won't take a minute. I'll get a screwdriver out of the workshop." He turned towards the house.

Bagshott sighed. "Don't bother," he said in a dispirited voice. "I've changed my mind."

When their visitors had gone the two partners looked at each other and Forgan wiped his forehead.

"You nearly gave me a heart attack," he said, "offering to take those boards off for him."

"Only thing to do. He'd have got a policeman to do it if I hadn't."

"If he had seen 'Zee-Dee Furnishing Company' painted on the back he'd have eaten us alive. I've a sound respect for that chief-inspector," said Forgan.

"I'll take them off as soon as it's dark and scrape them clean," said Campbell. "I was a fool not to have done it before, but I never thought they'd pin it on us. Even now I can't think why. Or rather, how."

"I tell you," said Forgan, "that man Bagshott is nobody's fool, and Adam told us to beware of Hambledon."

The following afternoon the plainclothes detective on duty watching Forgan's shop was strolling along the Clerkenwell Road, wishing that something interesting would happen, when he was passed on the pavement by a large stout man with a sallow skin and black hair and eyes. He looked like an Italian or a Spaniard; though there are plenty of men in London of Mediterranean ancestry, this detective had a special interest in the Gatello gang and he regarded the man with curiosity. He did look very like one of the "wanted" men whose description had come from New York. The detective strolled after the man; when he turned into Forgan's shop, official curiosity was naturally intensified.

There was a constable on his beat approaching on the other side of the road and the detective crossed over to meet him.

"Better stand by," he said in a low tone. "I've a feeling we may be wanted in a minute."

"Over there?" said the constable, and looked at the model shop. "We'd better cross the road, perhaps, had we?"

He had hardly spoken before a fat little man in a raincoat, hatless, bald-headed and wearing gold-rimmed spectacles, bounced out of the shop door, looked wildly round him, and ran towards them.

"There now," said detective and constable simultaneously, and quickened their pace.

"Come quickly," said the fat man, panting, "there's a holdup in that shop—there's a man with a great big revolver—he said, 'Stick 'em up,' and the man behind the counter—oh dear—he put his hands up, but I was behind the bandit so I ran out—"

Detective and constable made a dash for the model shop and rushed in at the door to find Forgan behind the counter, duster in hand, rubbing up a polished brass boiler. There was no one else in the shop.

Forgan looked mildly surprised at their abrupt entrance but merely laid down the duster and asked what he could do for the gentlemen.

"We were told," said the detective, "that there was an attempted holdup in progress here."

"Holdup?" said Forgan. "Oh no."

"A man with a large revolver—"

"Oh no," said Forgan again. "No such excitement has happened here, I assure you. Look for yourselves, there's nobody in the shop." He glanced towards the window; an agitated face was visible at it, peering in through strong gold-rimmed lenses. "May I ask," said Forgan, dropping his voice, "whether the little bald-headed man outside told you this story? Yes? I thought so, poor man. I was afraid he might be going to trouble somebody with some such story when he suddenly dropped his notebook and rushed out at the door."

"Are you trying to tell me," said the detective, "that he suffers from delusions?"

"Only one delusion," corrected Forgan. "Such a nice fellow, too. Commercial traveler for a firm of small-tool makers. He was in the Spanish troubles; had a bad time getting out of Toledo. Came home with neurasthenia. Had to undergo treatment for it and then got this job. Oh, he's much better now, only gets these turns very occasionally, usually when the weather's extra hot; I suppose it reminds him— We all know about it—his customers, I mean. We don't take any notice. He'll be all right in a minute."

"Do you mean to say he imagines he sees a man with a revolver?"

"Just that," said Forgan, shaking his head in a pitying manner. "But he's much better than he was."

"But I myself," said the detective, "saw a man enter this shop only a moment before he rushed out. A dark man; looked like a Spaniard."

"Not 'enter this shop,' " said Forgan. "You see for yourself there's no one here. But no doubt that accounts for it. The man no doubt passed close to the window and possibly looked in—I didn't notice him myself—and our poor friend saw him and was reminded of Toledo. You said the man looked like a Spaniard, did you not?"

"But I saw him come in here," persisted the detective. "I don't suffer from delusions."

"No, no. But these small shops, so close together, it is easy to be mistaken as to which doorway a man has entered. To convince yourself, call my poor friend in, mention Toledo, and see what happens."

The door opened and the commercial traveler put his head in.

"Have you captured him?" he said.

"That's all right," said Forgan soothingly. "He's been taken away through the back yard to avoid a disturbance in the street. I was telling these gentlemen that you had had experience of holdups in the Spanish Civil War."

"That's right," said the little man, and came into the shop. "I was in Toledo; you remember the famous siege of the Alcázar, don't you? Hell it was, just plain hell. One evening—it had been pretty quiet all day for a wonder—four other fellows and I were sitting in one of those underground rooms you read about, when all of a sudden one of them looked up and there was a man standing in the doorway just as it might be here," said the commercial traveller, talking faster and faster, "not one of our men at all, but a stranger, and he—"

The detective glanced at the constable, who nodded and strolled away.

Three nights later Hambledon was in bed and peacefully asleep, not even—for once—dreaming, when he became aware that someone had switched on the light in his bedroom and was shaking him by the shoulder. He unwillingly awoke.

"Bagshott—what is it?"

"Angelo Gatello."

"What about him—have you arrested him—where is he?"

"Here," said the chief-inspector simply.

"In my flat?" said Hambledon, and was out of bed in one leap.

"Well, on the doorstep. Asleep. He's sound asleep, Hambledon, in"—Bagshott broke into one of his rare laughs—"in the famous gray velvet armchair."

Hambledon looked at him for a moment, sat down on the edge of the bed, and began to dress.

"He's been doped," went on Bagshott.

"Well, naturally. He wouldn't stay there if he wasn't. Do you mean he's on the landing outside the door of this flat?"

"No, not quite so near as that. He and the armchair were found in that outer hall—entrance lobby or whatever you call it—the space outside the actual front door of this block of flats. He was pushed well back into the corner, and it's dark there, of course. The constable on his beat passed several times before he turned a torch into the entrance and saw him. He—the constable—says there was nothing there when he came on his beat at midnight, because he looked. When he was passing two hours ago his attention was attracted by a faint sound."

"Don't tell me," said Tommy. "It was Angelo snoring."

"It was. He went to look and found a trampish-looking man sleeping in a particularly good armchair. Angelo has been living rough somewhere, Hambledon. He's got a three days' beard and streaks of dirt on his face, cobwebs in his hair, filthy hands, traces of brick dust and mortar and a few bits of straw on his clothes."

"Sounds like a cellar to me," said Hambledon thoughtfully.

"Yes. The constable tried to wake him up, thinking that he was drunk, and then noticed that he didn't smell of drink. There was the chair, too; he'd hardly have brought that there himself, sat down on it, and gone to sleep. In fact, he couldn't—one man couldn't—have carried it. So the constable rang up his station and reported, and in due course somebody spotted the missing armchair and informed me."

"On my doorstep," said Hambledon, knotting his tie. "Now, I wonder who put him there, don't you, Bagshott? He—and the chair—must have been brought in a conveyance of some kind. A small Ford van, do you think? Did any of the local constables see any such vehicle in this neighborhood at about that time?"

"There hasn't been time yet for the reports to come in."

"It doesn't matter. Angelo will tell us where he's been and who brought him here if—"

"If he knows," said Bagshott.

"What have you done with him—and the chair?"

"Gatello has been removed to a cell. I was so anxious that there should be no doubt about his identity that I had Giuseppe Mantani brought from retirement and shown into the cell without being told whom he was to see. The result surpassed my expectation. Gatello was still asleep; Mantani went and bent over him. The next second he took one leap backwards, cannoned into the station superintendent, dodged round behind him, shot up his back, and clung round his neck like a monkey with his favorite organ grinder. Talk about the Darwinian theory, I'm a convert. The super carried him out pick-a-back fashion; I peeled him off and asked him who that was. Even then he could only whimper like a puppy. He did manage to say it was Angelo Gatello and would we please shoot him before he woke up."

"There must be something forceful about Gatello, you know."

"The chair's in my office," went on Bagshott.

"There won't be anything in it now," said Hambledon gloomily. "Except stuffing and springs, of course."

"I don't know. If the money is becoming an embarrassment, Selkirk might take this way of getting rid of it. That's why I woke you up. I thought you'd like to find out."

"We'll have some coffee and go," said Tommy, "though I don't expect to find anything."

Hambledon was quite right about the gray armchair; there was nothing in it but springs and the customary kind of stuffing when the Hessian at the bottom was removed. There were clear indications that the Hessian had been taken off and replaced several times before; it was torn in one place and there were numerous nail holes in it.

"Nothing there," said Bagshott.

"A relief in a way," said Tommy. "I really expected to find a note telling me to go and boil an owl and put my head in the gravy. Well, now for Gatello if somebody can persuade him to wake up."

CHAPTER TWENTY
Mincing Machine

Gatello was awake when Hambledon and Bagshott were ready to interrogate him; he was even superficially washed and had had most of his dust and cobwebs brushed off. Coffee had been administered to complete the cure, and though he complained of headache he was evidently capable of answering questions. Bagshott began in the usual manner.

"Your name?"

"Alberto La Guardia," said Gatello.

"Angelo Gatello," said Hambledon.

Bagshott made an entry. "Age?"

"Thirty-eight."

"Nationality?"

"Italian born, naturalized U.S.A.," said the prisoner.

"Born in Argentina," said Hambledon, turning over some notes. "No United States naturalization."

"So smart you are," snarled the prisoner, "knowing all the answers, yes? I complain to my consul."

"To the United States consul?" said Hambledon. "Certainly, by all means. He's been looking for you for weeks."

Gatello hesitated and said: "No. The Argentine consul."

Bagshott looked up. "You said just now that you were a naturalized citizen of the United States of America. Do you still say that?"

Gatello did not answer.

"Where is your passport?"

"I have lost it."

"Oh. Cannot produce passport," wrote Bagshott.

"Now, Gatello—"

"I am not Gatello; I am Alberto La Guardia, me."

"You have been identified as Angelo Gatello," said Hambledon coldly. "You can take it that this ridiculous and unjustified assumption of a famous name will not help you in the least. You are here to answer questions truthfully, if you know what that means."

"Who identified me?"

"One who knows you well."

"I demand that I know who—"

"Angelo Gatello," said the chief-inspector, "you are being held for questioning in connection with the murder of Walter Race on Saturday, April the thirteenth, of this year in Marjorie Street, Soho. Also the murder of James Hyde at Putney on Tuesday, April the second, of this year." Bagshott picked up one of the telephones on his desk and told somebody to send up a shorthand clerk. There was silence till the man came in and sat at a desk in the corner.

"Now, Gatello," said Bagshott.

"This man at Putney—who?"

"James Hyde."

Gatello shook his head. "Even the name I do not know. And I was not ever to Putney, me."

"Gatello," said Hambledon, "on April the second, Manuel Varsoni, acting with your knowledge or under your orders, went to Putney and shot a man dead on the drive of the same house where your brother, Pietro Gatello, was killed on the night of April the eleventh. Now will you say you know nothing about it?"

"I know Varsoni shoot a man, yes. Not by my orders. Varsoni now dead. Not anything to concern me."

"Who did you think Varsoni shot at Putney?"

Gatello did not answer.

"Answer me," said Hambledon harshly. "Who died that night at Putney?"

"Varsoni come back and tell me he shoot Hugh Selkirk," said Gatello unwillingly. "I am not pleased, that is true. I want to—" His voice trailed off.

"You wanted to talk to Hugh Selkirk, didn't you?"

Gatello's face cleared. "That is so, yes. A private talk. A little matter of business between gentlemen."

"That's your story?"

"That is true, yes."

"Any questions, Bagshott?"

"Only one, at this stage. Who told Varsoni where to find this man you call Selkirk at Putney?"

"I do not know. My brother, perhaps."

"The one who is dead?"

"Yes."

"Very convenient that all the guilty members of your gang are dead."

"Turning to another subject for a moment," said Hambledon, "where have you been these last three days?"

"That's my business. I am not telling."

"Why? Do you know what happened to you? You were doped and left for the police to find."

Gatello scowled at his boots.

"Fast asleep, like a baby," pursued Hambledon. "Who did it?"

"I am not telling. I attend to my affairs myself. When I go from here I will see to that little mistake, yes. I pay my own accounts, me."

"Don't worry," said Hambledon. "You aren't going from here."

"What? You have nothing on me."

"What do you know about the murder of Walter Race?"

"Nothing. They tell Cesar Mariposa shoot him."

"Another dead man!"

Gatello nodded. "Very sad."

"Do you seriously think you'll get away with it on that story? You won't. You'll probably be sent for trial, Gatello, and it may take months. If you do get away with it, which I doubt, you'll be handed over to the United States. You'll never be free in London again. You'll never see Forgan and Campbell—"

Gatello sat up.

"So you may as well tell us all about it," added Hambledon.

"It was against the law, yes, what they do?"

"How can we know, if you won't tell us?"

The Argentine sat back and thought it over.

"If I tell, you punish, yes?"

"We make absolutely no promises," said Bagshott. "But if the law has been broken it is your duty to inform the police."

"Oh. Very well. I go to see Forgan about the same business I have with Selkirk. He is employ of Selkirk. I go in shop. Forgan there, I say hullo. Some man come from behind me run out of shop. I not know anything more. I wake up in cellar, hurt on head. I did not know Campbell there too, why not? I go in all innocent. I know now Campbell come up behind and bang on my head. That is against your law, yes?"

"Under normal circumstances, it is," agreed Bagshott.

"Very well. I wake up in cellar. I stay there many days."

"Three, to be exact," said Hambledon.

"They let down food through flap. I say, 'Let me out.' They say no. Against your law, yes?"

"We call that 'unlawful imprisonment,' " said Hambledon gravely.

"Good. That is right. Now you go arrest them. I am evidence."

"You haven't told us the rest of the story."

"No more story. They put down food, I say. I eat, I get sleepy. I sleep, I wake up here."

"And that's all you know about it?"

"That is all, señor."

Hambledon leaned back in his chair and nodded to Bagshott, who consulted a file of papers, cleared his throat, and began in earnest.

"You were the lessee of a flat above the Red Macaw night club in Marjorie Street, Soho? That means, you yourself took the flat and paid the rent for it. Is that correct?"

Question after question; continual reversion to previous answers wherever discrepancies appeared; dogged persistence whenever Gatello refused to answer; the interrogation continued for hours without a break. The Argentine stormed, cringed, turned sullen, and even wept; he lied and swore and was stubbornly silent by turns, but the steady bombardment of questions went on. Walter Race—who was with him—who was in the flat at the time—why did Race come to the flat—who brought him there and how—Cesar Mariposa—Ramon Jacaro—but you said just now—which gun was that, the .45 or the .32—you say Race was shot with the .45, you stick to that?—how do you account for the fact that—

At the end of three and a half hours Gatello, too strong to faint, went into violent hysterics and was removed.

"The doctor had better see him," said Bagshott. "I don't want him to crack up altogether; I haven't nearly finished with him yet."

Hambledon, rather white round the nostrils, wiped his forehead.

"That's the first time I've seen you really in action, Bagshott. Good lord, I hope you never get after me."

"We got some nice damaging admissions, didn't we?" said the chief-inspector cheerfully. "Lunch time, thank goodness, and I feel I've earned it." He got up and stretched himself.

"I keep forgetting to ask you," said Tommy. "How is Ramon Jacaro getting on?"

"Still pretty groggy. He collapsed after that interview we had with him the night of Race's murder and was removed to hospital. His skull was fractured and he was pretty bad. There was an operation, of course, and he survived it, but I haven't been able to question him again yet."

"Selkirk is a pretty hard hitter," said Hambledon, for Gatello had unwillingly described most of what had happened on the night of Race's murder.

"They don't seem quite certain now whether Selkirk is himself or a brother very like him, do they?"

"Reminds me of the schoolboy howler about whether the Odyssey was written by Homer or another man with the same name."

"Yes," said Bagshott vaguely. "Are you coming back this afternoon?"

"What for? To watch you putting Gatello further through it? No, thanks. You can send me a copy of the proceedings when you've finished him off."

"For the present," said Bagshott, "he'll have lots more questions to answer as the rest of the evidence piles up."

Hambledon looked at him with something like awe. "You know, British justice is a pretty terrifying business. A man-sized mincing machine. A colossal separating plant. Like a paper factory. You push a poor devil in at one end, the rollers chew him up, and he comes out at the other end wads of neatly typed statements."

"Eleven duplicates of them," said Bagshott. "You'll feel better after lunch."

Two days later Bagshott told Hambledon that Gatello had been brought before a magistrate, charged with murder in the case of Walter Race and complicity in murder in the case of James Hyde, and committed for trial. "I don't suppose we shall proceed with the second charge," he said.

"One is enough," agreed Hambledon. "Nobody seen Selkirk?"

"No."

"Are you doing anything about Forgan?"

Bagshott shuddered slightly and said that he was not. "I suppose we could charge him with unlawful imprisonment of Angelo Gatello, but it doesn't seem worth while. He did, actually, assist the police in the apprehension of a man for whose arrest a warrant had been issued."

"Isn't there a reward out in the States for the arrest of our Angelo?"

"I don't think so. For Varsoni and possibly Jacaro, but not Gatello so far as I know."

"Pity," said Tommy. "It would have been a simple and moving ceremony, you in your best utility suit with decorations presenting Forgan with a couple of thousand dollars in a gilt-edged envelope. But surely there was something highly improper about his dealings with that chair. Couldn't you pin something on him for that?"

"The hotel management have stated that, since they've got it back, no further proceedings are considered necessary," said the chief-inspector. "It didn't go down on the books," he added sadly. "I suppose Forgan is honest. If he ever comes before me charged with anything—"

"That's wishful thinking, don't yield to it. There are two other members of Gatello's party still loose, aren't there? What are their picturesque names again?"

"Tadeo el Caballero and Pacorro Pagote. We shall find them one of these days."

" 'And then there were none,' " quoted Hambledon. "We hope. But I still want to talk to Selkirk about that money. For one thing, he's broken several laws bringing it into the country; for another, I don't know anything about his political convictions. He may have stolen it from the Gatellos in order to present it to the Neo-Nazis or the Philosophical Rebuilders or whatever the blighters call themselves. I'm sure that's illegal, financing a political party in this country from a foreign source. Anyway, I've got to know about it, so I've got to find Selkirk."

"Yes," said Bagshott. "I want him too; he's a material witness in the Race murder, for one thing. I shall advertise, asking him to come forward, if he doesn't turn up within the next few days."

"If I were Selkirk desiring dignified obscurity," said Hambledon, "do you know what I'd do? I should call myself James Hyde, go down to Yeovil, and explain that the reports of my death were grossly exaggerated. Was it Mark Twain who said that?"

"He'd never get away with it among people who'd known James Hyde from boyhood. We know they're much alike, but they're not identical twins. Besides, he wouldn't recognize the people Hyde used to know, and that would be fatal."

"He may be confined to his room, suffering from a dislocated glottis or spots on the gizzard. If he tied his face up and explained that he'd lost his voice and his memory through overexcitement playing cribbage with a nice man he met in a train—"

"If he'd lost his voice, how could he explain?"

"In pantomime. In the deaf-and-dumb alphabet. On a slate. Not at all. Anyway, I'm going to Yeovil, Bagshott, are you coming? Do you good."

"You mentioned the Neo-Nazis just now," said Bagshott. "I received an odd report from one of my Special Branch men the other day."

"What was that?"

"On that list of missing Nazis wanted for trial as war criminals there is one named Hommelhoff, Konrad Hommelhoff. There's a photograph of him and quite a full description—"

"I remember," said Tommy, nodding. "He has a broken nose. He was trying to recruit men for their precious British Free Corps and he tried his persuasions on an Australian, which proved to be a mistake. Hommelhoff got his nose broken and the Aussie subsequently died. That is one of the things we want him for."

"That's the man. Well, this Special Branch sergeant was traveling on the Underground last Monday evening in the rush hour. Among the strap-hangers in the same carriage was a man who, my man thought, answered the description of Hommelhoff. He went out with the crowd at Oxford Circus; my man tried to follow but was caught up in the jam and missed him. The sergeant considered that it was very unlikely indeed that Hommelhoff should be in London, and his own errand was rather an urgent one, so he abandoned the chase and merely reported what he thought he'd seen. I think myself it was probably a mistake."

"So do I," said Tommy. "Although, you know, one of the few places where it wouldn't occur to you to look for a Nazi war criminal is Oxford Circus. Perhaps the man will be seen again somewhere and then you can clear up the point one way or the other."

They traveled to Yeovil on the following day and entered an obviously long-established tobacconist's to buy cigarettes for Hambledon and tobacco for Bagshott. They leaned on the counter like gentlemen of leisure and said that they were touring the country—very pleasant at this time of year, yes—visiting leather factories in different places to arrange contracts for export. There was a good old firm in Yeovil, wasn't there? Hyde & Son.

"Oh yes," said the tobacconist. "Very old firm, much respected. Started as a tannery only, but towards the end of the old man's time they began to manufacture leather goods as well, luggage and so forth."

"So there's a young man in charge now, from what you say," said Hambledon. "The 'Son' of Hyde & Son, I suppose."

"Well, no. Young Mr. Hyde sold the business when his father died and it became a company, but they kept on the old name. Young Mr. Hyde, I said— he's not so very young. Must be turned fifty, but he seems young to me who knew him when he was a boy. I'm seventy-five, gentlemen, last March quarter day."

Of course they congratulated him and told him he didn't look it. "It must be very interesting," said Tommy earnestly, "to live a long life in one place and remember all the changes that have been made and all the queer things that have happened."

"And it's even queer you should say that," said the tobacconist, "for one of the queerest things I ever remember has happened recently in connection with that same James Hyde."

"Do tell us," said Hambledon, "that is, if it's not a private matter. I like queer stories."

"When young James—I call him that from habit, gentlemen—when James left here and went to London he bought a house at Putney. He hadn't lived there a year when there was a murder in the very street he lived in."

"Good gracious," said Tommy.

"Yes, but the queer part is this, that the man who was murdered had the same name as himself, James Hyde. And lived in the same street. What d'you think of that?"

"Almost incredible," said Hambledon accurately.

"So of course all of us who'd known him all his life were very upset when we heard, as you may imagine. For, naturally, we thought it was him."

"Of course. Of course you would."

"You could have knocked me down with a feather, as they say, when he walked in here four days ago and called me by my name and shook hands with me, he did. Like seeing a ghost it was."

"Must have given you quite a turn, as they say."

"Yes. But he soon put that right and we had a good laugh over it. Very sad about the other poor man, of course; young James said he knew him slightly. But, young James said, it's an ill wind that blows no man good and he supposed there'd be no more trouble over getting their letters mixed up in the future as there had been in the past."

"What an extraordinary story," said Bagshott, not to be left out of it altogether. "I don't know that I ever heard its equal."

"They say coincidence has a long arm," said Tommy, "but she certainly stretched it that time. I suppose young James—I've caught it now—Mr. Hyde came down here to show his old friends he was still alive."

"Yes, and for a little holiday in the country. He doesn't like London in the summer; he says it's stuffy. So he's staying at the Spread Eagle, at the top of the town, for a week or ten days; if you drop in there for a meal any time I daresay you'll see him. A very pleasant gentleman, always, and looking so well. Not much changed, either, considering what a different life he's leading now."

"I think I must drop in at the Spread Eagle," said Tommy, "and have a look at the man who wasn't murdered. Eh, Bagshott?"

"Oh, certainly," said Bagshott. "Most interesting."

They detached themselves from the tobacconist and strolled up the street.

"Well, well," said Tommy. "What d'you know about that? I know I could say, 'I told you so,' but stupefaction is the word for what I feel."

"What I want to know," said Bagshott, "is how the devil he gets away with it? Talking to all these people—"

"Having lunch with the vicar who christened him—"

"Did he do that?"

"I don't know, but he's quite capable of it. You know, Bagshott, if it wasn't for two things I'd say we were making a mistake in identity; that it really was Selkirk who was murdered at Putney and James Hyde who is still alive and has taken his place."

"Two things," said Bagshott thoughtfully.

"Yes. One is that the man we're looking for now did quite recently show signs of having shaved off a beard. Selkirk had a beard; Hyde didn't. The body we saw at Putney hadn't lost a beard; we saw it ourselves. Therefore, the dead man must be Hyde and the survivor Selkirk. I did wonder once before which was which, until some witness—it was the garage proprietor who hired Selkirk the car that night Pietro Gatello was killed at Putney—he said the hirer had recently shaved off a beard. So that was obviously Selkirk, not Hyde. The other reason is psychological. Hyde would never do the things this fellow does. Remember Nairn's description of him? 'Curiously innocent,' he called him. 'Defenseless' was another word. 'Sair hadden down.' The gentle retiring man whose nose had been held to the grindstone by an autocrat of a father. Bullied by his housekeeper; remember Mrs. Watson, Bagshott? Asking advice about clothes and wines, buying a Victorian mansion at Putney. Now he throws gangsters out of fourth-floor windows—because you can bet that's how Varsoni went to his account—escapes from that murderous flat full of brigands, overpowers the hulk Jacaro with a gun in his hand, frightens Mariposa to death, though I don't know how, and generally leaps about like a combination of Harlequin and Bulldog Drummond. Gentle, defenseless Hyde? It doesn't make sense; it must be Selkirk."

"I agree," said Bagshott, "but that tobacconist shook me. Though he thought Hyde had altered a bit."

"People see what they expect to see, and perhaps our tobacconist at seventy-five doesn't see so well as he did. No doubt Hyde told Selkirk all about old days at Yeovil when they were swapping stories; he'd got nothing else to talk about, poor man. Would that be the Spread Eagle, do you suppose? Very nice, too. Too late for tea; we'll have something refreshing in the bar and an early dinner if the fates will let us. I could bear to spend a night here."

The Spread Eagle was a country hotel of the best type, plainly an old house carefully enlarged, with walls painted white, green louvered shutters hooked back from the windows, and a sweeping roof of ancient tiles. The house stood back from the street; a good width of gravel in front was marked off from the pavement by posts and chains. An elaborate wrought-iron bracket above the door upheld the signboard painted with an eagle holding up both wings in a gesture of wrath or horror. He shone with new paint, black and gold against a white background. "Argent," said Hambledon sententiously, "an eagle sable displayed, feathered or."

"That's the lounge on the left," said Bagshott, disregarding this exhibition of erudition. As they turned off the pavement an open car, enameled bright scarlet, roared in past them, turned sharply with a scatter of gravel, and stopped near the lounge door. The driver, who was the only occupant, a tall young man with untidy hair and a tweed sports jacket, leapt out of the car, leaving the engine running, and dived into the lounge. When Hambledon and Bagshott followed him in he was leaning upon the bar and ordering a gin and tonic water, "a long one, Charlie, I'm thirsty; and make it snappy, there's a good chap, for I've left the engine running and I don't want the police after me again."

"Would be a bit too soon, wouldn't it, sir? You think it best to let sleeping dogs lie for a bit?"

"Well, yes. I think a spot of tact is indicated. But was she a cow to start or was she! I don't want to stop her till she's warmed up a bit."

The bartender gave him his drink in a tall glass, a slice of lemon floating on the top with the bubbles fizzing round it. Hambledon ordered lager and looked appreciatively round the room, a paneled room, low-ceilinged, L-shaped, with the bar curving round the intrusive angle. Round the curve and almost out of sight were two men drinking sherry and talking to a big man with a waxed mustache behind the bar, probably the proprietor. One of the sherry drinkers was dark-haired and thin, with bright observant eyes; the other was shorter and stouter, with fair hair turning gray and a particularly pleasant expression.

Hambledon looked across and met the eye of the brown-haired man regarding him with unmistakable interest immediately concealed.

"Bagshott," said Tommy quietly, "those two fellows over there, are they our men?"

Bagshott turned and looked across; at that moment the men they were watching put their glasses down and moved out of sight round the corner; the next moment a door shut with a soft thud. Hambledon put down his untasted lager and turned to follow them. Quick footsteps crushed the gravel outside, a car door slammed; the regular murmur of an engine ticking over rose to a roar and immediately began to recede in the distance.

The young man in the sports coat dropped his glass with a crash and rushed to the door just as Bagshott and Hambledon reached it; they impeded each other in the doorway and burst out together just in time to see the red car go roaring up the street, snaking between lorries and cars and making pedestrians leap for their lives. The next moment it was out of sight.

"Oh, damn it all," said the exasperated owner, "those two blighters have gone off with Bloody Mary!"

CHAPTER TWENTY ONE
Unwilling Journey

"Well, that's settled one point," said Hambledon in a low tone to Bagshott; "that wasn't Hyde. Not young James upon his native heath." He turned to the landlord, who had joined the group on the gravel. "Who were those two gentlemen?"

"Mr. James Hyde and his friend Mr. Adam."

"You know Mr. Hyde personally?"

"Lord, yes. Known him for seven—no, eight years."

Hambledon looked at him as one who beholds with pity the onset of senile decay, and Bagshott asked the red car's owner for its number. He gave it, adding, "I'd better ring up the police about it. For one thing, the insurance is limited to me only; they aren't covered, not even third party. I mean, if they're going to drive like that, I should think they'd soon want it, what? And I want to tell the police it isn't me driving; you gentlemen are witnesses to that. I mean, the police know that car and if they see a scarlet streak flashing past they might not see it wasn't me. I mean, I don't want any more unpleasantness—" His voice trailed off and the landlord came to his rescue.

"Mr. Curtison has been rather unlucky lately," he explained. "One misfortune after another. He is understandably anxious not to have any further—er—contention with the police."

"Besides, I want my car back. Can I use your phone, Milligan?"

"Certainly," said the landlord of the Spread Eagle, but Bagshott cut in.

"I think I'll ring up the police, if you don't mind," he said. "I will make your innocence quite clear to them."

"Frightfully good of you," said young Curtison, "but why should you bother? I can perfectly well—"

"I want a word with the police about this matter on my own account," said Bagshott, and showed his card.

"Oh, golly," said Curtison in an awed voice. The landlord whistled dolefully and showed the chief-inspector the way to the telephone. The Yeovil police were asked to trace the missing car and detain the driver and passenger on a charge of driving it away without the owner's consent. The number was so-and-so and the car was an open two-seater painted bright red.

"Oh, Bloody Mary," said the desk sergeant unguardedly. "We know her."

"Actually," said Bagshott, "I am anxious to interview both driver and passenger about another matter," and he gave his name and rank. "I don't think they really meant to steal the car; I think they just wanted to get away in a hurry."

"Like that, is it?" said the desk sergeant, deeply interested. "You can identify the men who took it—do you know their names too?"

"Mr. James Hyde and his friend Mr. Adam."

"Mr. James—did you say Mr. James Hyde?"

Bagshott said that that was, indeed, the name.

"Good gracious. Well, we'll do our best."

Bagshott came out from the telephone cabinet to face the landlord, hovering in agitation; young Curtison, plainly curious; and Tommy Hambledon with an expression of deep amusement.

"Your name is Milligan, I think?"

"Captain Milligan, at your service," said the landlord.

"Captain Milligan, I should like a word with you in private."

Curtison removed himself with noble self-denial, and Bagshott asked such questions about the Spread Eagle's late guests as occurred to him. Nothing of any fresh interest repaid him for his efforts; it only became increasingly clear that James Hyde was accepted as James Hyde among men who were neither failing in eyesight nor naturally credulous. Bagshott gave it up, and Milligan sighed with relief.

"Believe it or not," he said, "this is the very first time I've ever been questioned by the police. I think that the man who gets the better of you deserves his freedom. Will you have dinner, gentlemen? There's a saddle of Wiltshire mutton. . . ."

In the middle of dinner a message was brought to the chief-inspector. The red car had been found abandoned beside the main road to London just short of Shepton Mallet. No one had seen the driver or passenger at any railway station, nor traveling upon any local bus.

"They've thumbed a lift in a passing car," said Hambledon. "Either all the way to London or to any railway station within a fifty-mile radius. Or even more."

"They may not have returned to London," said Bagshott gloomily.

"If the last remaining two of the Gatello gang are still in London, they will. Can't you serve a witness summons on Selkirk-alias-Hyde?"

"Of course I should, like a shot, if I knew where he was."

"Send it by post, c/o Forgan, Clerkenwell Road, with 'Please Forward' in the top left-hand corner."

"You can't serve witness summonses by post."

"The law does make things difficult, doesn't it?" said Hambledon. "You'd better advertise. 'Will Mr. James Hyde-Selkirk please call upon Chief-Inspector Bagshott at his earliest convenience to blow the gaff upon one Angelo Gatello, as the said Bagshott wants to hang the said Gatello.' It might fetch him, you never know."

"I shall advertise," said Bagshott, "though not in those words."

"And suppose he doesn't arise? Can't you subpoena him?"

"Your ignorance of English law is abysmal. A subpoena must be served personally, and if we can't find him—"

"You go on looking, that's all," said Tommy cheerfully. "Don't be so downcast, something will doubtless occur. As for English law, I find it best not to know exactly how many laws I'm breaking. It cramps my style."

Bagshott sighed, and they returned to London by the first available train. Here they encountered the first piece of good news they had had for weeks; Pacorro Pagote and Tadeo el Caballero had been located.

"You haven't arrested them, have you?" asked Hambledon anxiously.

"No, sir," said Detective-Inspector Ennis. "They are being kept under observation pending your return. They are living in a boardinghouse just off Lisson Grove; they have a double room at the back of the second floor and are keeping very quiet. They come out once in the mornings to buy cigarettes and a newspaper and have a glass of wine at the Good Intent, and again in the evening for another glass or two. Yesterday afternoon they went to the nearest cinema. They look worried."

"Continue to keep them under observation," said Hambledon to Bagshott, "and at the first indication of the arrival of Messrs. Hyde-Selkirk and Adam, let us be informed. We didn't have our journey to Yeovil for nothing, you know; these eyes have actually seen the objects of our desire. Of course, they won't go near Forgan and Campbell; they're much too intelligent. The Pagote and El Caballero won't do anything all by themselves. I am really quite sorry for them. They must feel like lost dogs."

"If I were in their place," said Bagshott, "I should throw my hand in and go back to the Argentine."

"If they move," said Detective-Inspector Ennis, "they can always be apprehended. There is a warrant out against them for complicity in the murder of Walter Race."

Hambledon nodded, and Bagshott said that it was not to be executed at the moment unless the men tried to bolt. He then gave a description of Hyde and Adam in the police manner, the first really good description the police had obtained, and a further period of waiting began.

Some days later a letter came from Captain Milligan of the Spread Eagle at Yeovil, saying that he did not know whether Chief-Inspector Bagshott would be interested, but Mr. Curtison had received a communication from Messrs. Hyde and Adam about the red car. They apologized handsomely for having borrowed it so unceremoniously, but their need was great and urgent. They hoped that their action had not inconvenienced Mr. Curtison and begged his acceptance of the enclosed sum as compensation for any such inconvenience, which they sincerely regretted. Ten pounds in one-pound notes was enclosed in the letter, which had been addressed to Curtison c/o the Spread Eagle. The letter was postmarked Oxford on the day after they left.

"You can enquire at the Mitre or the Clarendon," said Hambledon, "but it won't be any use."

"As a matter of routine, I shall," said the chief-inspector, but Hambledon was right.

He had also guessed correctly about the manner in which Hyde and Adam had made their escape. They drove the red car out of Yeovil in the first direction which offered itself, dodged about in country lanes to confuse their line of flight, and emerged upon the main road just west of Shepton Mallet. Here they abandoned the car at Adam's suggestion.

"This—this curricle is much too conspicuous," he said. "Once seen, never forgotten and much too easily described. Enquiries after us are now with every policeman for miles around; we should never get through another village without being stopped."

"Well, it's a nice day for a walk," said James cheerfully, "and we have no luggage to carry."

They walked past the gray walls of Shepton Mallet and continued for another three miles beyond it before they attempted to get a lift, being anxious to dissociate themselves completely from the red two-seater. Soon after this they were fortunate enough to stop a car going to Oxford and returned to London by train the following morning.

"There's only those two other brigands to deal with," said Hyde, "and then we can hand over the money and retire. Do you think they'll give much trouble?"

"I shouldn't think so. They are minor villains."

"What do you suggest that we should do with them?"

"I think it would be a friendly gesture if we put them in a taxi and sent them to Scotland Yard," said Adam. "I feel sure that Hambledon is a man to appreciate helpful courtesy."

"What—do you mean tied up and gagged?"

Adam laughed. "That would give the taxi driver a thrill, wouldn't it? No, I really meant that we might persuade them to go quietly. I don't know whether they know that Angelo Gatello has been arrested; if not, no doubt they're wondering what has become of him. If they do know, they must be feeling rather lonely. We could explain to them what a serious matter it is to be involved in a murder in this country; they probably don't realize that yet. When they do, we can tell them that their only chance of survival is to turn King's Evidence. These men would sell their grandmothers for the price of a drink; they'll certainly sell Gatello to save their skins. It might work."

"We could promise to pay the taxi fare, too," said James kindly. "My only regret is that we shan't be there to see that chief-inspector's face when they walk in. Where do they live?"

"In one of those streets between Lisson Grove and Edgware Road, in a boardinghouse."

"Unless, of course, the police have arrested them while we've been away."

"They may have," admitted Adam. "Forgan will know. We'll ring him up as soon as this train gets in."

"We'd better not go to Forgan's, had we?"

"We mustn't go near the place. We'll buy some more luggage, secondhand if possible, and a few necessaries, and find a hotel. There used to be plenty in the Paddington district, and it's handy for Lisson Grove. We'd better not be seen wandering about London until this business is all settled up."

"How do you propose—do you know what plan Selkirk had in mind about the money when it was all over? You said something about sending it to the Chancellor of the Exchequer."

"I think we'd better consult Hambledon, if we can arrange an interview with him."

"I should think that would be extremely easy," said Hyde. "He's been chasing us long enough. In fact, it would be only civil to go and call, wouldn't it?"

They bought such things as were necessary in shops near Paddington Station, and even found a couple of small rooms in an obscure hotel. After which they telephoned to Forgan and heard all the news. Forgan had only written to them at Yeovil in the vaguest and most general terms; in fact, so deep was the studied obscurity of his narrative that they were not at all sure what had really happened. "The Big Bad Wolf," wrote Forgan, "fell asleep in a cellar and woke up in a cell. Too bad. The furniture deal went through as planned. Campbell and I are quite well; we have had a few visitors lately, but nothing interesting happened."

He told them the story in fuller detail over the telephone. "I am only sorry," he said, "that Bagshott went off with your good kit bag. He said he'd send it back, but he hasn't done so."

"It doesn't matter," said Hyde. "I'm getting used to losing luggage."

Forgan said that Pacorro Pagote and Tadeo el Caballero were still at the same lodging house. He thought it probable that they knew of Gatello's arrest since it had been reported in the papers, also the fact that he had been sent for trial on a murder charge. "They can read English without difficulty," he said, "especially Tadeo. He fancies himself as a linguist. I imagine they've got the wind up; they stay indoors most of the time. Second-floor back, you know the address."

Shortly after ten o'clock on the following night the police watcher, loafing in a doorway near the lodging house, saw a taxi drive up to the door and two men get out. They went up three steps to the door and rang the bell; while they waited for the bell to be answered the loafer strolled past. The two men were admitted, the taxi waited, and the loafer, quickening his pace, departed for the nearest telephone box.

The two foreign gentlemen were at home, second-floor back; Hyde said there was no need to show them upstairs, it was only giving unnecessary trouble, they would find the room without difficulty. No doubt the landlady had quite enough of running up and down the stairs without doing so unnecessarily. They could let themselves out, too, couldn't they?

They walked up the two flights unattended except for the landlady's gratitude; on the second landing Adam slipped past Hyde, murmuring: "Better let me go in first." He tapped at the door and was answered from within; he opened the door and entered quickly, with Hyde at his heels. In the hands of both were serviceable revolvers.

"Hands up!" said Adam sharply, and the men, taken by surprise, obeyed. One was lying on the disheveled bed and the other sprawling in a basket chair. Hyde kept them covered while Adam removed their firearms.

"There," he said mildly, "that's better. Do you know you could be arrested in this country for carrying those things?"

Pagote told the visitors what he thought of them in words which were almost all completely new to Hyde, while El Caballero called upon his Maker to redress the outrage.

"No outrage at all," said Adam. "A kindness, if only you knew it. I will explain." He delivered a short lecture on the severe view taken of murder in England, including the theory of Principals in the First Degree and Second Degree, and of Accessories Before and After the Fact. "If you were in the room when a man was killed, and if you helped the murderer in any way—by preventing the victim's escape, for example—you are a Principal in the Second Degree and will probably be hung."

"What, if I hadn't even got a gun on me?" asked Pagote.

"I've never known you without one. But, yes, even if you hadn't."

"Say," said Tadeo, "they are very strict in this country, I say."

"If you did nothing to prevent the murder—if you weren't even in the room at the time but helped the murderer afterwards—if you helped the murderer beforehand by bringing the victim into danger—"

"I seem to remember," said Hyde, "being hustled up the stairs past the Red Macaw by five men. I remember their faces quite well," he added, looking from one to the other. "One is dead, two more are in jail, and now there's only you left."

"And the police are after you; they'll be here any minute," said Adam, more truly than he knew.

"And you'll both be tried and probably hung," said Hyde cheerfully. "Because you were both in the room when Race was shot, weren't you? The only one who wasn't there was Jacaro, who was with me."

"So you're in rather a spot, aren't you?" said Adam.

The two Argentines looked from Adam to Hyde and back again during this antiphonal jeremiad, and their faces lengthened.

"I didn't have no quarrel with the guy that got shot," said Tadeo. "I hadn't ever seen him before, I say."

"Yet you shot him," said Hyde.

"No, I say. That was Gatello."

"And Gatello will say it was you. Then the jury will say, 'They were all in it together. Hang the lot.' "

There was a melancholy silence which Pagote broke by saying in a pained voice that he understood the visitors had come to do them a kindness and he'd like to see it. "Can't you get us out of this, señor? We will work for you faithfully forever for very low wages. Very low, just enough to buy bread, señor."

"I wouldn't have you anywhere near me if you paid me for it," said Adam briskly.

"Besides, we couldn't," said Hyde virtuously. "It would be illegal."

"This kindness," urged Pagote.

"Is a little good advice, that's all. Go at once to the police, give yourselves up, and offer evidence against Gatello. That is called 'turning King's Evidence,' and if you speak the exact truth you will probably get a lighter sentence," said Adam.

"And not be hung after all," said Hyde.

"But you must go at once, before they come here for you. It must be your own doing."

"We have a taxi waiting at the door; you can take that."

Pagote turned to his friend and spoke in Spanish. "I think we go, yes? This hanging—" He shivered.

But El Caballero was made of firmer stuff. "It is all lies, what you say," he declaimed. "The police, they cannot find us, I say. So you come here and you persuade us to walk into jail like the stupid beasts into the cannery. No, I say, no. We will not go."

"I think you will," said Adam, and leapt at him. He caught the Argentine by the wrist and pressed the muzzle of the revolver into his ribs. "Now then, down the stairs. March! You bring the other skunk," he added to Hyde. "And no tricks from either of you or I'll drill you so full of holes your coffin'll be drafty. Get on!"

They went down the stairs close together like friends. "Remember the Red Macaw?" said Hyde. "Think of me on staircases in future."

Tadeo opened the front door and Hyde shut it after them. They went down the steps, across the pavement, and entered the taxi.

"Tothill Street," said Adam to the taxi driver. "St. James's Park Underground Station will do." He got in and the taxi drove away. The interested loafer, inconspicuous in an adjacent doorway, heard the words and took the car's number. He came forward as they turned a corner out of sight and was standing on the edge of the pavement when another car arrived a minute later, a black Vauxhall full of policemen.

"They've just gone," said the watcher rapidly, and gave the taxi's number. "St. James's Park Underground, they said."

The police car accelerated and went off in pursuit.

CHAPTER TWENTY TWO
Tadpoles to You

The taxi drove on down Seymour Place and paused for traffic lights; Pagote looked out of the window and said, "Where?"

"Marble Arch," said Hyde.

Tadeo el Caballero, who had been sunk in reflection, woke up at this.

"It is an outrage," he said.

"I don't care much for it myself," admitted Hyde, "but it's nicer than the Albert Memorial."

Adam laughed, and the taxi proceeded down Park Lane. Tadeo shook his head angrily.

"It is your doings that are an outrage, I say, not your Marble Arch," he explained.

Pagote intervened to keep the peace. "What is it for, your Arch?"

"I really don't know," said Hyde. "I must find out one of these days."

"You are a fool," snarled Tadeo.

"Who, me?" asked James. He and Adam were sitting on the small seats with their backs to the driver, the two Argentines in the back of the cab.

"You, Pacorro," said El Caballero.

"I like the quiet life," said Pagote frankly.

"Just as well," said Adam. "I expect you'll get a lot of quiet life in the future."

The taxi crossed Picadilly at Hyde Park Corner and turned down Constitution Hill.

"Soon," said Hyde helpfully, "we shall pass Buckingham Palace on our right. Have you seen the changing of the guard?"

Tadeo leaned forward to thrust his face within a foot of Hyde's, opposite to him. "You make a mock, I say," he began, when Adam hit him hard on the head with a slim weapon which had appeared unexpectedly in his right hand. Tadeo grunted and keeled over forwards; Hyde pushed him back again into his corner, where he lay still.

"You have kill him!" said Pagote.

"Oh no," said Adam. "Only put him to sleep; he was becoming tiresome. This wouldn't kill anybody unless you hit 'em behind the ear."

"What is it?" asked Hyde.

"Only a bit of rubber tube with a lump of lead in one end."

"Oh. I thought something was going to happen when you changed your gun over from one hand to the other."

Pagote looked at them with increased respect, and the statue of Queen Victoria appeared to smile faintly.

"Look here, Pagote," said Adam. "I'm going to serve you the same way. These fellows can't have any grudge against you if you are knocked out too. If you go willingly to the police, the gang might get you for it one day."

Pagote thought it over during the transit of Birdcage Walk and made up his mind.

"It is just, señor," he said. "More, it is kind. Not this side," gesturing towards his right ear. "I have an old head wound there. On the left, if you please."

He set his teeth, shut his eyes, and leaned forward; Adam put him scientifically to sleep in the corner opposite to Tadeo.

"I wonder he swallowed that story," said Hyde critically. "Rather thin, wasn't it?"

"So is his intelligence," said Adam, putting away his gun and the rubber pipe. The taxi turned into Tothill Street and the driver leaned back, opened the door a crack, and said: "This do, guv'nor?"

"Very well, thanks," said Adam. Hyde got out and Adam, after adjusting Tadeo's hat for him, followed. Adam told the driver to go on to Scotland Yard. "Inspector Tadeo—a foreign police official—has business with Chief-Inspector Bagshott. Drive straight in."

"Righto, guv'nor," said the taxi driver, and went on along Tothill Street. A black Vauxhall came up past the Underground Station, and keen eyes within it saw the number of the taxi ahead.

"That's the one, Coram. Close up a bit. They're still inside; I saw a head pass the back window."

The taxi led them across Parliament Square; police interest passed through surprise to incredulity when the cab drove straight to Scotland Yard and turned in without hesitation. The constable at the gate stopped it; the police car drew up behind, and its passengers alighted in haste.

The constable asked the taxi driver where his passengers wanted to go, and the other police closed up to hear the answer.

"Inspector Tadpole to see Chief-Inspector Bagshott," said the taxi driver.

"Tadpole?"

"Some such name. A foreign gent."

The inspector in charge of the Vauxhall party opened the taxi door, and Tadeo el Caballero immediately rolled out in the road.

" 'Ere," said the taxi driver, "what's all this?"

"Tadpoles to you," said the inspector, turning El Caballero face upwards.

"Here's the other one, sir," said a constable, opening the other door. "He's out, too."

"You had two other passengers," said the inspector briskly. "Where are they?"

"Got out in Tot'ill Street. St. James's Park Station, they said."

The inspector murmured something which might have been a blessing, and the taxi driver asked who was going to pay his fare.

"There's an envelope stuck in this hat," said a policeman, picking up Tadeo's black felt. The envelope was a small one inserted in the ribbon; upon it was written: "Taxi fare and tip. Thank you."

"Oh, Caractacus," said the inspector, and the constable told the driver that it looked as though he'd be all right.

"Which is more than we shall be," said the inspector to his senior constable, "when Bagshott hears of this. We've got the cheese and lost the mice. Bring them in, men," he added aloud.

The inspector was quite right; Bagshott was so angry that he almost gibbered. "We had these men," he said. "We could have got them two days ago if we'd wanted to. Now they've been picked up under your noses and thrown at us, and the other two are as far away as ever. Why was the police car two minutes late in Lisson Grove? No, don't tell me, I'm not interested in excuses. What did you take, the Vauxhall, or a wheelbarrow and two bath chairs? Flying Squad, huh? One more break like this and some of you will be pounding a beat again. Go to St. James's Park Station and see if you can pick up any trace of them. Somebody might have noticed them; it's a quiet station at this time of night. Of course, you may find everyone who's supposed to be on duty is sound asleep. In which case you can sympathize with them, can't you? What are you waiting for? Get out of my sight."

The inspector fled.

Bagshott picked up the telephone, dialed Hambledon's number without reply, and then remembered that Tommy was dining out and did not expect to be home much before midnight. He sighed and replaced the receiver. It would be no use ringing again for three quarters of an hour at least. In fact, it was not very clear what would be gained by ringing Tommy up that night at all since the morning would do perfectly well, but Bagshott was in that state of irritability where it would be a relief merely to pass on the vexation to somebody else.

A constable came in and said that the prisoners had recovered consciousness if the chief-inspector wished to interrogate them. Bagshott said the constable could take them away and drop them down a well, and the constable said: "Yes, sir," in a wooden voice. The chief-inspector took a pull on himself and told the constable to put them in cells for the night; they could be charged in the morning. The constable said: "Yes, sir," again and left the room. He was just giving his co-mates a vivid description of Bagshott's state of mind when the inspector came back from St. James's Park and heard the tail end of it. He straightened his back with an effort and went up to give his report.

Two men answering the descriptions of Hyde and Adam had been seen at the Underground Station at the time mentioned. They did not take tickets at the office; they obtained them from the automatic machine. The porter couldn't say what price ticket they took; it might have been a twopenny or a threepenny, or even a fourpenny. They went off on a westbound train. Did the chief-inspector wish further enquiry to be made?

"In view of the fact," said Bagshott, "that they could change at Charing Cross for any one of fifty-seven stations in six different directions, no."

"Very good, sir."

"That will do."

The inspector retired thankfully. Bagshott looked at his watch and decided to give Hambledon another ten minutes before ringing again. If there was no reply this time he would give it up and go to bed. That, at least, was there when one wanted it.

He lit his pipe and looked through some papers for a few minutes. He was just on the point of picking up the receiver to call up Hambledon again when the telephone bell rang.

"Chief-Inspector Bagshott," he said curtly. "Who is that?"

There came a slow and pleasant voice from the other end. "My name is James Hyde," it said. "Er—good evening, Chief-Inspector."

Tommy Hambledon found his evening's entertainment disappointingly dull; he made an excuse and returned home rather earlier than he had intended. He walked across St. James's Park in the summer dusk. Big Ben struck half-past eleven as he put his latchkey into the lock of his front door. The flat was full of shadows but not dark since the blinds were not down, the hour was only ten-thirty by true time, and there was a clear moon to help the street lights. It was perfectly quiet in the flat, yet Hambledon stiffened and a little prickle ran up his spine. There was somebody there; the place did not feel empty. A man does not go armed to an official dinner in London if only out of regard for the sit of his dress clothes. Tommy made a silent rush into his bedroom, opened a drawer, and remedied the omission. He was a man who had made many enemies in the course of his life, and one never knows.

From the sitting room there came the sound of a remark in a low tone and somebody laughed quietly. Two of them, two at least. Hambledon glanced at the telephone by his bedside; at the other end of that wire were innumerable policemen, and the bedroom door could be barricaded. But what a fool he would look if there were some simple explanation—Reck come back, for instance. Reck had a latchkey. It was a very grim-faced Hambledon who confronted his visitors, having switched on the sitting-room light with his left hand since his right was otherwise engaged. He looked from one to the other as they rose at his entrance, and his expression gradually relaxed.

"Mr. Hyde-Selkirk and Mr. Adam, I believe," he said.

"Yes—er, that is—do let me first of all apologize," said Hyde, "for entering your flat like this in your absence without permission. We did ring the bell several times, and we were so anxious to interview you without being—er—intercepted, that we thought it wiser to wait for you inside. I hope you will forgive this unpardonable—"

"Intercepted?" said Tommy. "By whom?"

"The police," said Hyde simply.

Tommy's mouth twitched. "It was just possible, you know, that you were referring to the Gatello gang, or what's left of it."

"There isn't any left," said James. "We sent the last two to Scotland Yard in a taxi this evening."

Hambledon thought of Bagshott's arrangements for just this contingency and said: "But didn't you see any policemen?"

"Policemen? Only the usual ones on point duty."

Hambledon broke down and laughed aloud.

"Poor old Bagshott," he said. "Well, do sit down, gentlemen. Just a moment and I'll get the whisky. It's always a help, don't you agree?" He put down his automatic on the top of a cabinet and took out glasses and a decanter. "You must excuse my greeting you with that thing," he added, indicating the gun. "You see, I didn't know who was here. Well, here's luck. I hope you've come to tell me a long and interesting story."

"Good health," said James. He sipped his drink and put it down. "Actually, it would save a lot of time telling the same story twice over if Chief-Inspector Bagshott were here too. Do you mind if I ring him up? He won't be at Scotland Yard so late, I suppose?"

"I should try there first," said Tommy gravely, and told him the extension number. Hyde made a long arm for the telephone—Hambledon had one in the sitting room as well as beside his bed—and was put through at once. Hambledon could hear a squeaky noise as Bagshott answered.

"My name is James Hyde. Good evening, Chief-Inspector. I am speaking from Mr. Hambledon's flat, and I wondered— Yes, Mr. Hambledon's flat. . . . No, we came here of our own accord; in fact, we arrived first and had to wait for him. . . . Yes, Mr. Hambledon is here. . . . Certainly, by all means. Just a moment. . . . He wants to speak to you," added Hyde, addressing Tommy and offering him the receiver.

"That you, Hambledon?" said Bagshott.

"Myself in person," said Tommy cheerfully.

"And those two blighters are there in your flat—are they both there?"

"Yes. Why don't you come along and join the party, Bagshott? It looks as though it might be amusing."

"I'll bring a pair of handcuffs with me," growled the chief-inspector. "All right, I'll come. At once. Good-bye."

"He will be here," said Hambledon, "within minutes. It is quite a short distance."

"Yes, isn't it?" said Hyde. "Very convenient."

"Convenient?"

"If you want anybody arrested, for example."

"I don't know that I need arrest you two," said Hambledon thoughtfully, "but I warn you that Bagshott might."

"Oh, surely not," said James. "We haven't done anything."

Hambledon looked at him and laughed.

"Tell me how you got in here tonight."

"We opened the door," said Adam, speaking for the first time. "It's quite a simple lock."

"That's housebreaking, in case you don't know. No, since it was after 9 P.M.—did you arrive later than nine o'clock? . . . Yes, then it's burglary."

"No," said Hyde. "Seeking sanctuary. And bringing you something, not taking anything away."

"Ah," said Hambledon. At that moment there came a knock at the door and he went to admit Bagshott.

"Mr. Hyde-Selkirk and Mr. Adam," said Tommy, introducing them. "Chief-Inspector Bagshott."

"This is a pleasure," said Hyde.

"I, too," said Bagshott grimly, "have been looking forward to this meeting for a long time."

"But you must permit me to put you right about our names. I am James Hyde, as I told you just now, and my friend here is Adam Selkirk."

"What!" said Hambledon. "Then the man whom Varsoni killed at Putney was—"

"My brother," said Adam.

"But the Gatello gang never mentioned you."

"They didn't know who I was. I am the brother who lived in Spain for so long, for whom they mistook Hyde here, on account of his likeness to my brother Hugh. Hyde is our cousin, actually. I came to Argentina at the end of the war to lend Hugh a hand over that money of Ribbentrop's, and we thought it would be useful if they didn't know I was a Selkirk too. So I passed as his valet."

"And where is Ribbentrop's money now?" asked Hambledon.

"Here," said Hyde. He slipped his hand under the chair in which he was sitting and brought out a brown paper parcel. "Three million dollars in negotiable securities and two diamond necklaces. Will you take charge of it, Mr. Hambledon? The chief-inspector is a witness that we have handed it over."

"But—but what d'you want me to do with it?"

"My brother Hugh," said Adam Selkirk, "realized that it would be impossible to trace the original owners of the money, though possibly the necklaces are identifiable. He thought the money should be applied to the relief of some of the suffering the Germans have caused. His own suggestion was that it should go into the funds at the disposal of UNRRA. Would this be possible, do you think?"

"I don't know," said Tommy rather breathlessly, "but I will find out. The suggestion seems to me to be just."

"Thank you," said Adam.

"It is a relief," said James, relaxing comfortably, "to have handed that over to the proper quarter. I must admit that it rather weighed on my mind at times."

"Why didn't you bring it in before?" asked Bagshott.

"Because, if we had, the Gatello gang would have heard of it and gone home, and we wanted to deal with them. It was the halter we held them by, you see," said James. "By the way, 'halter' is rather an appropriate word, under the circumstances, isn't it, Adam?"

"I cannot think of a better. Would it not be advisable for Mr. Hambledon and Mr. Bagshott to check the contents of the parcel together?"

It did not take long, since even vast sums can be concentrated into compact form. They repacked the parcel and Hambledon made out a receipt to Messrs. Adam Selkirk and James Hyde. "I'll find out as soon as possible what can be done about this," he said, "and let you know. Bagshott, will you take charge of it for tonight? I'll put it in safe-deposit tomorrow morning, since my flat seems to be rather too easy to enter."

"I'll take it with me," said the chief-inspector. "I've got a police car outside, so it should be safe en route."

"Well, now that's done," said Hyde, rising, "we need not detain you from your—"

"Here," said Tommy, "if you suppose you're going to walk out and leave us guessing all the lurid details, you're wrong. Have a heart. You're as bad as Forgan. Start at the beginning and carry straight on."

Adam Selkirk told the first part of the story; how the loot came to the Argentine, was stolen from the Germans there by the Gatello gang, and taken from them again by his brother and himself. Tommy listened attentively; much of this he had already heard from official sources, and it was evident that this man was speaking the truth. After the account of how Hyde and Selkirk changed places and Selkirk was murdered, the story became a duet by Adam and Hyde, with an occasional question to clear up a point here and there.

"We were mistaken about who was murdered at Putney," said Hambledon, "but we did know Varsoni had done it. I suppose you threw him out of the window, did you?"

Bagshott looked horrified, but James answered simply that they had not touched him. "He just looked at me, turned white, and fell backwards. He took me for a ghost, no doubt."

When the whole story was finished Hambledon and Bagshott looked at each other.

"Well?" said Tommy. "Our friends' behavior has been highly irregular, no doubt, but I don't know that they've done much actual harm."

"They've broken about sixteen laws at a moderate estimate," said Bagshott.

"We did help you, didn't we," said James apologetically, "to clear up the Gatello gang?"

"Having enticed them to this country in the first place," said the chief-inspector.

"If we hadn't," said Adam, "those Germans would probably have got the money in the end. The Gatellos were no match for them."

"There is that," admitted Hambledon. "It is at least safe from the Germans now."

"Yes, but look at all the proceedings you've involved us in," said Bagshott. "Three murders, two cases of sudden death, the larceny of that chair—"

"We only borrowed it," said Hyde meekly. "And we didn't murder anybody."

"Their real offense in your eyes, Bagshott," said Tommy, "was introducing you to Forgan. By the way, Hyde, your lawyer friend Nairn will get rather a shock, won't he?"

There came a knock at the outer door, and Hambledon, saying, "Who's this at this time of night?" went to open it. He left the sitting-room door ajar, and a subdued murmur of voices floated in from the tiny entrance lobby. Then the sitting-room door opened slowly and Hambledon came in backwards. His guests noticed with a shock of surprise amounting to disbelief that he was holding both hands above his head. He was followed into the room by a tall man with a square, lined face and a nose which had been broken at some time. He was armed with a heavy German automatic.

He barked an order for them to put up their hands, adding: "Get back against that wall, you!" to Hambledon. "Not near your gun, no."

"O.K., Frankenstein," said Tommy, unwillingly obeying.

"And I will have no insolence."

"Oh dear," said Hyde, "I did think this rather trying business was all over."

"It is only now beginning," said the man with the gun. "You think because you deal with those contemptible petty gangsters you have things all your own way. You have now met your better. I have come for my money, and I think it that parcel on your imitation mahogany table, yes?"

This stung Hambledon, since the table was genuine Queen Anne. "You be-sotted fool," he said, "what do you take us for? You'll never get out of the country with that. Or even without it."

"At least I shall have time to burn it. You, to dare to touch what is ours. I waited only for you Selkirks to destroy the Gatellos and take the money; you did not know you do my work for me. Now I pounce."

"Meow," said Tommy.

"I punish insolence, I warned you earlier. For that, you hand over the parcel yourself. Come forward. To the table; that is right, good dog."

The back of Hambledon's neck turned scarlet, but he came forward slowly.

"Now pick up the parcel, good dog. Bring it here to me. Stay still, you," he added as Bagshott made a movement. The gun in the German's hand was still weaving from one man to the other as Hambledon picked up the parcel in both hands and advanced slowly with his eyes fixed on the German's face. There was a rug on the floor; Tommy reached it and appeared to stumble. He dived forward headfirst, butting the German violently in the stomach, and instantly the scene changed. The automatic went off as its owner doubled up with a grunt; the bullet smashed one of the windows. Bagshott leapt at the German, and the three men went down in a heap on the floor with Hambledon gasping and struggling underneath. Adam caught the hand with which the German was trying to strangle Bagshott, bent it back to the floor, and knelt on it. Hyde yelped as one of the flailing feet caught him on the shin, and the table went over with a crash. He dodged round it and, with some recollection of dealing with a struggling horse, sat down heavily on the German's head, adding con-siderably to Hambledon's inconvenience. The door burst open as the police driver and constable escort, who had heard the shot, rushed into the room. They seized the German by the wrists, disarmed him expertly, and dragged him to his feet. The rest of the mess sorted itself out, with Bagshott patting his pockets in search of something.

"Take that man," he gasped. "Could have sworn I brought some handcuffs."

"I have, sir," said the constable, and moved aside to show the prisoner al-ready handcuffed to his wrist.

"I know this man," said Adam. "One Hommelhoff," and Tommy nodded.

"Quide righd," he snuffled, with a handkerchief to his nose, for it was bleed-ing. "They wand him in Gerbady, they'b beed looging for him." He gulped and continued more clearly. "A little matter of a prisoner of war who died, Hom-melhoff, do you remember? I suppose you got away to the Argentine in that submarine which was alleged to have rescued Adolf and Consort. Whad a wasde of pedrol. Oh damn," he said indistinctly, and retired to the bathroom.

He returned a few minutes later to find that the prisoner had been removed. Adam, having picked up the table, was gathering broken glass from the carpet, and Bagshott was being official over the telephone.

Tommy addressed Hyde, who was tenderly exploring his shin.

"Tell me," he said earnestly, "what, if any, are your plans for the future?"

"Oh, I don't know," said James vaguely. "I shall go out to the Argentine with Adam for a start, I think. I've always wanted to travel."

"Quite a good idea," said Hambledon. "You'll have the Gatello gang's relations to keep you from getting bored, won't you? When you've come to the end of them there's another scheme that might occupy your peculiar talents to advantage."

"What's that?"

"It is estimated that there is a million pounds' worth of looted gold hidden in Germany; you might like to hunt for it. Over there," added Tommy, after a short pause filled with no particular enthusiasm, "you wouldn't be able to worry Bagshott."

The End

About the Rue Morgue Press

"Rue Morgue Press is the old-mystery lover's best friend,
reprinting high quality books from the 1930s and '40s."
—*Ellery Queen's Mystery Magazine*

Since 1997, the Rue Morgue Press has reprinted scores of traditional mysteries, the kind of books that were the hallmark of the Golden Age of detective fiction. Authors reprinted or to be reprinted by the Rue Morgue include Catherine Aird, Delano Ames, H. C. Bailey, Morris Bishop, Nicholas Blake, Dorothy Bowers, Pamela Branch, Joanna Cannan, John Dickson Carr, Glyn Carr, Torrey Chanslor, Clyde B. Clason, Joan Coggin, Manning Coles, Lucy Cores, Frances Crane, Norbert Davis, Elizabeth Dean, Carter Dickson, Eilis Dillon, Michael Gilbert, Constance & Gwenyth Little, Marlys Millhiser, Gladys Mitchell, James Norman, Stuart Palmer, Craig Rice, Kelley Roos, Charlotte Murray Russell, Maureen Sarsfield, Margaret Scherf, Juanita Sheridan and Colin Watson..

To suggest titles or to receive a catalog of Rue Morgue Press books write 87 Lone Tree Lane, Lyons, CO 80540, telephone 800-699-6214, or check out our website, www.ruemorguepress.com, which lists complete descriptions of all of our titles, along with lengthy biographies of our writers.